THE LONG DROP

A top-secret Commando raid into German occupied France.

French resistance fighters uncover the position of a secret German store containing files and reports of vital information on the movement of troops. The details are passed to British intelligence, who formulate an ingenious plan – to break into the heavily guarded store and steal the information – thus gaining the upper hand for a precious few hours. This was a job that demanded a tough, ruthless, highly trained band of men. Men who could parachute into enemy-occupied territory and efficiently carry out an operation that depended on split-second timing, and get out again – men like those of commando unit Special Group 404.

THE LONG DROP

THE LONG DROP

by

Alan White

Magna Large Print Books
Long Preston, North Yorkshire,
BD23 4ND, England.

British Library Cataloguing in Publication Data.

White, Alan
    The long drop.

A catalogue record of this book is
available from the British Library

ISBN   978-0-7505-3075-0

First published in Great Britain in 1969 by Herbert Jenkins Ltd.

Copyright © 1969 by Rhetoric Ltd.

Cover illustration © mirrorpix

The moral right of the author has been asserted

Published in Large Print 2009 by arrangement with
Alan White, care of Watson, Little Ltd.

Magna Large Print is an imprint of Library Magna Books Ltd.

Printed and bound in Great Britain by
T.J. (International) Ltd., Cornwall, PL28 8RW

for Mike Legat

Roget Belfière was short and fat, but despite his bulk he could move swiftly, silent as a lizard. He needed to. There were twenty German soldiers within a spit of him, all armed and bored. Last week Jean Postif had been caught and the German soldiers poured more than a hundred nine millimetre bullets into him. Artoise crawled up behind Roget and touched his boot. The door to the concrete building was open; they had only the next four minutes. 'A' Troop was going off duty, 'F' Troop coming on. Kranstalt was in charge of the hand-over, and that meant the complete military ritual. Here in Liège, most sergeants would have let the men relax a little. Artoise nodded, smiling at the progress of Kranstalt's tireless rigmarole. Roget beckoned for her to take shelter beside the break in the wall. She reached under one of her several jumpers and pulled out two grenades. She settled herself into the angle of the wall and Roget went, skittering over the pile of rubble with barely a sound to the doorway into the building. He rose to his feet and stepped inside. Artoise listened as Kranstalt ploughed his way laboriously through the routine, checking each man's weapons, ammunition and stick grenades. Each man must not only declare he still was 'in possession' of his active service issue, he must also produce it for Kranstalt actually to see. The hand-over was half way completed but there was no sign yet of Roget's return. Artoise felt again that familiar stab of anxiety. The operation had been timed carefully, but one of the soldiers could have left just one stick grenade inside the concrete building; Kranstalt would certainly send him to get it and Roget had no back way out, no bolt hole. Artoise glanced at the door though her main preoccupation was with the soldiers; let one of them come round that corner and she'd have him playing hopscotch with a four second fuse. On each occasion they had timed this hand-over Kranstalt had taken four minutes minimum, even five on one of his finicky days. Siegermann, the youngest sergeant on this post, took only long enough for each man to answer the roll call. Still no sign of Roget. Now Kranstalt was three quarters of the way through; within such a short time 'F' Troop would pour through that door loosening tight belts, taking off packs, starting the coffee for the short vigil before they went off duty at midnight and the locked door made entry impossible. 'This is always the bad bit,' Artoise thought, 'the jobs Roget and I do together, alone, the jobs where Roget takes a chance while I watch, and keep him protected with my hands full of grenades and my throat dry as talcum powder.' Kranstalt was about to end the parade. Damn him, he's missed off the inspection of rifle barrels. Damn him. 'Roget, you're cutting it too fine.' Three minutes and forty-five seconds since the hand-over started; and suddenly Roget came back, a barely discernible blur in the lighted doorway, now you see him, now you don't, moving quickly over the stones. He dropped down beside Artoise. She, thrilled with relief and pride, reached out her hand and touched him with the back of her knuckle where it clenched, white, around the grenade. He was excited by the folder in his hand, and stuffed it into his pocket. Together they backed into the gloom of the corner and over the first low wall. Kranstalt gave the final order to dismiss; 'F' Troop broke ranks and clattered into the concrete building. Now it was safe to rise. 'A' Troop marched the other way heading for barracks and bed with never a

11

backward glance. Kranstalt would keep them at attention, eyes forward, all the way home. For Artoise and Roget, the long climb, over the second wall, past the oil drums, the rear of the vehicle park, up the high wall into which Muette, dieu te garde, had rammed the climbing pitons, over the roof gully between the two long buildings, down into the carpenter's yard, out through the gate and along the alley-way. Now it should happen; everything so far has gone too well and the night has that smell of sour death. Now comes the stupid mistake you can't plan against since you can't anticipate it. Two bicycles had been left for them in the carpenter's yard. They wheeled them along the alley-way. Now comes the moment for one of the cycles to have a puncture, and you can't ride with a puncture, can you? Not that you mind damaging the tyre in your compelling haste to get away, but because it would look so damned suspicious to ride along on a flat tyre, with inner tubes practically impossible to replace. There's nothing. Roget would have sniffed it, and he's plodding along like a man who's just finished a work shift and is in no hurry to get home. There's no better man; Artoise would not have served any other but Roget. At the far end of the alley-way they mounted the bicycles and cycled away, talking quietly to each other of work time banalities, a conversation designed to deceive and soothe any chance listener.

They arrived at the granary, a mile out of Liège on the Ardennes road, without incident. In it, among the several machines for grinding corn, was an electric motor Pieter had adapted. A coil across the terminals and other gadgets only he could understand emitted a silent radio mush whenever this motor was used. It scattered the sound of frying eggs onto any radio reception or transmission within half a mile. The Belgians cursed its interference when they were trying to listen to Radio Liège, even though the station had been taken over by the Germans and broadcast mostly propaganda and 'acceptable' German military music. There would have been no complaints from the Belgians had they known the motor effectively prevented the German direction finders plotting the location of the clandestine radio Roget kept in the roof of the granary. As soon as he saw them arrive, Pieter switched on the motor master switch and remained below on guard while they climbed the stairs to the small room in the joists where the corn hoist was kept. He didn't speak to them, and only when they were sitting beneath the corn hoist did they speak to each other of where they had been.

Roget took the folder from his inside pocket and handed it to Artoise, who could read German as well as he could. The starred TOP SECRET classification was known equally to both. Inside the folder a single sheet of paper carried a list of numbers with dates and times next to each block of five. The paper had been crumpled ready for the shredder. Artoise whistled, silently.

'It's all like that,' Roget said, excited as a child with a new toy, 'filing cabinets all round the wall.'

'An information centre?'

'The Signals Data Storage Unit for the entire Western Army.' He got up, walked about, couldn't contain himself. Artoise cast an anxious glance below, but Pieter was still on guard. 'Important, eh?' she said. 'Important – it's the most exciting thing we've come upon so far. When I think what is contained within that one small building...'

'But what can we do?' she asked, practical as ever.

'I don't know, but whatever it is, believe me, it will be the most substantial thing we have ever done,' he said.

'Kranstalt is only on duty once each fortnight on the late watch, and he's our only chance of getting in and out.'

'We can't do anything in four minutes, believe me. You'd need an hour to clear that place. There's so much stuff, there's so much, Artoise,' he said, his excitement rising again.

'Surely anything we take they will miss?'

'Burn the lot, that's what we could do. Incendiaries, timed to go off after twelve o'clock. Think what a mess that would make of their communications systems? It would bring them to a virtual standstill for six or seven days.'

'Yes, it would. But what then, Roget? They'd duplicate the system and start again.'

'They'll always start again. We can't hope anything we ever do will prevent that. The job of the resistance is to cause delays and upheavals. We can't win the war. The Allies will do that, with their armies. We can only skitter about beneath the surface, like rats polluting the water. There'll always be something for us to do, Artoise, until the war ends. There'll always be a train to blow, a railway line to cut. Don't despair.'

He had mistaken her mood. Too excited to sit down, he paced up and down. 'I know

15

there'll always be another job,' she said, quietly, 'but what happens when one of us makes that mistake, when they catch us, you or me?'

He walked to where she was sitting, a bulky shapeless mass beneath her coats and sweaters. No-one could have called her handsome. Roget knew he could do nothing without her. He reached out and seized her hand. She gripped him with familiar vigour.

'At least,' he said, 'they'll catch us both.' In any other man it would have been a terrible selfishness; she knew it for a reassurance that whatever might happen to her, he would hope to be there. 'L'absence est le plus grand des maux,' he said; and he was right; there is no greater evil.

He switched on the radio transmitter in the small black wooden box, hidden behind the dusty wall panel. When the needle registering anode current had reached its maximum he nodded and she flipped the switch that controlled the grinder. When the grinder had run for about a minute, sufficient time to persuade anyone accidentally listening to the frequency to tune away, she switched off again, and he started to tap the morse key. 'Hello England, Hello England, Rainbow calling...'

Across the Channel, he knew not where, someone was listening…

Steele was a brigadier when war started. There had been innumerable attempts at promotion, all successfully resisted. Brigadier Steele was sitting in his office in a house in Maida Hill overlooking the canal. He was awaiting the arrival of another brigadier, from the War Office. What a bloody waste of time on a summer's day. He watched the large green Humber pull up on the road outside the house two doors further up the street. A civilian-clad figure climbed out of the back seat when the driver had opened the door. The uniformed driver saluted, got back into the Humber, and drove it up the street.

'Bloody pantomime,' Steele growled. Damn it, they'd been told not to send official cars here time and again. What was wrong with taking a taxi, except you don't get a poncy salute when you climb out! He pencilled a note on the top of his day pad. 'Security of Premises?' It would remind him to pretend to an appropriate display of anger. It took the other brigadier five minutes to get through Steele's underground defences; good, that'd show the bastard a thing or two about security. Finally, Major Heseltine opened the door and admitted him. 'Brigadier Forbes,' he announced, as if he were a toastmaster at a Masonic dinner. Forbes came in, rush and bounce, pink fingernails, stiff collar, mouth full of teeth. 'My dear Steele!' he said, pronouncing the last 'e' as a 'y'. Steele waved him into an arm chair. 'My dear Forbes,' he said.

Forbes gave him a slip of paper. Steele signed it, handed it back. Mumbo-jumbo land. Forbes gave him a folder tied with thin yellow string and sealed. The walls of the tents he and Emily used in the Lake District were tied with that colour of string, back in '35. He broke the seal after giving it a cursory examination, opened the file. In it was a transcript of Belfière's message. He glanced at the datetime, only three hours previously. 'Not wasting time, are we?' he said. When he had read the message, and the notes scrawled on it, he put the signal back into its folder and retied the string. He took a wax wafer from his top drawer and pressed it on the knot. He took the metal insignia from its chamois leather cover in the special pocket of his trousers, placed it in the sealing machine, switched on, allowed a few seconds for the machine to warm up, then pressed his insignia onto the wafer. 'What are you going to do?' he asked as he examined the wafer. 'Are you going to give them the incendiaries they ask for?' He handed the file back to Forbes who placed it back on Steele's desk.

'We're going to send in some men,' he said, quietly.

'S.O.E.?'

'This isn't a job for S.O.E., old man,' Forbes said. 'They need someone they don't mind losing. Some kind of person up there has wished this job, I'm afraid, onto you!'

Brigadier Steele and Major Rhodes were sitting in the front room of a boarding house in Sittingbourne, Kent, the only house in the street which led to an Army barracks of hastily constructed Nissen huts. The camp was a known training ground for infantrymen who had passed the first six weeks of Army indoctrination, and there was a constant flow of all ranks and officers up and down the road. No-one would have spotted the few men walking towards the barracks who turned off into the drive of the boarding house. The same War Office tabulator that had sifted the personal details of these men also prepared a schedule of their arrivals. All were on time to within a minute. Since the Brigadier and Major Rhodes were dressed in civilian clothes, few of the men knew their rank; one or two faces, however, were well known to the Major and received a special smile of recognition. By the end of the day the Major had seen all he wanted.

'I could do with a drink now,' he said.

Together they drove up the A2, then turned off the road into the old world village of Bredgar. It would be their last moment of intimacy until the job was completed.

'Why do you always give me these jobs?' he asked. 'Why don't you go yourself? You're a damned sight better at this sort of caper than I am, and a trip abroad would do you good!'

'Chains of command. Some high-and-mighty in the War Office sets it up, I get you to knock it down. You set things up, and any one of twelve men, selected by tabulator, knocks 'em down again. Believe me, it's a great temptation to do everything oneself. Don't think I enjoy sitting here while you swan off abroad. It's hell sitting here, wondering if you're bungling something I could have handled perfectly myself. Same way it's hell for you to watch one of your lads make a balls of something. But that's the way it has to be.'

'Why can't the S.O.E. do this one?'

'I asked that, but you know what they say, S.O.E. men are in too short supply, too valuable, too specialist, for this sort of job.'

The time had come to break off their intimacy. 'What are we calling this caper?' Rhodes asked.

'404, that's the job name. You'll be Special Group 404. Good luck. We'll give the men you select a pay parade and let them make their way to your training camp after seven days' leave. You come to my office when you're ready. And let me repeat it.'

'What?'

'Good luck. This time, I get the feeling you may need it.'

The barbed wire eight feet thick stretches to each side as far as the eye can see; not that there is any time for the eye to wander with machine-gun bullets flipping through the air three feet above your head, tracer every tenth round for which Thank God since it places the trajectory of the other nine killer rounds.

The barbed wire was six feet high, a rolled concertina mass as dense as tangled hair. The sergeant major said, 'I want you so low on the ground you'll need to look up at the worms!' For a thousand years a herd of cattle had munched this field contentedly, every one a Carnation Milk factory. Each in her turn had been eaten, and the signs of their passage long ago were caked deceptively, crusted firm as stone mushrooms. Until you slide over one. 'The things I do for England, home and beauty.' He reached the front of the wire and cautiously extended his hand to lift the strand of the first coil. The wire was cold and damp and though it had started to rust it sprang back when he released it. Damn! Slowly he dragged his body forward through the cowpat to the wire, then, working with his hands close to the ground, he sprang the wire and cut it strand by strand using the short-handled cutters from his belt. Alf worked methodically beside him, matching him snip for snip. Slowly they advanced, cutting the wire and pulling it back, trying to make certain it wouldn't spring back onto their bodies.

Roger's hands are lacerated and bleeding; so numb he hardly feels the slash of the baleful spikes. As Alf works he mutters. Both are nervous; but only Alf shows it. The machine-gun fire increases in intensity through the wire.

There was a 'whang' as bullets screamed in new directions, ricocheting off the steel knots of the barbs. Suddenly Roger felt the sting on his neck and when he pulled his fingers away, they were sticky with blood. Alf heard Roger exclaim as the ricochet hit him. He put his finger to the wound, about an inch and a half long, the thickness of a pencil. A neat sliver of flesh had been gouged from Roger's neck an inch below and behind his ear. He felt the bone behind Roger's ear. No sign of injury.

'You all right?' he whispered. This was no time for first-aid.

'Yes. They ought to pack that up; it could be dangerous!'

Roger worked his head from side to side, risked lifting it three inches off the ground. Remember when Nobby got one in the buttocks and jumped up cursing? That finished him. They all missed Nobby, the section joker. Seventeen when they started; how many left now? Five, including Alf. Alf's all right, he'll make it. It took ten minutes to cut six feet of wire; and then they were enclosed by it.

'There's a mine under that cowpat,' Alf said.

Suddenly you didn't hear the machine guns, the whang and whistle of bullets above you. Suddenly you didn't hear a bloody thing! There was a mine in front of you, under a cowpat.

'Are you sure?'

'Wherever did you see a cowpat that wasn't stuck to the ground?'

'Hey-ho,' Roger said. 'Off we go again. Shall we lift it, or cut round it?'

Alf had had enough of cutting wire. 'Lift the bloody thing,' he said.

'Whose turn?'

'I'll take it if you like?'

'They've run out of medals!'

'I'll buy one in the N.A.A.F.I.!'

The mine had been buried in the top soil and the crust of a cowpat placed over it. You wouldn't know it was there, except the cowpat was not sitting squarely on the ground and that's against the laws of nature, isn't it? Alf snipped the barbed wire on the other side of the mine, taking care the wire didn't spring back and clout the top of the cowpat. Gently, he lifted the hardened ring of crust. It was about ten inches circular, the size of a dinner plate: not that they'd eaten off a plate for a long time. He laid the cowpat on the ground as if it were Crown Derby. There it was, a dirty khaki paint-on-brass plunger, like a big nipple. Alf dug with his fingers around the sides of the mine, in the earth. 'Watch out for wires,' Roger whispered. Sometimes they wire them up in series, so that anybody setting one off will fire a couple more for good measure. No wires. Wiring takes time, and this bugger's been put there in a hurry, hence the cowpat. Alf eased the soil from around the mine with his finger. The mine itself was about six inches long, and four inches wide. An old friend, Mark Two. Written on the top of the mine, incongruously, was the word Achtung. 'We are achtunging, you silly sod!' Roger muttered. The spigot sat proud of the centre of the mine, in a loose collar. It didn't matter which way you moved that spigot, it would still get you. Alf took a grip on the collar with his thumb and forefinger. 'Let it be easy,' he begged out loud. He turned the collar and a watchful God for once said okay. The collar unfastened easily. He unscrewed it carefully, the thumb and forefinger of his left hand on the spigot itself, to prevent bending its knuckle joint. Slowly he pulled upwards with his left hand as he unscrewed the collar with his right. After five complete revolutions of the collar the spigot moved off its seat. It wasn't until that moment that Roger felt the sweat pouring off his forehead. He pushed his head down onto the ground to wipe his forehead on the wet grass.

'I'm doing the work and you're sweating.' Alf smiled at him.

Roger's face was not fifteen inches from the mine. 'If that bugger goes off,' he said, 'it won't matter which of us is doing the work.'

Alf looked down at the mine. The collar had turned five turns, the spigot was loose on its seating. In theory, the collar and the spigot should now come out together. He looked at Roger, who nodded. 'Lift the bloody thing,' he said, 'and let's get it over with.'

Alf lifted the collar and the spigot together. Both came free. He pulled them upwards and there was the quite audible sound of a click.

'It's booby-trapped,' Roger yelled.

From the bottom of the spigot two wires trailed inside the mine to the booby trap fuse that lay below.

Both tried to stand but couldn't for the wire. Alf threw the mine but it hit the tangled wire and bounced back.

'Three second fuse,' Alf shouted, his face

twisted with terror.

Roger scrabbled in the ground to press himself backwards, but the barbs of the wire snatched his clothing and his pack. Alf thrashed about trying to clear the wire from his back, but became more and more entangled. In the last second, both realised they could not get away and turned their backs to the mine awaiting the blast. Is it true all your life flashes past your mind's eye at such a moment?

The mine exploded.

'Dammit,' said Company Sergeant Major Ben Bolding, thirty yards behind them. 'That's two more we've lost. The Major will be livid.'

The Major *was* livid. 'Damn it all, Ben, they've been taught booby traps over and over again.'

'They get nervous, Major.'

'I can't take nervous men on this trip.'

The C.S.M. hesitated.

'I was wondering, Major, if you'd care to speak to them before they leave. Give them a bit of a pat on the back, if you see what I mean. One of 'em got a nasty wound on his neck.'

'He should have kept his head down.'

'He did, Major. A ricochet off the barbed wire got him.'

'Ah, well, that could happen to anybody. Where are they?'

'I imagine they're scrubbing off!' The C.S.M. chuckled. A low level charge planted in the casing of practice mines that exploded with the force of only a Guy Fawkes night penny banger, but was surrounded with liquid methylene blue dye impossible to wash off. Sometimes it seemed the men were more scared of the dye than of live explosive.

Smithells and Burdon had stripped when I went into their barrack hut, and standing on a towel each by the stove were scrubbing themselves with soap and Vim. Smithell's wound had been dressed, but his neck had started to stiffen.

They both tried to stand to attention when they saw me.

'I'm surprised at you, Smithells,' I said, 'I never thought you'd let yourself be caught by a booby trap.' He looked shamefaced. 'We forgot, Major, in the excitement.'

The whole of one side of Burdon's face was tinted blue. I had to restrain an impulse to laugh. 'And you, Burdon, the best man we've had so far with explosives, what about you?'

'He's right sir, you do forget. You're so bound up in what you're doing, you forget the details.'

I felt sorry for them. It was the end of the road so far as they were concerned. There was a strict rule in camp – one failure and you were R.T.U. – returned to unit. But, dammit, these men were volunteers for the Commando, they'd suffered a basic training that crippled a merely average man and yet had re-volunteered for Special Group 404. Not one of them had any idea of what 404 meant to do, but still they volunteered.

'You'll be returned to your units,' I said, 'I'm afraid I can't help that, but we shall see you get leave before you go back. You are both first class men, and I'm sorry you're not staying with us; but when we get into Europe a simple thing such as forgetting a booby trap would wipe out not only the men who forget, but probably the rest of Special Group 404. That's something I will not risk.'

'Don't worry, sir,' Smithells said. 'We knew what we were letting ourselves in for the first day. We're sorry we didn't make it.'

I turned to go. At the doorway I stopped and looked back. How vulnerable they seemed, the white flesh of their naked bodies contrasting with the wind tanned hue of their limbs, the blue stain on their faces. 'This is something I tell only to the good ones,' I said, trying to smile. 'Get yourself a bleached blonde, and use her bottle of peroxide to wash yourselves. Both will do you some good, the bottle and the blonde.'

They both grinned. I turned to go. I had no grin in me. Everyone so far who had failed had qualified for the bottle and blonde tip. They had all been good men.

'I think that bugger's almost human,' one of them said, unaware I could hear him. Yes, I was almost human, and that was something to watch. Humanity and weakness go hand in hand; many men have been 'understood' and killed. Only by holding to inhuman standards could I protect the safety of all these men entrusted to me. I had to be a bastard to cut out human weakness.

It was not a pleasing prospect. This would be my fifteenth job. I'd had enough.

Special Group 404 had taken over a deserted village on the moors of North Yorkshire. There had been a street with six houses, a pub, a village shop-cum-Post Office with a battered enamel plate advertising Hovis bread and Horlicks, and a large brick misery-faced Methodist Chapel. All the buildings bore the scars of war. Not a half pane of glass was left in the window frames, and more than one door was propped with a stick. Gardens that once had been tended cottage-style with proud-headed Chrysanthemums, Michael-mas Daisies, Sweet Williams, now were rank with nettles and head-high Golden Rod. Roses, Clematis, Wisteria and Honeysuckle, no doubt thriving on the nitrate in cordite, rampaged over the walls of houses and the Post Office. Amid the couch grass you would have found self-seeded Pansies and Poly-anthus struggling bravely against the on-slaught of total war, but you never had time to look. On each side of the street concrete observation posts had been erected, black-eyed, cavern-mouthed silent watchers from another world. The village had formerly been a rendezvous for Saturday afternoon cyclists and hikers up from Timble. Mrs Tannin in the fourth cottage down from the Post Office had once a modest mouth-to-ear reputation for ham-and-egg teas, eight around the big table in the front room and no space if you arrived late. Mrs Tannin now made muni-tions in Bradford, and her boys had gone to war, along with the cyclists and the hairy stockinged, knobbly-kneed hikers.

Once upon a time you couldn't walk up that village street on a Saturday or a Sunday if you came from Bradford without meeting ten men you knew. Now, with concrete clad watchers permanently on guard, it would be a good man who'd get up that street even under cover of darkness, without a bunker spitting bullets, grenades, thunderflashes and militarised nastinesses at him. Sometimes the blank cartridges were replaced by live rounds and tracers; the observers were all marksmen with a military licence to shoot to wound. Of the hundred and three men who had volunteered for Special Group 404, three had been killed by accident and twenty-two had been wounded. The remainder had heard the hungry whisper of live ammunition, the impact thud of nickel plated lead seeking flesh to slap against the stonework walls. Selection by elimination, training by doing, each error costly, each failure final; it was that kind of unit. Special Group 404 had a quiet, night-time, ruthlessly efficient job to do and there was no room for mistakes.

I waited with C.S.M. Ben Bolding in a pill box concrete bunker overlooking the Methodist Chapel. It was getting on for midnight.

The year, nineteen forty-three. That morning early it had started to pretend to snow, and the ground was covered in dark grey slush; the month was November.

My name is Robin Rhodes and I stand six feet two, a height that can be a damned nuisance jumping out of a plane with a parachute strapped to your back. In the old hole-in-the-floor tail jump days of bombers hastily converted for drops, many times I had scythed forwards through the hole 'ringing the bell' as they called it, smashing my face against the badly protected rim. Now a nose permanently bent to one side adds to my attractiveness or so they tell me! I was a seasoned campaigner of twenty-eight. They promised me this was my last job. C.S.M. Bolding was a thin rat-faced Yorkshireman, lean as a ferret. He had a thin rasping voice that could never have cleared a barrack square, but he never needed to. He was a corporal when he joined Lieutenant Rhodes in nineteen forty-one in one of the first of the Special Groups. Since that time we had always been together. Ben Bolding had only one ambition, to survive the war.

'Why did *you* join the Special Services?' I asked him.

'Destiny's a deceitful bitch,' Ben Bolding

said, 'and I want her in my own two hands, where I can see what she's doing. None of this "once more into the breach" lark. If I've got to fight, I'll do it independently. Just me and a few people about me I can trust. That's my style.'

'You trust me?' I asked.

'Until the Lady Destiny tells me not to.'

'And if I say jump, you'll jump, every time?'

'Ah, now that's another matter. You're an officer, and I'm a sergeant major. Yes, Sir, I'll jump, Sir! Lead me to the edge, Sir! But you and I, Major, we've soldiered often enough together to know that there comes a time, perhaps only one occasion, when you'll say jump, and I might not go. I might think about it first.'

'And you'll be dead.'

'I know I will. That's what I mean by trust. If I could guarantee to jump that one time, I know I could stay alive. I think that, if you're the one telling me to jump, I'm more likely to do so than if it was any other officer I've served under.'

'Flattery will get you nowhere.' I had to laugh at him. We were standing relaxed in the concrete bunker. Over at the far side of the bunker, a corporal sniper couldn't hear what we said; he probably wasn't interested.

'It will, you know, Major. It'll get me over there, wherever we're going, because you're the only officer I could say a thing like that to and that in a way is trust.'

What a strange man he was, Ben Bolding, how well and how little I knew him. I knew all his physical mannerisms, I could detect him instantly in a crowd of men by no more than the style of his movements. I crawled through a field with him and though six feet away felt him tense when he spotted a sentry. I always knew, instinctively, which way he would move in an attack. Never any need for me to say, you take the left, I'll take the right. And yet vast depths of his mind I could never hope to fathom. I didn't trust him at all. I knew his motives were based on self-interest and survival. For some reason he had come to believe he stood a better chance of survival with me. I didn't trust him always to tell me the truth, when the truth was important to someone else; I knew he'd always follow a straight line of expediency, no matter the cost.

One time two of our men were picked up, drunk and disorderly, in Hurstpierpoint. We were due to start training for a job; it was the last night of liberty for a long while. The men were wheeled in front of me. I didn't want to sentence them but there is a very straightforward code of discipline and the military police wanted them punished. 'Were these men drunk?' I asked the sergeant major. 'I was with them all evening, sir, and can swear they never touched a drop of intoxicating liquor.' That was a lie I was able to accept. No, I had no trust in Ben Bolding, but a faith that whatever he did it would be for the ultimate good of himself, and the immediate benefit of our particular objective. He knew damned well that having those two men could have meant the success or failure of the job we were about to do. He wanted the job to succeed, that was the immediate objective. But he wanted to get out of it alive, and that was the real motive behind his lie.

'What do you think about this lot, Ben?' I asked him.

'Not much. We'll be lucky if we get a dozen.'

I was bound to agree with him. 'Where've they all gone?' I knew where they'd gone. We'd lost them on jobs. Over forty men in a year, good men, all gone.

'They all forgot to jump,' he said.

At the far end of the street a lorry pulled

up and men started to disembark.

'Time to go back to war.'

As we walked out of the pill box, the corporal with a sniper's flash on his arm took his place at the pill box aperture.

'Live ammunition tonight,' I reminded him.

'Yes, Major.'

We walked down the street together. At the far end, large wooden hoardings were mounted on steel wheels; some had windows cut in them, others had doors. I referred to the drawing in my map case and then men from the lorry pulled the hoardings down the street, erecting them in front of the existing buildings by the lorry's lights. When they were in position, what had formerly been a village street now appeared as the corner in a town. It was a startling transformation.

Six men and an officer had stayed in the back of the lorry. The vehicle was driven a quarter of a mile down the road and the tense silent group disembarked. I walked after them, found them grouped round the officer in a tight circle. All wore denim trousers and battledress jackets; their faces had been blackened with burned corks, and on their heads they wore the traditional green beret of Commandos. The officer saluted while his men stood to attention.

'You've been briefed, Captain Derby?' I asked.

'Yes, Major.'

The odds against survival were great. Possibly one would get through, possibly two. Certainly no more. The course was the toughest I could devise, and technically the most difficult.

'You get a half hour for this phase,' I said, 'and remember we shall be operating at all times under actual field conditions. That means the ammunition we shall be firing at you will be live, any men you might encounter will carry out their instructions to immobilise you by any means possible. As far as the War Office is concerned, this whole area is designated a battle zone, and any man who dies tonight will have the sole satisfaction of knowing his next of kin will be informed he has been killed in action.'

'Do we get a stripe if we're wounded, sir?' one of the men asked cheekily. It was Bates. He already had three red strips sewn vertically down the arms of his 'best' uniform, souvenirs of Dunkirk and a couple of 'moonlight' jobs in France.

'I'll sew it on for you personally, with a machine gun,' I promised.

'I want you off at exactly 0300, Captain Derby,' I said and left them at once.

Dodger Bates shivered, and that wasn't solely on account of the coldness of the night. Walking into live ammunition was never something you took in your stride; nothing sounded so evil as live bullets punching the air about you. Taking apart a mine or a grenade was simple by comparison; a purely technical task you learned over and over again, until if necessary you could do it blindfold. There is a lot of free air about your head, and a bullet is small. The mathematical chances of being hit are negligible. When a man is firing at a hundred yards, his sights need only be off by a cat's whisker and he can miss you completely. But somehow, despite the mathematical possibility, Dodger had already been hit three times by bullets. Jokingly the fatalists among them said, 'If it's got your number on it, you'll get it.' It had to be something like that, since the mathematical possibilities were against it. It had to be predestined, guided by some all seeing eye. It had to have *your* number on it.

The night was cold, the sky overcast. Thank God for that. At least they'd have a dark walk up that long street.

'Let's go,' said Captain Derby. Each man knew exactly what to do. Dodger Bates was first. He started slowly forwards down the road, keeping twelve inches away from the hedge. Two men came behind him, the Captain, the other three men, each man twenty feet behind the man in front. It was a risky grouping, but one they would need. They couldn't afford to be further apart than that, and to be closer would be suicide. Fifty yards, then stop. Freeze into the side of the hedge. Listen! Not a sound. Look! Nothing in sight. Glance back. Next man ten feet behind. Advance. Fifty yards, feet down flat, weight on the balls of your feet ready to jump in any direction. The first mortar is always short of target. They do it deliberately. It's easier and more accurate to lift a mortar than to drop it, so they take the first sighting short a fraction, ready to lift. Trouble is, they aim for the centre of a patrol, and the short shot gets the front man. Weight on the balls of your feet and listen for the crack. That gives you one second before it drops down out of the sky at you. Remember Knocker, at Dieppe? Bashing 'em back like cricket balls, despite the impact fuse. Asked him how he managed it afterwards. 'Well,' he said, 'you take care not to hit them on the end, don't you?' That he hit them at all was a bloody miracle. Poor old Knocker, his parachute didn't open on that job in Holland. He candled, went down like a stone, in the long drop. Is that somebody standing with his back to that wall, there, twenty yards ahead, just by the first building? Crafty sod; he's standing back from the corner in the shadow. That's a joke, the whole bloody place is a shadow. Strange how much you can see though, at this time of night. Or is it morning? That wall's just a fraction lighter than he is, and he stands out like a shadowgraph etching. I'll have that bugger. Dodger was carrying a Thompson sub machine gun – well, if it was good enough for Al Capone, why not – though he had to admit it made him feel like a gangster. Thank God they'd done away with the circular magazine; they'd got this clip beneath the butt and that was a lot happier, wasn't it? And you could carry ten clips in your pockets. Patch of shadow ahead; into it, and go sideways. Look back. Next man's seen the sidestep. Good, he's lifted the barrel of his gun and they'll all know, or those who can see him will know, something's wrong. Now sideways into the shadow. I bet that sod by the wall has lost me. Right, quick nip right, still in shadow, round the back of the building. Yes, there's room to get round between the building and that hedge. Go along the side of the building to the corner. Number two will have moved up. Let's pray to God he spots the man against the wall. Right, flat on your face. Best way to look round a corner; they never look at foot height. Yes, there he is, in the shadow. Not moving either! That sod's a damned sight too still. Ten feet to go to get to him. Can't be done. Right, down the leg. Steel rod fifteen inches long, three sixteenths thick in the centre, sharpened to a point at each end. Could throw it, but oh the risk if it misses. Right, down the other leg. Steel caps and a wire between them. Put the steel caps one on each point of the steel rod. Flex it. That works a treat. Same leg, steel pin ten inches long. An arrow. Watch the point, sharp as a virgin's teeth. Marvellous how they make these arrows solid at the tip, and a tube all the way down to keep the weight forward. Put the arrow against the wire of the bow, pull back, aim, let go.

The arrow sped across the short space to the throat of the waiting figure, and there it stuck, through the neck, into the wall behind. I heard the whang of the arrow and

42

smiled. That Dodger, you couldn't fool him! The figure was a booby-trapped dummy. If Dodger had dashed across the space to tackle it, he'd have stumbled across a trip wire that would have sent a flare sky high. Lesson number ninety-seven or thereabouts – watch a motionless figure, ten to one he's a booby-trapped corpse. No live human can stay so still for so long.

It must have taken the courage of a conviction, however, for Dodger to risk firing an arrow into what could have been the throat of one of his Army mates. Teach them inhumanity.

Dodger had seen the trip wire, and was dismantling the mechanism that would have fired the flares.

Now they were back in formation, going up the street.

Dodger would drop to the back, behind Lance Corporal Levine, and number two would take his place.

Damn that number two. Where the hell does he think he's walking, down Brighton Pier? Doesn't he realise he's crossing an open strip, with the light from the sky behind him? The Corporal sniper was itching to shoot.

'Seen him?'

'Yes, Major – I've had him for the last five paces.'

'Then why the hell haven't you fired?' Ben Bolding snarled. He too was disappointed. The sniper took aim again, and squeezed the trigger. The shot must have passed a quarter of an inch from the soldier's ear. He dropped to the ground. RTU. He was lucky to get away with his life. Two more men had been eliminated by the time the patrol reached its objective, the fourth façade down the street, and the face of Captain Derby was grim. He took his position by the side of the wooden wall and waved Dodger Bates forward. They were all belly flat, crawling through the slush and crystalline snow. Dodger grinned cheerfully across the small alley. Lance Corporal Levine was crawling behind Dodger. Together they crossed the yard between the two cottages behind the wooden façade. Captain Derby crawled after them, keeping them in sight. The other men had crawled round the building, and by now would be in position on the corner. There had been a pig stall under the cottage on the left, and flagged steps led down to it. Dodger went first, his pack off his back hanging in his right hand. Lance Corporal Levine unslung his pack, and crouched on the edge of the stairs.

There might be someone in there, there might not. The cellar door could be booby-trapped, but that'd never deceive Dodger. If there was any reason he couldn't just walk through that door, he'd find it soon enough. Meanwhile, it was Captain Derby's job to make certain no-one came into this yard, that no hidden gun barrel poked itself out of one of the top windows. Dodger found the charge in the hinge of the door. Open that door and the hinge would crush the detonator and they'd all be in kingdom come. An old rusted spade was by the back door. Dodger examined it carefully, then picked it up. It had not been booby trapped. He inserted the blade of the spade under the door and lifted gently. The door rose gradually. The lintel above the door was loose. Dodger let the door down again, then used the spade to prise out the lintel. He passed the balk of the wood back to Levine. Then he lifted the door again and took it off its hinges. The door started to fall outwards, but Dodger caught it and swung it aside. There was no-one in the cellar. It was a risk he had had to take. The detonator was set on the outside of the hinge – the door had lifted past it not a quarter of an inch away. Almost contemptuously, Dodger lifted the detonator off its

45

wiring, and showed it to Sam Levine. He buried the detonator in the soil beside the top of the flagged steps leading down to the cellar, then together they went inside.

A concrete slab floor had been poured into the ground floor room of the cottage. There in the cellar they were beneath it. Dodger's task was to blow a hole in that concrete slab, about two feet across. Once the hole had been blown, they had to climb through it. The 'exercise' finished when they were all knocked out, or when they were standing in the room above that cellar. They had a half an hour from start. Twenty minutes left. Now they were inside the cellar, Captain Derby crawled back to the wooden façade and took up a position where he could see down the street, ready for any simulated attack I might mount. In the cellar, Dodger and Sam Levine would be preparing the charge for blowing. Now that Alf Burdon had gone, RTU'd with a blue streak down his face, Dodger Bates was the best explosives man we had. Tonight it had better work. Someone was creeping down the side of the façade, on the other side of the cellar steps. In his mouth he held a thunderflash, a large 'banger' that, in the confined space of that cellar, would blow the senses out of Dodger and Sam

Levine. Captain Derby cursed under his breath. That man, whoever he was, had just passed a so-called sentry, posted to prevent him. The sentry must have been knocked out. Damn. That left only Dodger, Sam Levine, and Captain Derby from the original seven. The Captain went stalking. Slowly he crept forward along the buttress of the wooden façades. When he had gone fifteen feet, he was slightly to one side of the crawling intruder, who had at least twenty feet to traverse before he could get close enough to lob his thunderflash. Whoever it was he was good. You could hardly see his movements as he crossed the ground. The Captain knew he would never be able to overtake him moving at that speed. He rose up into a crouch. He took a large stone, and lobbed it over the head of the crawling figure to the far side of the small space between the cottages. The stone clattered. The crawler stopped. In one bound Captain Derby leaped across the intervening space and landed with his knees in the small of the crawling figure's back. The crawler gasped, and slumped even flatter on the ground, unconscious. Captain Derby turned him over. Another lad for RTU – Brian Johnson, one of our best signallers. Captain Derby dragged him back against the wall of the wooden façade, away from the bomb blast due in exactly three minutes. Suddenly he detected the faint sounds as Dodger and Sam Levine came scrambling back up the cellar steps. They flattened themselves against the wall and edged to the corner, dropped to the ground and waited. Five seconds later, there was an eardrum shattering blast as the explosives went off, and a puff of black smoke edged with the yellow tongues of the explosive flame rolled up the flagged steps. No sooner had the shock wave subsided than Dodger and Sam Levine dashed back again into the courtyard down the cellar steps, Captain Derby at their heels. A large scab had been scooped from the concrete bed. It had not been pierced. Most of the blast had thrust itself downwards and sideways to the walls, all of which had cracked. A hole three feet across and two feet deep had been blown in the cellar floor, and all the wooden joists on which the concrete floor had been laid were snapped at their ends. The mobile generator outside was switched on, and with the wander light in my hands I walked down the cellar steps and into the cellar itself, the light illuminating the crestfallen faces of the three men. They were covered in dirty slushy mud, shivering with cold and disappointment. I walked across to the scab chopped from the concrete.

'Didn't get through, eh?'

'No, sir.' They shook their heads, looking miserable. I didn't tell them that I had been testing that explosive up in the moors for over a week, and had not cut concrete with it. 'Don't worry,' I said, 'it's not your fault.'

'If only we could double the amount, Major,' Dodger Bates suggested. You can't tell a man too much; some don't complete the training, and your security is shot to hell. 'Believe me, Dodger, if we could use another spoonful, I would. But this amount has been calculated for us, and we shall just have to make it go through.' Dodger's face was glum. 'I thought it wouldn't be like that in the Commando,' he said. Captain Derby made a motion to stop him, but I put my hand on Peter's arm. 'No, let him speak; you thought what wouldn't be like what, Dodger?'

He was our most cautious man, a loner, a man apart. Dodger thought things out for himself. It could be dangerous, for often the discipline we needed was purely instinctive. Often I'd see Dodger mulling a thing over in his mind, and then, when he had been able to accept it, become a demon in its execution.

49

'When I first volunteered for the Commando,' he said, starting slowly, 'I worked it out that with a force like this, we'd get the best of everything to work with, I mean. I was fed up with the stuff they'd been handing out to us in the Fusiliers, rusty shovels, picks with broken handles, all that sort of stuff. Now here we are back at the same situation. We've got to blow a hole through a piece of concrete, and it won't work because the equipment we're using isn't right. We need sandbags to tamp that explosive flat against the concrete. We need air drills to start us going with a few sinker holes. We need blast runs to crack the concrete. What do we get? Slap the stuff up against the roof and put a detonator in it and blow. No wonder half the puff goes up the steps outside, wasted force.'

He was right, of course. He couldn't know that not all the instruments and equipment in the world would help us. We had to get into 404 with limited help, we had to do it quickly, and get out again; for once it was most important we got out. Usually, once we'd done a job, blown up a power station, derailed a train, knocked out a gun battery, our own importance had vanished. Getting the men who did the job back home was an act of military charity. They didn't need us once the power station had gone sky high. This time, we had to get in and get out again. But I couldn't tell Dodger, not yet. There was, however, something I could tell him.

'I don't want this to go any further, Dodger, but I think it's safe to say that you, and Sam Levine, will be on the next job with me.'

They looked relieved. Dodger put his doubts away, momentarily. 'You all did an excellent job of getting here – it wasn't your fault you couldn't complete the assignment.'

Even Captain Derby was liable for the RTU penalty should he make an error, despite his rank and seniority. He too looked vastly relieved. 'Off you go,' I said, 'back to camp and into bed. We don't want you catching pneumonia, not if you're coming looking for Germans.'

Switching on the generator was always the signal for the end of an exercise. An ambulance parked outside the village was brought in to take out any casualties. Brian Johnson was carried aboard. Captain Derby, Dodger and Sam Levine cadged a lift and away they went.

It was still snowing, that heavy damp snow that soon turns to mush. I shared the thermos of brandied coffee with Ben Bolding.

Somehow, I had a disinclination to go back to camp. We talked over the exercise as we always did, going over each point of the route and the performance of each man. We were both agreed that Dodger and Sam Levine would come with us, and Captain Derby. The village was now peaceful and all the staff men who helped set up these exercises had gone back to warm billets. The war had ended for a few hours. In the distance, over the moor, searchlights licked the low clouds probing the skies above the towns of the West Riding. German bombers were out. Occasionally we could hear the dull crump of shells, see the white hot fire of incendiary explosions. A fighter screamed low over the moor, one engine flaming. On the ground, all was peaceful, the tick of our jeep the only sound.

It was November 1943. For a short time I was out of the war.

Finally I told the driver to take us back to camp, the lid of the thermos clasped in my hands. The night air had cleared, the snow had stopped, and now I could see over the stretch of moors, down into Wharfedale. My Professor of Organic Chemistry used to live down there, in a large house with a large garden. I took packets of examination papers out to his house, and his wife gave me tea on the lawn. There'd always be a package to take back, but it would never be ready. I enjoyed tea on the lawn with the Professor's wife. I learned from her those standards of womanly charm and grace I would never forget. I hated the packets of examination papers. Even in those days of peace I handled them as if they were explosive.

Brigadier Steele looked after me at the War Office. I was a hybrid, neither army, navy, nor airforce. Even though the military mind had organised skulduggery into commandos, special air services and combined operations, apparently there was still room between the interstices of legitimate warfare for bastard outfits such as mine. I knew the reason why; we were on the strength of no unit, and could be written on and written off with equal facility. We belonged to no-one; no-one could be charged with responsibility for us. Brigadier Steele had promised this would be the last job. 'The invasion's bound to come soon, Rhodes, and then you can go back to being a soldier.'

He was in no position to make such a promise. I was prepared to accept what the Brigadier must tell me to do in the name of expediency; I didn't expect always to be told the truth, and didn't therefore object if he should occasionally tell me expedient lies. But I had a right to demand that the mechanicals of our bastard existence, on which so much depended, would be impeccably effective. Tomorrow, I would go to London, to the War Office, and there play merry bloody hell. I was going to have the biggest row over that explosive they'd heard in a long time.

The amount Dodger had used should have blown a hole neat as a can opening, but it hadn't. Just what the hell did the boffins think they were playing at? The prescription had been quite specific; for once we had an exact description of our target. There was no reason at all why they couldn't turn up an explosive that would do exactly what we asked of it. Or so I thought.

I was going to take a troop of men into Europe to do a simple job. Every second we were over there those human lives would be under risk. We had planned everything, of course, but who has ever seen a paper plan that works exactly on the ground as you have drawn it on the board? I'd had enough of cock-ups.

'Remember Liebville?' I asked Ben.

He chuckled. 'She was lovely!' he said.

'Not that, you randy devil!'

Liebville is in the south of France, and the Maquis had discovered the Germans were making small parts for bomb fuses in a factory. We went over, Special Group 22. On the way across, the plane developed engine trouble and dumped us in the sea. We were supposed to meet a leader of the Maquis. Incredible though it seems, he overslept. Perfectly normal human error. He overslept. It threw the whole operation into chaos. We never did get to the factory, and were lucky to get out through Portugal. We were holed up in Lisbon, waiting for a plane to Ireland. Ben Bolding had been hidden in the home of a fado singer. As he said, she was lovely. He was glad to get out of Lisbon for a rest.

I was determined that 404 would not be another Liebville.

Up here on the moors, I was testing men's spirits to ensure they were of the finest calibre available. The boffins had nothing else to do but supply us with explosive that worked. What the hell did they think they were playing at?

'How thick will the concrete be?' Ben asked. His mind had been turning on the same problem.

'It was twelve inches thick when it was laid in 1941 – they might have poured a screed on top of that; the maximum thickness will be fifteen inches.'

'We'll never do it,' Ben said, 'and then we shall look like silly buggers, shan't we? It'll all be wasted.' 'We will do it,' I said quickly. 'You trust me... I'll make such a stink tomorrow.'

Ben smiled, relaxed on his seat. He'd heard me making a 'stink' in the past. 'Any coffee left, Major?' he asked.

With the Brigadier was Professor Challoner of Birmingham University, F.R.S.; a nervous little man called Sewidge from I.C.I., with picric-acid-stained fingers, halitosis, and the degree of Doctor of Science; and a full Colonel from the Royal Engineers with letters strung behind his name like bunting. 'The problem couldn't be more simple, it seems to my lay mind,' I said when the introductions had been completed and I had read their impressive qualifications from the typewritten sheet an A.T.S. girl had placed before me. The Brigadier wanted no nonsense – my little B.Sc. looked miserable in such a constellation. I was no more than a technician; my job was to see their laboratory experiments were made to work. They just damn well would *not* work! Not up on the Yorkshire Moors. There was a helluva lot of talk across the table about thrust and pressures, moments of forces, but when they got to electron parameters I'd had it. I daydreamed. Smoked. Drew bosoms of impossible size on the top page of my doodle pad. It was Doctor Sewidge who first observed my lack of interest.

'Can we ask the Major to contribute his thoughts in the matter?'

'It doesn't work. It's as simple as that. I'm not concerned to do a long involved research into why it doesn't work – I only want something that will work, and I need it soon!'

'We all accept that,' the Brigadier said, crisp as burned bacon rind, 'but we want to know what you suggest?'

'On the question of explosives, if this distinguished gathering has no suggestion to make I'd be foolish and presumptuous even to try. But here's a thought I've had. What do we usually do in the Army when we want an outrageous job done?'

The Brigadier smiled. 'We get an outrageous man to do it. That's why you're here!'

'But outrageous though I may be, Brigadier, I have no specialised knowledge of explosives and concrete cutting, and that, it seems to me, is vital. I've blown down bridges, blown up culverts, cut railway sleepers and lines, brought down overhead telephone systems, but I'VE NEVER CUT A HOLE IN CONCRETE!' I said each word slowly and carefully. All right, let them charge me with dumb insolence.

'I can see what he's getting at,' Professor Challoner said to relieve the tension. 'We ought to forget our theories, and look for someone who's had practical experience in civilian life of cutting holes in concrete with explosives. It should be easy to find such a person from the staff of one of these larger construction companies.'

But it wasn't, as they discovered. It was very easy to find men who'd mixed concrete under oil and water emulsion fifty fathoms deep in the Persian Gulf while smelling of Attar of Roses. But all the concrete had been *laid.* No-one had ever, it seemed, needed to *cut* it precisely and swiftly. We could find a hundred men who specialised in jack hammer techniques for *smashing* concrete to little pieces – but that took a compressor and a jack hammer, daylight in the middle of the High Street stuff. That early in the war, it seemed nobody had needed to *slice* concrete, swiftly. The military system boasted it could find anyone to do anything – poachers could cross country silently and I had my share of them. I had men could climb buildings – former steeplejacks. I had men could smell Germans a mile away. Ferrets give off a slight odour when they detect a rabbit – a ferret handler develops a nose on him like a bloodhound. Safe makers crossed the line and opened safes, motor mechanics dismantled vehicles, watch makers made sense of even the most delicate mechanism. We were trained to throw knives by a lad who'd thrown 'em at his wife for a living, and I once was taught to fall by a stunt man who'd worked with Charlie Chaplin and Buster Keaton, out in Hollywood. But we didn't have anyone who could blow a neat three foot diameter hole in concrete in the conditions under which we had to work.

I went back to Yorkshire.

'When we've worked it out or found someone,' the Brigadier promised, 'you can come back.'

PETER DERBY

Notice in a public lavatory – 'My Mother made me a queer.' Beneath it the words, pencilled in, 'If I send her the wool, will she make me one, too?' Not very funny, is it? My name is Peter Derby. I've got a million of them, all about queers. Like the Jews we seem to destroy ourselves, because we are what we are.

I don't know how *I* got to be this way. My private parts are possibly a little on the small side, but not noticeably so. Certainly at school no-one ever laughed at me or ridiculed me because of them. I've never been over-dominated by women – my Mother was a marvellous person and we got on very well together; but then my Pa was a marvellous person, too, and we got on very well together, too. Of course, he thought I'd done all the usual things, and so I imagine did she. He thought it very wise of me not to get married early, to wait until I came into a bit of money, from Grandpa's estate.

I know lots of girls. I played tennis with them, danced with them, even necked with them, but do you know, I just don't like the taste of a woman's mouth. It's as simple as that. I've explored their bodies to see what happens, to them and to me. Clinically speaking the experiment has been interesting. But nothing ever happens to me, if you know what I mean. Well, assuming you don't object to the anatomical details, I never get an erection. Not with a woman. I've had girls in my room at The House, and no fear of anyone coming in since we weren't that kind of family, and I've taken off all their clothes and really explored them. But nothing has ever happened to me. One time, I tried to put myself in. I wasn't hard, but I tried to get in thinking something might happen when I was inside. But I couldn't get the damn thing in. She was very understanding. Said: Don't worry, we'll try again some other time. We never did, of course. Yet the first time I saw Jamie Morrison in the shower I was as hard as a stallion. Now how do you account for that?

No traumatic experiences when I was a baby, no nanny forcing me back on to the pottie, no dominant mother, absolutely no desire to wear girl's clothing and yet, with a girl nothing, with a boy an indecent stalk!

Everything was fine, just fine until I met John. He owns a garage and Pa lent him money when he wanted to expand. John was not the sort of fella I'd take to socially. A bit common, if you know what I mean, though he did his best to hide it. I happened to meet him one day up at The House when he was talking to Pa, and frankly that was it. I really fell in love with him, in the most dreadfully sensual way. I wanted to hold him, fondle him, stroke him, I wanted to be with him all the time. We used to talk together on the telephone for as long as ninety minutes. Luckily he felt exactly as I did, though he'd been wise and had taken a wife for the sake of appearances. We used to meet all the time. Pa still thought I was being sensible protecting his investment. Well, then the war came and I knew I'd have to go, and so I joined the County Regiment. It meant I could live in the local barracks and still get in a bit of hunting from time to time. Pa was very good about the wine cellar and pheasants and things, and since John failed his medical (he had a flutter in his heart and I teased him it was love!), I had the best of both worlds, the new Army life and the civilian comforts I'd left behind.

Of course, we all thought the war would be over in fifteen months. One day John was at The House seeing Pa; Mother was there and had a few people in for bridge; I was orderly officer and would be going along later. During the afternoon the gas main fractured, or so they said at the inquest, and The House just blew up. Of course everyone thought it was a bomb and the anti-aircraft battery opened fire until they ran out of shells. They were all killed at The House.

I went wild for a month or two. In London. With guardsmen and sailors and anybody I could pick up.

Then I met this M.P. chap, who had me transferred to a job at the War Office – that's how I got my captaincy – and by that time I had become what the French call a pederast.

One night my M.P. friend had arranged a party. Six of us for dinner at his place in Victoria, and afterwards some new films he'd just acquired. They'd been smuggled out of Sweden by an escaping prisoner-of-war. My date couldn't come to the dinner party and one of the boys there rang someone for me. 'You'll love him,' he said, 'he's a virgin and he needs the money!' When the boy turned up, it was like seeing John again, John all over again. Love at first sight, I suppose. We had the meal and I noticed this boy Philip was drinking practically non-stop. We settled down with the brandy and watched the films. Afterwards we all went to bed.

Now, let me explain something. Whatever two adult people may want to do together is all right by me. I believe in freedom. Some of the things men and women do together I consider infinitely more degrading than the things two men or two women do together. And there's a lot less love about it. It happens that I prefer men to women, boys to girls. I find boys more attractive aesthetically than women. I think the male human form is much more beautiful than the female human form with those great bags of flesh hanging from her chest and wide hips. Breasts I find absolutely revolting. The whole point is freedom of choice. If a man prefers that sort of grossness, then let him. I don't. So you see, I don't feel guilty about being a homosexual.

It's important to understand that.

The following morning Philip woke up, as I had told him he would, with a terrible hangover. I gave him my cure, two eggs whipped up in milk with a large brandy, and he seemed better after that. We stayed in bed for a while caressing each other. I was reluctant to leave the bed, reluctant to let him go back to his barracks. Eventually he got up and I persuaded him to have a shower. He had such lovely feet, I'd spent hours just caressing his toes. After the shower he put on that terribly rough uniform, and had to go. Of course, I gave him a little present, but that's not important. I was convinced he hadn't been with me for the money – I was alive again and in love again, and all the horribleness of the last few months had disappeared. I still missed John, of course, I was still shaken by the loss of both my parents, but I knew that with Philip, some of the less creditable excesses of the past few months would be forgotten. I determined to take him to my tailor to have a decent uniform made. I made all sorts of wonderful and exciting plans.

That evening the police went to the flat in Victoria. They'd traced Philip there since he'd written down the address when he took the telephone call in the guard room, when we had telephoned to ask him to come to the party.

When Philip got back to his billet he took his rifle, loaded it with a bullet he'd been keeping as a souvenir, put the end of the barrel in his anus, and pulled the trigger. With his toe.

The M.P. had it hushed up, of course. He was very good at arranging things. He even got me into the Commandos. I felt I had to go somewhere to prove I was still a man.

I had no need to go back to the War Office. The War Office came to me in the person of Lieutenant Arthur Sywell, aged forty-two, heavily built and thick-set.

'It takes all sorts to make a world,' Ben Bolding commented, as we watched him climb out of the car bringing him from the station.

Arthur Sywell had policeman written all over him. One thing you couldn't tell about him on sight, however, was that he was a Bachelor of Science of Manchester University. He'd also made all the most difficult climbs in the Lake District, on Ben Nevis, and Snowdon, and was the country's leading expert on explosives, the illegal uses of. He was all copper!

Brigadier Steele spoke to me on the telephone, an hour after Lieutenant Sywell arrived.

'Where is he now?' the Brigadier asked.

'With the sergeant major, getting kitted out.'

'Good. Have you had a chance of a talk with him?'

'Yes, Brigadier, though only briefly.'

'What's your reaction?'

'A bit slow.'

'Don't be deceived. I wanted to send him up as a technical expert. He refused to come on that basis. Said he'd join you as a volunteer, just like the rest of 'em, subject to the same disciplines. If he's good enough, he stays with you to do the job. It's your decision. I think you might find him useful. If not, send him back. I can use him elsewhere.'

A transformation had taken place when Ben brought Lieutenant Sywell back from the quartermaster's. He was wearing a denim outfit, like those we all wore, without badges of rank. On his head he wore a woollen comforter. He had Innsbrucker boots, well broken in, and gaiters. In the sheath of his trousers, he carried a regulation knife. Now he looked less like a copper, more like a killer. I didn't hope for too much: it's no easy matter to break habits of a lifetime, and he'd been brought up on the lawful side of the book.

'It'll be a change for you,' I said.

'The other side of the fence?'

'Yes.'

'I can adapt to it, sir.'

'Can you adapt to this? I call you Arthur, you call me Major. You call the men by their

Christian names – though the use of the word Christian is purely academic, and they call you whatever they think fit, but, I hope, sir.'

'I get that, Major.'

'Brigadier Steele tells me you know a thing or two about explosions?'

'I've seen the results of a few.'

'Safe breakers? Bank robbers?'

'That's right.'

'Well, there's one fundamental difference, Arthur. A bank robbery, correct me if I'm wrong, usually takes place over a week-end, and the men give themselves ample time to prepare. We shall have exactly half an hour.'

'It makes a difference.'

'What's wrong with the explosive?'

'Nothing, Major.'

'Where does the fault lie?'

'With the men using it,' he said simply. This was not a man I'd rattle quickly. He was sitting on a hard chair across the desk from me, not moving.

'What's wrong with the men?' I said, pride offended.

'They don't know enough about explosives.'

'And *you* do?'

'I think I do.'

'Right, you get half an hour, anything you ask for that can be carried, and I shall expect to see a three foot hole in that concrete.'

Sam Levine and Dodger Bates went out of camp that evening; they returned with a sack and stains of undergrowth on their elbows and knees. In the sack were seven cock pheasants and a partridge. 'Got to leave the hens alone, haven't you, or there be no young 'uns for next year,' Dodger said. Sam had been an apt pupil. Even Harry Landon, and he had lived among game for years, approved of the birds.

'Going to eat or sell 'em?' he asked.

'What use is money where we're going? I need the energy.'

Dodger and Sam were sitting on their bunks plucking pheasants into a satchel when Lieutenant Sywell opened the door of the Nissen hut and stood there coughing tactfully. 'May I come in?' he asked Alf Milner, nearest the door.

'Watch it, coppers...' Sam said, his voice east end, low down.

Within seconds the pheasants and the sack were under the bed, the satchel of feathers hanging in a locker. Lieutenant Sywell walked slowly up the hut. At the far end

Corporal Taffy Andrews and Harry Landon had pushed their beds parallel to the wall to provide more space. Each was wearing blue PT shorts, socks and plimsolls. Each had a commando knife in his hand; they were practice-fighting.

'Don't let me interrupt anyone,' Sywell said. He stood near the stove watching Andrews and Landon as they crouched defensively. Harry moved small steps never off balance. Taffy moved larger, occasionally pouncing, hoping to get round the knife Harry held by its handle now down. It could slit a gut when it came up, and Taffy knew Harry was totally ruthless once he had it in his hand. All the boys knew that one day they may have to face a German ruthless as Harry, without mercy. There could be no better training. Harry, small steps, crowding Taffy back towards his bed, an inch at a time. Taffy knew it, darted to Harry's right side, but the low knife point still faced him on a hand and arm firm as a piston rod. Taffy danced left; Harry deftly flicked the knife across to his left hand.

'Stand still, you're not in the bloody ballet!' he said.

Sweat stood out on Taffy's brow as he crouched, right hand holding the knife

70

forward, left arm extended.

'If you think you're going to use that left hand to push my knife to one side I wouldn't bother,' Harry said, grinning. Then he pounced. His right arm swept up, across, round and down; pace forward faster than Taffy's eye could see, movement a blur of speed that left him gripping Taffy's hand carrying the now useless knife trapped clenched to his side iron hard. Harry's knife point was between Taffy's legs, the edge of the blade against his testicles.

'Want to become a choir boy?' Harry asked, still grinning. A shout of approval from the lads watching the fight. Dodger stood beside Lieutenant Sywell. 'Nobody can take one of Harry Landon, sir,' he said.

Harry pulled himself away from Taffy who stood there looking ruefully at his useless knife. 'You've got to develop your speed, Taffy,' Harry said kindly, 'and watch it when a man starts talking to you. The expression of his lips while he's talking hides what he's going to do.'

'You're too good for me.'

'Harry's too good for all of us,' Dodger said: but then he turned to Sywell, a crafty look on his face. 'Why don't you have a go against Landon, sir?'

Sywell glanced around, quickly. All had heard. No-one spoke, but each face carried the same statement: 'Yes, copper, let's see what you're made of.' He looked at Harry standing there supremely confident, and at that moment Taffy Andrews pushed his knife, handle first, into Sywell's hand. The circle about them was a ring of expectation. Harry tensed, ready, his hand dropped, blade point aimed at Sywell's middle, his left hand forward, his arm bent, rock steady iron hard.

Without appearing to look upwards, Sywell flicked the knife point first into the beam above his head. All eyes went to it in admiration. Sywell dived in under Harry's arm, twisted it palm uppermost, banged his shoulder into Harry's chest and pulled with all his strength. The cantilever of Harry's elbow was in the wrong direction for Harry to escape; he was carried helplessly forward up and over Sywell's shoulder in the oldest police throw of them all. As he went down Sywell straightened holding to Harry's wrist and Harry's shoulders and back hit the floor flat with a sound that reverberated through the hut. He plucked Harry's knife from his fingers, leaned across with his knee paralysing Harry's arm muscle and placed the point of the knife at Harry's throat.

'I was taking cutthroat razors off race gangs in Brighton long before this war,' he said quietly. He stood upright, flicked again, and Harry's knife stuck in the beam not an inch from that of Taffy Andrews. Now the men were all grinning at him; he'd won his crown of laurels. But for the grim look on his face, several would have slapped his back in approval.

'I came looking for a couple of volunteers to help me blow a hole in concrete,' he said. They all volunteered. He accepted Dodger Bates and Harry Landon.

'Now you can get back to plucking your pheasants,' he said to Sammy Levine, 'and the word is policeman, not copper!'

Together we drove out to the village in the jeep. Arthur Sywell examined the hole scabbed out of the concrete. I went and sat in the jeep. I would not be the one to blow the hole in the concrete on the job; let him do it first, and then he could replace the man who was to do the job. Dodger Bates was explaining to Arthur exactly how they had tried to blow the concrete.

When they were ready, I pulled them back out of the cellar.

I started my stop watch. 'Right, just the two

of you, and you have exactly thirty minutes starting from now.'

If any man was going to criticise my lads, he would need to justify that criticism by actions. 'Put up, or shut up,' that was my motto. Or as Ben Bolding liked to say, 'Piss, or get off the pot!'

They took twenty-five minutes to set the charge; four minutes longer than the previous slowest time.

When the explosion came, it was louder than anything I'd ever heard any of my men achieve. I looked at Ben. He shared my feelings. An almighty cloud of smoke came billowing out of the cellar, and fierce tongues of yellow and red flame. I waited until the smoke cleared, then went into the cellar. The scab he had blown in the ceiling was fifteen inches in diameter, six inches deep.

'Not much of a hole, is it?' I asked.

Arthur Sywell kept his temper. We drove back to the camp in silence.

'Do you still think the men are at fault?' I asked him when we were back in my office. He was furious, but had the sense not to show it. He knew, as I did, that he was on probation.

He asked my permission, then got on to the Ordnance Depot at Pateley Bridge from which we obtained our explosive supplies. Through them, he spoke to Dr Sewidge and the man at I.C.I. who had manufactured the explosive. He gave him the batch number, and the man checked his files and test reports.

'I guarantee that explosive is perfectly sound,' the man said. Arthur Sywell had asked me to listen on the extension earpiece. Like all boffins he was mortally offended we should criticise his work.

'It isn't all right,' Arthur insisted – 'it doesn't do the job, and that's the only criterion of what's all right and what isn't.'

'Look, you have two requirements. You want penetration, and you want silence. What Dr Sewidge and I have given you is a compromise, I'll grant, but it will still do the job.'

Together we set up explosions on the concrete 'tables' that had been erected, there above the Yorkshire Moors. We tried the explosive all ways. I tried, Dodger tried, Arthur Sywell tried. The only conditions I imposed were that the task should be completed in a half an hour and the only material to be used should be portable and relatively easy to procure.

We didn't pierce a single table.

Two days after the telephone call to I.C.I.,

I called a meeting in my office of Arthur Sywell, Peter Derby, the sergeant major, Dodger and Sam Levine. 'The purpose of this meeting is to try to find any reason I should not suggest to the War Office this job be cancelled. The boffins can plan as much as they like but unless we, the men actually involved, can do the job with the materials available in the stated time, the job should be cancelled. No-one likes to be a pessimist; especially when I've watched all you men putting so much effort into preparing yourselves; but I would be a fool to take you over there on the pious hope that everything will go all right.'

I looked around at them, one by one, inviting each to pluck from the air the one possibility I had overlooked. It was a forlorn hope.

'Couldn't we use twice the quantity of explosive,' the sergeant major asked, 'and take a chance on getting out?' It was a thing we'd done before, and the chance had come off. We blew a bridge an arms train was due to cross near the Dutch railhead at Genepp. As luck would have it, a plane came over as we were preparing the blow, and dropped a few bombs. The rail guards thought the explosion they heard was yet another bomb, and never guessed until it was too late that we had split the rails. We couldn't rely on bomber support for this job. 'Believe me, Ben, the quieter we are the better. This job depends on it. It's got to be as quiet as if we were blowing the High Street branch of the Westminster Bank on a Saturday night.'

We discussed several alternatives during the next twenty minutes; always we came back to the same snags. No noise, fast penetration, men in and quickly out again. I said it again – 'this time, we've got to be in and out again as quietly as if we were blowing the Westminster Bank.'

I saw a look come to Arthur Sywell's face. 'What is the deadline?' he asked, quietly.

'In forty-eight hours I have to tell the Brigadier to cancel the job, otherwise he will assume it's still on.'

'Give me that forty-eight hours?' he asked. 'If I can blow a hole in that concrete within forty-eight hours under the conditions laid down, can the job be put on again?'

'If you can do that, the job will never be off.'

'Give me the forty-eight hours, Major.'

He had something in his mind he didn't want to talk about, not at that meeting. I wouldn't press him.

'Right,' I said, 'you can have it.'

The meeting was adjourned, and we returned to basic training. Arthur Sywell made a call to the War Office, to Brigadier Steele, and within the hour the Brigadier called him back and gave him permission to carry on. Still I asked no questions. He left the camp in my own jeep, wearing the denim outfit in which we had tried the abortive explosive experiments. There was nothing military about him as he drove out of the gate; he looked more like an engine room stoker than an officer and a gentleman. I had a full report from him later of what happened. Apparently, he drove like a madman over the moors to Durham. The Military Police stopped him once and called the camp to verify his story – they assumed he had stolen the jeep and was AWOL.

Five hours later he was being shown into the Governor's Office of Durham Prison. Waiting for him, as he had requested, were Fred Pike and Joe Stanhope. As soon as he arrived, again as he had requested, the Governor left his office and shut the door behind him. Arthur Sywell sat on a hard chair in front of the Governor's desk. Both men were looking warily at him. They were old sparring partners.

Fred smiled at him. 'Good afternoon, Mr

Sywell,' he said, 'fancy seeing a nice girl like you in a place like this, and what lovely weather we're having for the time of the year!'

'That job you did in Hatton Garden, Fred? How did you get through the walls? You're the only two men in the country could cut through concrete like that!'

'Where's Hatton Garden, Inspector?' he asked, a look of cherubic innocence on his face.

Both men were in their early thirties, two of the best safebreakers in the business. Arthur Sywell had put them inside when they tried to 'do' a woollen mill in Bradford to get the payroll.

'I've got a job for you lads,' he said, 'if you're both man enough to take it. Mind you, it'll need guts.'

'What's in it for us?' Fred Pike asked. Of the two men he was usually the leader – he'd had a rough and tumble upbringing in Bristol by the docks, and this had given him a fierce independence. Joe Stanhope, on the other hand, had come to crime from greed. His family life in Crosby near Liverpool had been eminently respectable, and he had lacked for nothing.

'There's a decent life for a start, and there's a free pardon. You can walk out of this prison with me today, and if you do this one job, that's your lot as far as the past is concerned.'

'And the job, is it straight or bent?'

'It's a war job.'

'That means it's bent!'

Joe Stanhope was smiling. 'You know, Inspector,' he said, 'you ought to try it in here sometime. We have a marvellous life. Three squares a day, and all found. Our own air raid shelter. Sometimes I think of those poor devils conscripted into the foot sloggers, marching up and down a barrack square with a sergeant major bellowing at them. I'm quite happy to be here in my little nest.'

'Hang on a minute … this job, where is it?' Fred asked.

'In Europe, that's all I can tell you.'

'Where the Germans are? You must be out of your mind.' Joe laughed. 'I'll stay here, thank you.'

'Hang on, will you?' Fred said. 'What kind of a job is it? Obviously, it must be a safe or something, otherwise why should they need us. Is it a safe?'

'I can't tell you.'

'Is it a bank vault?'

'I can't tell you.'

'Well, you'd better make up your mind,'

Fred said. 'We're not going to take part in something unless we know all about it, now are we? So you've either got to open your trap a bit wider, or shut it completely.'

'It's a vault.'

'A bank vault?'

'Sort of.'

'What do you mean, sort of? Is it a bloody vault, or isn't it?'

'Yes, it's a vault, but not a bank vault. There's a bank next door, but we're going into the vault behind it.'

'Pity. If you'd said we was going into the bank, we might be interested. Any money in this vault?'

'I don't know.' Could he risk a white lie? By the time they found out, it could be too late. 'There might be.'

'"There might be." What do you take us for?' Joe asked.

'Well, I'll tell you what I take you for, since you ask me. I take you for a couple of fellows who've gone wrong in the past, and since that time have worn a badge that says "criminal – keep away." I think that if you had a chance to get rid of that badge once and for all, you might enjoy doing so. I think you're also a couple of Englishmen and you might, just for once in your life, enjoy doing something on the right side.' He stopped. Joe had extended his left arm, and was moving his right hand across it as if playing a violin. 'Hearts and Flowers, Inspector,' he said. 'We're branded, and you know it. We're criminals, lags, gaolbirds – and we always will be.'

'I'm giving you the only chance you'll ever get to wipe that out in one go,' Arthur Sywell said.

'Bollocks!'

'No,' Fred said, 'let him talk – I think he's got something.'

'But I don't want anything. I'm very comfortable in here, thank you, living in the style to which I have become accustomed, as they say.'

'We get a free pardon, Inspector?' Fred persisted.

'That's right, and we tear up the files. Born again.'

'Just one job in Europe somewhere?'

'Just one job.'

'And you get us there, and bring us back?'

'That's right.'

'And when we get back, we get a discharge from the Army – I gather we'd be joining the Army or something?'

'If you wanted one, we would give you a discharge. Or alternatively, you could stay in a cushy number in the Army, in the R.A.S.C. driving lorries, or something like that.'

'This job, what does it involve?'

'That's something I can't tell you, except that it means blowing a hole in concrete.'

'Is that all?'

'That's all.'

Fred thought about it for a long minute. Then he took hold of Joe's arm and walked him over to the window. There they talked together earnestly in low voices. From time to time Joe would look round at the Inspector. Arthur Sywell was glad he had not put on his full military uniform. He had guessed, correctly as it turned out, they would have had a bellyful of uniforms and might welcome seeing him dressed as one of the boys.

Finally they turned round.

'It's like this,' Fred said, 'we'd like to do it but we can't make up our minds if you're on the level about the pardon. We'd hate to do the job and then find ourselves whistled back inside. If we get the pardon first, we'll do the job. And we want a lawyer to draw up the agreement.'

Arthur Sywell could have laughed out loud. Two convicts, without a notion of legality between them, a totally amoral pair of ruffians, and they wanted an agreement drawn up by a lawyer! He walked across and opened the door. The Governor was sitting in his outer office, his face thunderous. It was quite apparent he didn't like this intrusion.

'I'd like them released right away,' Arthur Sywell said.

The Governor was cold and formal. It was only because he had received a telephone call from the Home Office that he didn't make his feelings more clearly known. 'Full cooperation' the call had requested. Right, full cooperation it was. Arthur Sywell left the prison fifteen minutes later in a jeep with the two men, without a guard. Fred Pike and Joe Stanhope, however, were handcuffed to each end of a chain which passed through the bed of the jeep seat. 'Since you want to play it legally, Arthur said, 'that's the way we'll do it. I'll take the cuffs off when we've worked out a legal agreement with your solicitor. You can take the cuffs off to sign the contract, and that's the last you'll see of them.'

The prison governor insisted he sign for the handcuffs.

I was outside my office when the jeep came in through the gates with its two passengers, and Arthur Sywell driving. The guard on the gate stopped him when he saw the two strangers, but Arthur vouched for them. I had spoken on the telephone with him before he left Durham, and as requested had brought a solicitor from Ilkley, and a Colonel from the Judge Advocate's Department.

The jeep drove across the camp square and stopped outside my office. The two men in the back didn't look around them, uninterested in their surroundings. Arthur jumped from the driving seat and bent over each passenger's lap. They rubbed their wrists as he released them, and I caught a glimpse of the handcuffs. I had a moment of misgiving – other men walked into this camp as volunteers; these two, doubtless former 'associates' from Arthur Sywell's police past, had the appearance of being shanghaied. He refastened the handcuffs before he led the men inside my office. I didn't like it, didn't like it at all. Unless he was prepared to remove those handcuffs I had no intention of meeting the men. If they joined the unit they must do so willingly with no physical restraint. I couldn't spend my time in Europe locking and unlocking handcuffs. Nor could I afford the time it would take to have them watched. If they came with us, they'd travel as we did, free as the air.

The troop was on the short range at the

bottom of the camp, practising knife throwing, bows and arrows, steel pin throwing. I went down and watched them. They were all becoming remarkably proficient. There's a technique to throwing a knife or a steel needle completely unlike dart throwing. You throw the knife or needle point first, but your hand moves in a flat trajectory, and the final jerk just before you release the projectile is the one that gives speed. Accuracy is something you can't teach. Men either have it or don't – something to do with the coordination of the eye and the arm muscles. If you have that coordination, with practice you'll hit the target every time in a circle not more than two inches diameter. If you haven't that ability, you might as well pack it in. No man could qualify for 404 without that ability. Silence was going to be of paramount importance, the silence that only a knife can give.

I arrived back in my office as the men were signing the agreement the two solicitors had hurriedly drawn up. It had been typed by my own orderly, who was an A.T.S. girl seconded from the War Office. Later that day, an official from the Home Office would arrive in camp, and another officer from the Judge Advocate's department, an impromptu

'Court' would be held, and the whole matter would be legalised.

I stifled my grave misgivings about the two new men, and prepared to keep an open mind until I had seen them in action. That came at six o'clock on the same evening. Pike and Stanhope were shown the concrete floor of the village house, and their eyes lit up when they were handed the plastic explosive. Pike chose a fresh section of the concrete and made ready his charge. Then he asked us all to leave the cellar, except Joe Stanhope.

'If you see how I do it,' he said, 'you won't have any use for me, will you, and I could be back in Durham before bedtime tonight.'

I saw the logic of that and ordered all the men out.

Pike and Stanhope walked leisurely out of the cellar ten minutes later. They'd cut five minutes off the time it normally took Dodger and Sam Levine to prepare. They walked to the corner and there they stood, away from the blast. When it came, the sound was considerably less than the previous explosions, more a low crump. No black cloud of smoke billowed out of the cellar, and there were no tongues of yellow flame. I was the first inside the cottage – a gaping hole was in the floor, two feet six at least in diameter, easy to get all the men through. The ground floor room was a shambles where the concrete lumps had been projected against the ceiling and the walls. Very little damage however had been done in the cellar.

The other men crowded into the cellar. I looked down on them from the ground floor room. Fred and Joe both looked modestly at their efforts; Dodger and Sam were full of enthusiastic approval, pumping them on the back. I caught the Lieutenant's eye, anxious still and questioning.

'Okay,' I said to him, 'the job's on.'

The whoop from the cellar almost brought the remains of the plaster from the ceiling.

I called for the records of all the men, all the notes the training officers and I had made of each man's successes and failures, and settled down to make my final selection. After the first initial excitement a pall of gloom spread over the men's quarters. One Nissen hut had been set aside as a canteen for the men. It contained a billiard table and a dartboard, and was served by the N.A.A.F.I. and volunteers from the W.V.S in the nearest village, Grimsback. A few men wandered over to the hut through the dark of the camp, but there was no joy there. One of the W.V.S. normally would have spent the evening fending off the good-natured suggestions of the soldiers. Not one of them made a pass at her this evening. Supper was served in the mess hall at seven o'clock – liver, onions, mashed potatoes, and suet dumpling for sweet, covered in treacle. The men sat toying with their food. At eight o'clock I switched off the light in my office and went out. The Officers' Mess occupied one end of a Nissen hut, the other end being our kitchen. A further Nissen hut contained sleeping quarters for all three officers – the training officers were based on the camp outside Ilkley. As I walked through the ranks of Nissen huts to my own quarters, the men drifted out onto the street. In my hand I carried a buff folder which each of them knew instinctively contained a list of the selected names. The C.S.M. occupied half of the Nissen hut nearest to the Officers' Mess. He too was sitting in the doorway. As he saw me coming down the street he got off his chair and walked outside. He was not wearing a hat. As I came past he stood to attention. Looking up the street you could see the silent knots of men, all standing rigidly to attention.

'When will you tell them, Major Rhodes?'

the C.S.M. asked softly. 'They won't get any sleep until they know.'

I stopped. This was part of the job I hated. How do you distinguish between the men who, on the surface, have been trained to the same pitch of perfection? How do you tell a man 'No, I don't think your temperament will fit in with what we have to do'? Damn it, these men were all volunteers, they all wanted desperately to come with me. Of course, there were simple rules – you don't take a man who wants to go for the wrong motives – you avoid the Oxbridge Death or Glory boys, the sadists, the brutes, the cowards who didn't yet know it, the men whose wives exerted an extra pull on their loyalties. But how do you tell the good man he isn't quite good enough? How do you tell the eager man he isn't quite adept enough? I turned round and faced them. The C.S.M. moved his hands quickly and all the stationary figures jumped suddenly to life, running into a half circle in front of me. There was no disorderly scramble. All stood 'at ease', but not 'easy.'

All, I noticed, were wearing the coveted green beret. Ben Bolding had donned his too.

'I can only take twelve men with me,' I

said, as soon as they had formed up. 'But I've selected twenty from which to pick that final twelve. I shan't do that until just before we leave. I'd like to keep you all, but from now on the training has to be so intensified I can't afford the time to deal with more than twenty. All you men are good,' I said, 'and that has made my job of selection harder than I've ever known it to be. The ones I haven't selected must not feel that, in any way, I am saying they were inadequate to the job we have to do. I merely think the twenty I have selected will do the job more safely, more quickly, more effectively.'

My voice carried on the night air. Fred Pike and Joe Stanhope had been put in a barrack room with six other men. I could see them standing among the six men, a part of the entire group of men before me. Faces leapt at me in the gloom, incidents from the arduous weeks of training, names of men, personal foibles I had found in them.

'Now, as to the future. The men I have selected will stay here in the camp with me, the other men will be sent home first thing in the morning on leave. Any man who wants to go on leave tonight can do so, or there's a dance down in Timble – there will be transport laid on. The selected men, of course, will not leave camp, since the training resumes at five o'clock in the morning. I'm not going to give you any pep talk. I shall merely say thank you for volunteering for this assignment. Sergeant Major.'

'Yes, sir?'

I opened the folder. 'This is the list of men who don't go to the dance in Timble,' I said. The crowd tension was broken, and faces cracked in smiles.

'Right-o, you lads,' the sergeant major called, 'now listen to me. I'll read the list once, and once only, so pin your lugs back.'

The company sergeant major knew what he was doing; in a flat military voice he called out without pause a list of twenty names.

'Right-o, you lot,' he called out when the list was complete, 'fall out and double away to bed. And keep your hands above the blankets. The rest of you, how many want transport to a dance in Timble?'

Without exception, they raised their hands.

'Rendezvous at the top of the camp by the guard room in thirty minutes, okay. Right, dis-miss!'

I turned to go into my quarters.

'Do I go dancing, Major?' Ben Bolding asked.

I took another sheet of paper from the file

and handed it to him. It was headed OFFI-CERS FOR 404. On it was my own name and that of Captain Derby, Lieutenant Arthur Sywell, and Company Sergeant Major Ben Bolding, MM. 'Get back in time for parade at five o'clock in the morning and the night's your own,' I said.

DODGER BATES

Bates, Dennis Geraint Roscoe, only son of a Maidstone butcher and his wife; conceived within a week of his father's return from the First World War in 1918; celebrated his twenty-first birthday in a N.A.A.F.I. can-teen in Dover, waiting for a boat to take him to France with the British Expeditionary Force in early December, 1939.

Dennis Bates went to Maidstone Gram-mar School, and took a school certificate and matriculation with six distinctions. On the day he was due to return from summer holidays – they'd all been to Scarborough for two weeks – to start his two years of studying for the higher school certificate, he went to the side of the old Maidstone coaching road with no more than he stood up in, as they say, and thumbed a lift to London. He never returned home.

When the Salvation Army eventually traced him he was sailing as a deckie out of Fleetwood – trawlers for the Grimson Line – earning four pounds a week including his share of the catch. Since he refused to attend night school while ashore, refused to study in his few brief hours off-watch on board, he had no chance of getting a mate's or a skipper's ticket. 'Bloody waste,' Old Grimson said, each time he signed him on again for thirty-eight days as a deckie.

His mother and father travelled all the way to Fleetwood in the desperately gay summer of 1939 to try to persuade him to return home. A friendly dockside radio operator keyed the message to the skipper of the *Marigold,* and Dennis jumped ship at the harbour mouth. He never collected the few belongings he kept in digs in Aisley Road, Fleetwood, never claimed his pay nor share of the catch money, and was never seen in Fleetwood again. His mother and father waited forty-eight hours, then returned home with the money in an envelope. When they arrived in Maidstone his father cleared the room that had belonged to Dennis, and burned everything in it before turning it into a workshop for his marquetry. Until Dennis's mother died two years later his name was never mentioned in that house. When Mrs Bates died – of a broken heart the neighbours said – Mr Bates paid for a personal message in the *Telegraph, Express* and *Mail.* 'Dennis Geraint Roscoe Bates. Regret to inform your mother passed away. Father.' He never got a reply. He had installed a walk-in fridge in his butcher's shop in Maidstone in 1939 – one of the many improvements against the day he hoped Dennis would take over. In 1942 he stumbled in the fridge late one evening, the door closed, and they found him next morning frozen to death.

In 1942 Dennis was in the Royal Fusiliers stationed at Brixham. In the interim he had travelled to France, returned in a small boat, and was now taking a course as a driver. Dodger, as he was now known, was six feet tall and weighed eleven stones. His fair hair defied combing, and he had grown a blond moustache. He was good at throwing a dart, at drinking, at boning boots and blanco-ing equipment. He had an enormous appetite, an immense stamina arrived at and cultivated on the four hour dog watches trawling off the coast of Iceland, and a slow temper. He was a pathological outsider. He talked to no-one in the barrack-room, answered in the briefest possible way when asked a direct question, and never volunteered information about himself.

When the M.T. course was finished, Dodger was posted to a unit of the Royal Fusiliers at Crossgates near Leeds in Yorkshire, whose main task was to guard a munitions factory into which parts of the Woolwich Arsenal had been evacuated. Dodger's job kept him away from the other men of the unit. He sat perpetually behind the wheel of a lorry. Even when Dodger had no official assignment, you would very often find him up there, just sitting. Whichever lorry he took over was always the cleanest and best maintained lorry in the unit. The Army has a maintenance system for its vehicles, and a driver can usually run through the procedure in a matter of minutes each day. When Dodger wasn't driving or sitting in the cab, he would be going through the maintenance drill, point by point. After a spell on the heavy lorries, Dodger was given the pick-up trucks to drive. He didn't much care for this, since it put him in more intimate contact with passengers, many of whom insisted on talking to him. Best of all he liked to drive the Commanding Officer, a Lieutenant-Colonel dredged up from between-the-wars retirement. The Colonel never talked with the drivers. The others resented it – to Dodger it was paradise. The Colonel began of habit to select Dodger to drive for him, and Dodger's immaculate pick-up truck, which shone like a civilian car despite the coarsely applied camouflage paint, was frequently to be seen parked outside the Commanding Officer's billet.

Everything would have been fine if human nature hadn't been as it always is – if the silent colonel and his equally silent driver could have been left to themselves to travel the byways of wordless thought. But the other drivers saw in Dodger's preferment a threat to themselves and their positions.

Dodger was never miserable or dour; he carried a tireless smile that gradually imposed itself on all the other drivers. He was regarded, at first, as being a 'bit thick'. This gave way to an accusation of 'slyness'. It came to a head one Sunday, when Dodger had been warned by the Commanding Officer they would be taking a trip to Selby. The pick-up was ordered for 1400 hours. Dodger parked it outside the Commanding Officer's hut at 1345, gleaming bright. The tank was full of petrol, the sump full of oil, the radiator and battery filled with water. The spark plugs and points had been cleaned with meticulous care, the pressure of each tyre exactly matched its opposing one. At ten to two another driver came alongside in a fifteen hundredweight lorry.

'You've left your work ticket on the bench behind the door in the garage,' he said.

Dodger patted his top pocket. 'Pull the other one!' he replied, his smile never varying.

The second driver came along on a motor bicycle. 'Thank God I caught you before you left,' he said. 'You forgot to sign the petrol requisition and the M.T.O.'s hopping mad.'

Dodger merely smiled and shook his head.

The driver smiled and shook *his* head in imitation. 'You'll be for the high jump,' he said, 'if you don't get back and sign it.'

Dodger shook his head and smiled.

As the driver rode away on the motor-cycle he called – 'Your nearside back tyre is down, you know.'

Dodger smiled.

He wouldn't have smiled if he had seen the third driver standing by the back of the pick-up while the second driver had been talking to him. The third driver poured a half a milk bottle of piss into Dodger's petrol tank.

The Colonel was furious when the pick-up broke down ten miles on the way to Selby, with the nearest telephone box over a mile away.

The next day Dodger put in his application to join the Commandos. The first initiative test that Dodger was ever given, by a million to one chance, was to break into the Ordnance Factory at Barnbow near Crossgates. The unit of the Royal Fusiliers was located within the Ordnance Factory barbed wire perimeter. Dodger broke into the factory, stole the day's production log as a souvenir, and paid a call on the cookhouse of the Royal Fusiliers detachment Motor Transport Pool.

Once in there, he unbuttoned his trousers over the porridge that would be heated for breakfast for the drivers. There was a lot of piss – he'd been saving it!

Special Group 404 had been designed and trained for one job. All the signals data for the German Western Army were stored in one centre in Liège, Belgium. In one vault were all the code systems, code books, code machine lock-systems, frequencies, and special transmission setting patterns of the entire Army. The vault was part of an innocuous-looking building on the outskirts of the town. Down the road was a small underground ammunition dump, and a barracks containing well over a thousand German Occupation troops. The area was industrial with a large number of factories engaged on munitions and other engineering works. Before the war this area had been industrial on one bank of the river, residential on the other, with the homes of the industrialists on walled family estates. Now the estates were commandeered for occupation by the officers of the German Army, for hospitals, Signal Centres, Army Headquarters. The whole area was a complex of military activity. At the very heart, absolutely impregnable or so German Intelligence thought, was the Signals Data Storage Centre. It had been constructed of concrete four feet thick, poured over one inch thick prestressed steel braces set one foot apart; the box had been constructed on two floors, with the storage vaults below, the offices above. The work of constructing the vault had been carried out in 1941 by a forced Belgian labour gang, shipped off, immediately the job was completed, to Germany. One of them, however,

Roget Belfière, escaped from the German labour camp in 1943 and made his way across country back to Liège. When he arrived he got in touch with the underground.

Early in 1941, Roget Belfière had gathered a small group of partisans who refused to surrender with their country to the Germans. One night they penetrated the outer perimeter of a forbidden zone in which a number of Belgians were working in forced labour gangs. Belfière's plan was to steal petrol, stored in a shed within the perimeter. All went well and they established a line passing the five-gallon jerrycans out of the storage shed and into a pit dug by the forced labour gang for an unknown purpose. They planned to take the cans the rest of the distance during the following night. According to the leader of the forced labour gang, no-one had been near this pit during the previous four days. It was just his bad luck that the following day, the German Workmaster ordered them to pour the pit four feet deep with concrete, with one inch steel rods laid in the concrete to strengthen it. The Belgians were left on their own to do the job, and the petrol cans were piled in a square in the centre of the pit three feet high and twelve feet across, and wet concrete was poured on the tarpaulin that hid them. When the German Workmaster came to inspect the job, he saw a depth gauge at the side of the pit marked to a depth of four feet. He probed the concrete round the edge with an iron rod, and pronounced himself satisfied.

Four hundred five-gallon cans were hidden under that concrete, enough to keep the partisans up in the hills of the Ardennes going for six months or more.

Later that evening, the same work gang planted a bomb under the petrol store from which they had taken the cans; the Germans never knew that four hundred cans were missing.

It had been their intention to lift the petrol cans out of the still wet concrete during the night, but this proved impossible, since work on the wall had already started. By the next day, the concrete had set, and the petrol cans were sealed in, or so they thought, for ever. The knowledge of the whereabouts of the petrol cans was carried to Germany with the forced labour gang. Roget Belfière was taken not a month later.

When he returned to Liège in 1943, he told the underground this story, and a tunnel was constructed under the floor of the building which by then had grown on the site. Once under the building, it was a simple matter to dig upwards until they came to the petrol cans and remove them one by one. It was not important to the partisans at the time that the floor out of which they picked the petrol cans was only fourteen/fifteen inches thick in its centre and contained no steel bars. It wasn't until Belfière learned late in August 1943 of the significance of the building, that he began to plan a way into it. Through its soft underbelly via their tunnel was the obvious route, if only they could blow the concrete.

Let the Germans know that vault had been blown, and confusion would certainly be caused to the entire German Western Army signals system. But, if someone could get into that vault and out again, without the Germans knowing, if only for a few hours, the information could successfully be used to eavesdrop on a thousand coded conversations. The disposition of the entire Western Army could be uncovered. Those few hours between the vault being blown and the Germans discovering the loss were vital.

Special Group 404 was the instrument chosen to carry out that plan, and I was chosen to lead it. The first detailed briefing took place in a house along the canal in Maida Hill, in the part of London some joker euphemistically had called Little Venice. We got into and out of the house two doors further up and walked through a long corridor built below ground. The four times I went there, that corridor was an inch deep in canal water, and rats scuttled along it. The briefings themselves took place in the first floor drawing-room; deep magenta velvet curtains, and window frames that would need a blowtorch to burn away the accumulated brown and bottle green paint of ages. The room cried out for long light curtains, a dry clean carpet, furniture hand-picked from auctions held in country parsonages all over the country, and a cool slim lady. It got perspiration, fat A.T.S., unnameable cigarettes and the lung gasping odour of boffins' curly cut tobacco. It also got Sandy, a young R.A.M.C. captain psychologist, five feet four inches of real woman.

Many men have started a dynasty on a shorter experience. The first official meeting lasted five hours. I was conscious of them all appraising me throughout it. Brigadier Steele's protégé, I was unknown to them except by his recommendations, and that didn't mean a great deal to these back room theorists. What they wanted was a text book hero, stock answers to typical situations, the Higher National Certificate mentality. Every statement was a loaded question, every question a psychological death trap. They were father and mother to 404; I felt like its untried nanny. I answered their questions the only way I knew how, bluntly and from my own personal experience. When the session ended, they scurried away to their gnawing boards. Brigadier Steele and Sandy stayed behind.

'I thought that you and Captain Noble here might take a bite with me?'

He lived in a charming house in Wellington Square, off the King's Road. It was a tall house, with an elegant sitting-room on the first floor. The dining-room was on the ground floor at the front; the kitchen behind it. His batman served as a butler; his batman's wife was cook to the household. We had a simple yet wholly delightful meal – a chicken cooked in wine with a tomato sauce, and vegetables brought 'from our place in the country'. And the choice of wine was superb.

The Brigadier's wife was totally charming, but I cannot even remember her face, so bemused was I with Captain Sandy Noble, R.A.M.C., whose face is etched in my mind with unfading precision; I can remember it exactly as if I had spent the intervening years gazing at a photograph. When dinner was over, we went out into gloomy London. There had been an air raid alert during dinner, but the Brigadier told us he always ignored them. Anyway, he wasn't going to have a lot of people camping out in his wine cellar, pushing up the temperature. I really think he meant it.

He had offered us the use of his Humber and driver. With a quick glance at Sandy, I said I preferred to walk a while. She immediately agreed. We walked along King's Road, into Sloane Square, towards the West End of London. We didn't talk. After about half a mile we held hands. I knew a bar in the Edgware Road. Part of a pub, not many people went into it. We stopped a taxi and he took us there. I ordered two beers, and we sat on a bench together, behind one of those small tables. Our knees were touching, so small was the table.

'Where will you stay?' she asked.

'I usually go to the St Martin's Hotel.' During the war it was a transit camp hotel for officers. The only snag was that it booked up early in the evening. The time was now ten o'clock.

'I have a flat in Warrington Crescent,' she said. 'You can stay with me if you want to.'

When the pub closed at half-past ten, we took a taxi to her flat. It had a very large sitting-room, a smaller bedroom at the back, and a kitchen and bathroom. In the sitting-room was the largest sofa I have ever seen.

We sat on it together. 'You had a bad day today,' she said, 'but you came through it well.'

'Load of bastards,' I growled.

'You're the most quietly aggressive man I've ever met,' she said. She traced her finger down the side of my jaw; I was scowling no doubt at the memory of the boffins. 'You mustn't mind them,' she said. 'It's a beastly life to compose a tune and see someone else go away to play it!'

'It's time they learned to get over it,' I said. 'For two pins I'd have told them what they could do with their job.'

'You're such a perfect subject for jealousy. You're tall, and most of them are short; you're very colourful, and most of them are pale grey; you're alert, strong, vigorous and most of them possibly wake up each morning with a hacking smoker's cough and heartburn.' My unpleasant memories of the day had vanished, soothed away by the touch of her fingers. I turned to her on the sofa. When we came in she had taken off her military jacket and tie and now was sitting there in her khaki shirt and skirt. She had kicked off her shoes and her knees were drawn up on the sofa. I put my arm about her shoulders and drew her towards me.

'I'll bet you're disgustingly healthy in the morning,' she said.

'Is that why you invited me to stay, so that you can give me a physical check-up after breakfast?'

'Not after breakfast,' she said. 'Before!'

Neither of us slept much that night. We went to bed early, but we spent most of the night talking together, and making love. It had never occurred to me before that making love would be a part of living. It had always seemed something you step out of life to do; something either transcendentally good, or brutishly abnormal. On the one hand you'd be so carried away by passion you wouldn't truly recall the details of the actual experience, on the other it'd be so sickeningly animal you'd long to scrub yourself in neat carbolic to wash away the vileness. With Sandy, it was neat, precise, totally satisfying but somehow pleasingly cynical. I had neither need nor desire to close my eyes while we loved; I wanted to see her face, to look into her eyes, to know her.

'You're a wonderful man,' she said once during the night. 'You have the strength of a lion and the tenderness of a kitten.'

I fell in love with Sandy during that night, and she, I thought, with me. Certainly I had never hoped so completely to explore nor to expose myself to any woman.

'There's a magic about two people together,' I said to her, 'that no one person can ever know. Hidden in the mind are so many small sacred recesses; that's something I imagine you as a psychologist know all about; but I'm not talking about the sicknesses, the miseries, the abnormalities, I'm talking about little quiet pools of possibility, like small water holes on the top of a moor; the heather and the gorse draw their nourishment from the rain, but they draw character and substance from the little pools of water. That's why the heather and the gorse are different on each part of the moor.'

Her face clouded. 'Robin,' she said, 'there's a war on, and you're in the most dangerous part of it. Don't let us go too far into each other.'

'You're like that with me, a pool from which I could draw substance. I didn't know you were there, on the top of the moor, but now that I know you I mean to drink deeply.'

She leapt upon me and forced me to make love to her with a new violence. Like a fool I imagined my words had caused the reaction in her; now I realised that all she wanted to do was to stop me talking in that way. Strength of a lion. I needed it that night.

We had breakfast early, and set off together to walk the few hundred yards to Little Venice and my first day of briefing.

It took ten of them. And Sandy. I could see that since the meeting the day before they had agreed to accept me. I had passed the viva examination, now we could embark on the practical.

The plan was simple, the way I liked them. I would be allowed ten men, and could make up my own mind what rank those men held. I could have a free hand in their selection provided I satisfied myself that each could fulfil at least three roles, none of which was particularly onerous. We would go in by parachute. 'You will appreciate,' the Brigadier said, 'that the number of ten men has been chosen to allow you to lose two,' as dry as his wine of the previous evening.

'We rely, of course,' Mr Stamford, the movement planner hastily added, 'on you not being one of those two.' A ripple ran across the table. Oh, hilarious bloody mirth, a boffin's made a joke.

The local unit of the partisans' movement, under the command of Roget Belfière, had promised to guide us into Liège.

'This partisan group,' I asked. 'They've been checked and double checked?' I once dropped into Holland to do a job with the aid of the local boys; one of their number was a traitor and I finished up in a small boat on the North Sea, more dead than alive.

'They've been checked most carefully; they'll be checked continuously until you arrive.'

We'd make our way by bicycle to the Signals Data Storage Centre. 'It's amazing how inconspicuous a man on a bicycle can be,' Stamford said in his thin, dry, high-pitched voice. I don't give a damn whether we ride on bicycles or elephants, just so long as we get there! He'd probably gone into a Yoga trance to work that one out. What has wheels and doesn't make a noise and is in plentiful supply in Belgium? That ruled out rickshaws.

'You can't miss the S.D.S.C.,' the buildings' boffin broke in. 'It's the ugliest building in Christendom. If you knew the agony

I've been through, just looking at the photograph.'

'I don't give a damn if it's turn of the century Georgian, with tessellated tiles in the hallway.'

I could feel Sandy looking at me, sense the warning.

We'd blow a hole in the floor, then leave the back way, again by bicycle. The partisans would pick us up in a lorry, and we'd be driven to a valley where a plane would land to bring us home. It would be a glorified Cook's tour! Ten men and me. When we got back to England, they'd turn the whole mess of code secrets over to the Intelligence, and we'd get breakfast with hot crumpets!

'This doesn't strictly concern you, old man,' the communications boffin condescendingly said, 'but we shall have an I and Sigs set-up waiting for you at an airport in Essex. They'll have been wire recording off the air for the previous twenty-four hours. Once they get hold of your information, they'll be able to read the whole lot like Winnie the Pooh. You won't forget to bring the papers back with you, will you?' I itched to commit him to a short course of surgery, with my hand wielding the knife.

'I'll try to remember,' I assured him.

It got a laugh. Sid Field would have died the death with such an audience.

My mind was storing the details of the plan as they outlined it. It was, as they had said, delightfully simple. I liked it chiefly because it depended on no one man.

'The actual explosion that will cut a hole in the floor is timed for four o'clock, in the morning,' the Brigadier said. I stole a quick glance at Sandy; she blushed slightly and looked away. She had woken me at four o'clock in the morning. 'Four o'clock's a terrible hour,' she said, 'when life's at its lowest ebb.' I comforted her, at her 'lowest ebb'. Later, during our fourth night together, she told me she'd never been able to sleep with me beside her, and always by four o'clock had been screaming for human companionship.

Sandy must have picked the time of the raid; after all, psychological factors were her pigeon, weren't they?

Once the general plan had been outlined, we went back over details. The tunnel had been blocked by the partisans but we could get in down a flight of stairs the Germans didn't know existed. We'd be under the Data Centre, in a hollowed out cellar. Once through the concrete floor we'd jam the door on the inside. It had a bank vault lock, apparently, and one they wouldn't open quickly. We'd leave the partisans to reconcrete the hole in the floor, and get out quickly. By the time the Germans got into the Data Centre, Intelligence would have been decoding secret conversations for anything up to forty-eight hours. With luck, we could have won the war!

'One flaw. When they know we've blown the floor of the Data Centre they'll change all their codes.'

'Of course they will, old man,' the communications boffin explained, as if to a child. 'But by that time we shall have been decoding at least twenty-four hours of top secret signals traffic. We shall know the entire disposition of the Western Army. However, we hope it'll be a long time before they do know, don't we, Harry?'

Harry was the explosives man. 'Precisely at four ayem,' he said, pointing with his pipe at a map on the table before us, 'you'll cause an explosion here. At the same time exactly, Belfière's men will cause an explosion here, two hundred yards away. Their explosions will be in an arms dump, and we hope it will be very loud, with clouds of smoke and flame. Anyone who feels the tremor of your explosion will see the flame and smoke two hundred yards away and think the tremor they felt has been caused by that explosion. They'll never notice your little lot.'

A thin faced, spectacled civilian now took over. I'd been introduced to him as Maurice, but guessed that was not his name. 'Belfière's men,' he said, 'will act as decoys all the time you are in that vault. They will provoke the Germans as much as possible drawing their attention away from you at the Data Centre. The only thing you must do, is to cooperate with them by remaining absolutely silent once the explosion has gone off, absolutely silent.'

'And that means,' the Brigadier said, 'no pistols, no rifles. You can take knives or any other silent weapons you need, but there must be no small arms fire, is that clearly understood?'

'What happens if we can't get out without using firearms?'

There was a sudden silence. 'I'm afraid you don't get out,' the Brigadier said blandly. There it was, the well-known principle of 'human expendability'. Hadn't Napoleon been the first to state it – well, the bastards in this room had learned it too. I looked around at them. He had just pronounced a

115

death sentence, and all they could do was to suck their pipes, fiddle with their flies, and twist their finger rings.

All right. You agree to go in, hoping the men who send you in will take some care to fetch you out. The papers we were going to fetch, however, were suddenly more important than we were.

Sandy was watching me, but professionally. Did *you* sit in at the meeting that agreed this plan of expendability? She must have done, the agreement was plain to see. They had all known of this condition before I had been selected. You've got the wrong officer, gentlemen – I almost said it out loud. I'm prepared to take my own chances to get in and to get out again, provided you don't tie my hands behind my back. No pistols, no rifles. It could be suicide.

'It's a challenge,' the Brigadier said.

They were all watching me. I could understand the reasoning. On no account must we let the Germans know we had been inside the Signals Data Centre. If we didn't get away with it, perhaps another unit could. Perhaps even now they were training some other unit to take over in the event we were knocked out. At all costs the value of the material we could take out of the Data

Centre was paramount. I could see that. It didn't stop my flesh crawling. I looked at Sandy. She smiled encouragingly at me. She was a doctor, I was her patient, going under. She didn't murmur any bedside platitudes. There was no point.

'It'll be less weight to carry,' I said.

The atmosphere in the room lost its electric charge, and in the aftermath of the spark they all began to talk at once.

On my next visit to London, in bed Sandy said, 'That was the most wonderful thing any man has ever done for me. As a person, I mean, not professionally.'

'What was?'

'I told the Brigadier to give you the information about the guns without any warning. Under stress, you looked straight at me. That was good. Under stress, when we have a choice, we always turn to those we love. That was a perfect psychological reaction!'

When I arrived back at camp in Yorkshire, Ben Bolding had been working with Fred Pike and Joe Stanhope, and they had been fitted with military equipment and uniform. They had been given woollen comforters, however, to wear on their heads, and not green berets. You had to earn a beret! The rest

117

of the troop had been left to our training professionals for final briefings in radio techniques and signals recognition. Fred and Joe had a lot of hurried training to do to catch up.

'They're as tough as two old boots,' Ben Bolding assured me.

'Prison life must have agreed with them!'

I was off-form after two days in the fleshpots of London. I always felt this way before a job, longing for the peaceful and well-ordered life of an infantry officer, or a regiment of field artillery. What a rest it would be under the Army's umbrella of command, where all actions are based on decisions taken higher up, where a chain of responsibility extends upward and downwards. Each of the men I would take with me had his own job, and his own responsibility, but all jobs and responsibilities were interchangeable, and all eventually became mine. These men entrusted themselves to my complete charge – the responsibility seemed awesome.

'How are you feeling after your dancing night?' I asked Ben.

'I shall live.' His smile hid a load of mischief. How well I knew him. Ben Bolding would dance only as long as was necessary to find a compliant companion. Who was I to blame him?

'Feel like tackling the Course?' The Course was our name for a special run we had devised to harden man's muscles. It covered twenty miles of rough moorland, with every possible terrain. We allowed ourselves only three and a half hours to cover it, and that meant we couldn't loiter!

'If you can do it after London, Major, I'm certain I can do it.'

I needed the Course to wash away the taste of cinders. The Sergeant Major went across to the men's mess hall and rousted them out on parade. Fred Pike and Joe Stanhope appeared to have settled in, but it's part of a criminal's ability to be a chameleon, to melt into crowds, to make himself inconspicuous.

There was a mock groan when the Sergeant Major announced the Course. The men had just eaten, but there'd be no pause for digestion over there. I could see Fred and Joe asking what 'the Course' meant, but had no time to watch their reactions.

I had set off, running.

The rest of them followed me in an orderly file of three ranks. The Sergeant Major, Lance Corporal Levine, and Corporal Taffy Andrews at the rear, Pike in the front rank of three, Stanhope in the last rank but one, Captain Derby and Lieutenant Sywell behind me.

The standard commando speed for movement across country was seven miles an hour. This killing pace could only be maintained by alternate walking and running. All men and officers were fully clothed and carried rifles and packs. I had a Bren gun slung over my shoulder to inspire them. I can still feel the bite of the steel magazine cover through my epaulette.

I prefer not to think about the first hour of sheer torture. A man can go out of training as quickly as fish can go 'off' – two days and one night in London, a few drinks before each meal, a couple of cigarettes, Sandy all night long, and I was puffing like a grampus. The first actual pains came in shin muscles pulled by the fast walking. After the first five miles, running became a pleasure to ease the muscle pains. Then came a stitch, a hard pain located somewhere under my ribs. I ignored it, waiting for the second wind to come, when the whole act of breathing could become subconscious. After an hour we stopped by a field crag on the moor overlooking Thornthwaite. Down below us was the Washburn and a pile of logs each fifteen inches in diameter, twenty feet long. The men not warned for duty flopped down on the side of the track, feet above their hearts to ease the pressure. The rest faced outwards. It's remarkable how effective a five minutes' rest can be with your body flat and your feet up. Joe and Fred were holding well, prison diet isn't designed to create fat, and both had the spare frame of typical endomorphs. But when we started off again after the five minutes' rest, I noticed Joe Stanhope was limping. I pulled him out of the file, sat beside him and made him take off his boots. A large blister on his left heel had burst and his foot was raw red. I held up his boot; though newly issued by the quartermaster it had been well broken in. I insisted on that. The boot was the usual Innsbrucker style, with thick cut rubber soles. Inside the heel, however, the raised back seam stitching had not been hammered down and waxed. Boots like that can rub your feet within a mile. I cursed! I always made a point of inspecting equipment issued, but I had been in London when Joe Stanhope drew these boots.

'Why didn't you tell me you had a blister when we rested?' He didn't answer, looked sullenly at me, as if I were blaming him for something not his fault. I'd need a special effort – I'd heard an account from Arthur Sywell of the prison interview and hoped Fred Pike had won him over. Apparently this was not the case. 'Don't be afraid to speak,' I chided him, 'no-one's going to bite you. If anything is wrong, tell me. We're not an ordinary army unit here, you know; you can forget anything you might have heard about army bull.'

I blamed myself. I had left the care of these two men to Arthur Sywell, since I had no experience of the criminal mind. Ben Bolding, however, had been responsible for the state of the equipment, and Ben was an old hand.

'Stay here,' I told him, and ran after the troop fast disappearing down the side of Thornthwaite Moor. When I caught up with them, I called the Sergeant Major away from them. They took the opportunity to flop down beside the track, feet in the air, sentries on rota facing outwards.

I drew the Sergeant Major out of their hearing. He could see how angry I was.

'Stanhope's boots,' I said, without preliminaries.

'I noticed he was limping!'

'And did nothing about it?'

'I thought he was trying it on.'

'Why?'

'Well, you know, Major, these ex-convicts, you know how they try to swing the lead...'

I stopped him. 'Now see here, Ben. As far as you, or I, or anyone else is concerned in this outfit, Pike and Stanhope are two soldiers. Where they came from is none of our business. As long as those men are with us, we forget where they've been and they get the same treatment as the rest of the men, is that understood?'

'Yes, Major.' His reply was clipped, his eyes smouldered. Ben didn't like ex-convicts, that I already knew. But 404 was too big a job, and was happening too soon, to coddle personal susceptibilities.

'Stanhope and Pike volunteered...'

'To get out of Prison, Major...'

'They volunteered, and I am not concerned with the reasons. I have never asked any man in any one of my troops why he volunteered. Not officially. I leave that to the psychiatrists on the selection committees. It's enough for me to know the men have volunteered, and therefore I can rely on them to do what I ask. In exchange, I give them every bit of help. And I ask – no damn it, I don't ask – I demand the same treatment from all my officers, whether commissioned or not. Stanhope needs a pair of boots to wear to finish the Course. I see he takes size eights, and so do you, and so do I, so what's it going to be, Sergeant Major?'

The devil smiled, Damn him, he smiled and charmed all the bad temper out of me.

'Permission to fall out, Major?' he asked, still smiling, still standing rigidly at attention.

'Off you go,' I said.

He ran away up the hill towards Joe Stanhope.

I got the men back on their feet, and we all ran off down to the Washburn, sparkling below. The river looked cold. It felt colder when four of us were standing in it up to our waists, manhandling the fifteen inch diameter, twenty foot long logs from bank to bank to make a bridge.

I let Pike and Stanhope stay in the shore party, keeping dry. No point in pushing them to the limit, not yet.

Scaling the twenty foot high wall of a barn near Kettlewell about fourteen miles from Thornthwaite, one of the men failed to balance on the top of the human pyramid we had created, fell sideways and landed on a rock, his leg splayed at a nasty angle. We left him lying there until we had crossed the wall, then doubled back. His leg was broken between the knee and the ankle. We made an improvised splint and bandaged him up with field dressings; I had morphia in my field dressing pocket which dulled the pain while Captain Derby reset the joint as best he could, and we constructed a stretcher of rifles and jackets on which to carry him the rest of the way. Looking at his face as he lay there being borne along at a slow run by a team of four, I got the feeling he had come to an end of his tether, and would be glad to be out of 404. I knew, almost from conviction, he had not fallen accidentally. Possibly he had been hoping to sprain an ankle. The human will is strong enough to carry you anywhere, to take you through any amount of fatigue and fear. Sometimes, however, the cord holding task and ability together strains that little bit too much, and can snap on the slightest provocation. There are no symptoms I could ever discern, though doubtless Sandy would see the tensions building up, would be aware of the growing strain and know what to do about it. Half of me wished we could take Sandy with us on 404. The other half, the 'whispers in the night time' half, knew the operation could never succeed if she were there, since I could never forget nor make adequate allowance for her disturbing presence.

It proved a bad day altogether. We lost two more men. We were on the long run home. The incident at the wall had eaten into our time, and we were trying to make speed down the Kettlewell to Skipton road. The troop was running along, in good shape. Joe Stanhope had stopped limping now he was wearing Ben Bolding's comfortable boots, and Ben, of course, had started. Each five minutes' halt he took off that left boot and tried to bang down the stitching with a stone – it didn't seem to be working very well to judge from the blood caked on his sock. Fred Pike was cantering along like a horse going back home to its stable and a feed of oats, with no sign of stress or strain. Corporal Taffy Andrews had weary lines down his face – at every halt he vanished behind the bushes and I guessed his trouble was digestive rather than muscular. Arthur Sywell looked drawn. Each time we halted, he fell to the ground and lay there inert until the time came to get on his feet again. His muscles, I could see, were not hardened, and dragging himself along must have been agony for him. I knew the feeling well; I had it in smaller amount each time I came back from London.

The man with the broken leg had gone to

126

sleep. When it came to my turn to carry him, I noticed the leg had lost its redness. We would have to appoint Captain Derby our bone setter.

In action, of course, if any man broke a leg we would leave him behind. They all understood that; it would have been unnecessarily severe to leave him during training, though I'm convinced many of them thought I would do so.

It happened without warning. The man on the back of the stretcher on the right, simply keeled over and fell to the ground. I made a grab for the rifle to hold the stretcher, it part slipped from my grasp, but I managed to hold on to it and prevent the injured man from falling off. The momentum of the two front runners, however, jerked the stretcher forwards and I fell flat on the ground. I held tight to the stretcher handles and dragged the men to a halt. The stretcher flopped onto the ground in front of me. The men behind, unable to check themselves, were entangled in my legs; the whole column was in chaos. The Sergeant Major yelled 'Halt' and they all stopped and gathered round. 'Defensive positions,' I yelled. Immediately they all scurried off the road, leaving me, the stretcher and the unconscious man, lying in the middle of the road, while they scurried into the heather of the moor to take up an all round defence. The man who had dropped was totally unconscious, but whether from fatigue, or the end of his impulse to continue, it was impossible to say. When he fell on the road, he scraped the side of his face and nose against the tarmac. I wiped the grit from it, and dusted it with the anti-tetanus powder we all carried. I dragged him off the road and sat him with his back against the wall. His pulse was beating slowly, his face was white. The blood had obviously drained from his head while he had been running. I didn't care for the look of his lips; they were tinged with the blue I'd often seen in cases of overstrained hearts. His pulse was very slow, his breathing shallow. 'Frank Farleigh,' I yelled. The radio he carried was tuned in to our camp. He rose from the heather and ran to the road. There he flopped down on one knee beside me.

'Ambulance,' I said.

He clipped the throat mike round his neck, tuned the set, and started to speak our call sign. We had an ambulance constantly on the alert back in camp.

'Everybody on the road,' I yelled.

We carried on, leaving the unconscious

man, the man with the broken leg, and the signaller beside the road. There was nothing I could do for him, and the ambulance would get there as soon as possible. Farleigh would be glad of the additional rest – though we'd all taken turns to carry the set.

I was running along at the head of the troop about two miles short of Gordale Scar when Alf Milner increased his speed and ran along beside me.

'Yes, Alf?' I had long ago dropped my pretence of formality in these circumstances. They all called me Major, I called them by their surnames on parade, their Christian names when we were outside the camp. It seemed to work very well.

'I ought to have reported something,' he said.

'What, Alf?'

'Johnson has had stomach cramps for the last ten miles, but he refuses to report it. I think he's in real pain, Major.'

I wheeled off and let the troop pass me. I could see Johnson's suffering. He was one of those men whose faces are permanently set in a smile. You can rarely distinguish the true feelings beneath. Now the smile was a grimace, and he was holding his hand to his stomach.

I beckoned to him to leave the ranks. When he got to the side of the track he stopped, holding himself erect with difficulty. Then suddenly, he vomited. Appendicitis. The word jumped out at me. I don't know why, my medical knowledge is confined to broken bones and high temperatures.

'Sergeant Major,' I yelled. He halted the troop and ran back towards me. The ambulance would have come and gone long since, of course, back on the road we had left. Our radio man doubtless had ridden back to camp with it. I cursed myself for the simple weakness of having allowed him to stay with the unconscious man.

Now we had stopped Johnson felt a pain in his side so intense he was crying aloud. Ben Bolding came running up to us, stopped when he saw Johnson, and bent over him. When he looked round at me, I guessed he knew what was wrong.

We were in a long cleft running up to Gordale Scar. To our right the high moors rose and fell again to Threshfield; to the left they rose to Kirkby Malham. Either was three miles away as the crow flies, nearer four if you measured the actual tracks we would need to follow.

'Who are the fastest four men we have?'

'You Major, Landon, Garside, and yours truly.'

I had needed him to verify my own speed.

'Right, stretcher party.'

I instructed Captain Derby to finish 'the Course,' sent Sam Levine ahead of us to Threshfield to telephone to the camp, and within two minutes we put Johnson on an improvised stretcher of rifles and battledress jackets and set off across the moor. We had three miles to go and no time at all, to judge from Johnson's moans, in which to do it. I did not dare give Johnson any of the morphia since I did not know what effect it would have on an angry appendix. He sweated far more than we did. The first two miles we took at a cracking pace. The last mile I was running through a red haze. When we arrived at the roadside by Threshfield we put the stretcher down gently on the grassy edge. Johnson, silent for some time, had vomited twice. The pain was at the right side of his body; when I placed my hand on his stomach, the muscles were knotted tight and he flinched with pain. He had a high fever and didn't seem fully conscious.

Sam Levine had seen us at the road side. He came running up. Unburdened he had made good time to the village post office.

'The ambulance is on its way, Major,' he said. He looked down at Johnson on the stretcher. 'Do you know what's wrong with him?' he asked. 'I'm fairly certain it's appendicitis. You told the ambulance men he had stomach pains on the right side, and had vomited?' 'Yes, Major.'

'That should bring 'em.'

The ambulance was there in five minutes, skidding to a halt when the driver saw us beside the road. A civilian sitting next to the driver leaped from the cab and bent over Johnson. He felt Johnson's forehead and stomach, and then ran round and opened the back doors of the ambulance. 'Quick, lift him in here,' he shouted. We heaved ourselves to our feet, grasped the stretcher and carried Johnson into the back of the ambulance. The civilian shut the doors in our faces, or so it seemed, locking himself inside. The driver enmeshed the gears, and the ambulance drove rapidly away.

'They might have waited for us, Major,' Landon complained.

I had seen the look on the civilian's face – time and an appendix wait for no man. Medical men care for the dying, the living can look after themselves.

'Come on,' I said, 'we don't want to set

solid.' In single file we started down the long road home. 'Now we are only seventeen,' I thought.

Stanhope started malingering. When we had target practice, I could see him aim off deliberately. If he could prove how inefficient he was, he hoped I would throw him out of the squad. It didn't work. Ben Bolding and I took it in turns to explain to him how important practice was. We spent two hours watching him throw his knife into targets over and over again. We stayed with him when the rest of the squad went for meals. He'd last half an hour, and then hunger would take over, and guide his hand unerringly to the bull. When eventually he got to the cookhouse, his food was cold, and there'd be none of the special food I ordered for the rest of the men, high protein, high vitamins, thick juicy underdone steaks, liver, kidneys, fruit, hot house salads. There may have been a war on, but they could stuff their reconstituted eggs! We ate very little starch, though for a treat we'd have Christmas pudding and creamy rice pudding the men seemed to like. When Joe Stanhope arrived in the cookhouse, the steaks would be gone, and he'd be served corned beef, with mashed potatoes, and cabbage slimed in the way only army cooks can achieve. Every morning, as a matter of course, he reported sick. Every morning we had him examined by the doctor in camp, every evening we had to put in an extra two hours to make up for lost time. I told Arthur Sywell to leave him alone. I didn't think he would be able to help, since Joe Stanhope connected him with the police and civilian authority. Ben Bolding was our best bet; no lover of malingerers, he seemed somehow to find a special tenderness for Joe Stanhope, once I had broken his prejudice about the criminal past. All the N.C.O's ate with the men – a week before our own particular D-Day we moved out of that camp, and all lived together in a large barn up on Fountain's fell. I wanted to observe all these men's abilities as closely as possible. And all their little 'in camp' failings.

I put my sleeping-bag next to Joe Stanhope's.

On the third night when the rest of the men had fallen into a sleep of exhaustion I couldn't sleep. I was planning the training for the following day, wondering which one of them was going to break. Joe Stanhope wasn't able to sleep. I heard him toss and turn in his sleeping-bag, and then he sat up and I could hear the scrape of a match as he lit a cigarette. 'Got a cigarette to spare, Joe?' I asked him, as I struggled out of the folds of the sleeping-bag and sat upright, my head resting against the wall of the barn. He passed a cigarette in the dark; I had to feel around for it, and eventually found his wrist. His hand was shaking. I took the cigarette and he struck another match. Our sleeping-bags were only three foot apart; as he leaned forward to light the cigarette, I could see his face, white and drawn, in the glow of the match.

'What's the trouble, Joe?' I asked him. It was a gamble; maybe here in the dark, he might tell me.

'Nothing you'd know anything about,' he said.

'You'd be surprised what I know about. Anyway, even if it's something I don't know anything about, tell me and I might learn something.' I deliberately kept my voice flat and unemotional. He drew on his cigarette a couple of times; I drew on mine. I don't like smoking except socially, when I am drinking. The cigarette tasted like burned kippers up there on the moors. I deliberately looked to the front; I could feel his eyes on me each time I drew, but was in no hurry. I was prepared to sit up all night with him if necessary.

'I'm dead scared,' he said finally.

Thank God for that. Give me frightened men any time – I can't stand men who've never experienced fear. 'So am I,' I said.

He snorted in derision. Granted, I had always tried my best not to show it, and doubtless usually succeeded in conveying an air of absolute confidence to all the men. But inside, I was always as scared as he was. 'What are you scared of, in particular? The drop? The explosion? Being in among the Germans?'

'The whole lot.'

'Well, let's deal with it a bit at a time. The parachute jumping is easy. Later this week you and Fred and Sam Levine and Lieutenant Sywell will be taken for a short course. At the end of forty-eight hours, you'll know all about it.'

'Forty-eight hours?' he said. 'We'll be lucky! It must take weeks to learn to drop. The lads were telling me they get a three months' course in the paras.'

'When I learned to jump,' I told him, 'I was stationed in Maidstone. I travelled up overnight to Manchester to take the course. I wasn't due to report until the Monday, but I knew a girl in Manchester, and hoped she'd be free for the week-end. I arrived in the camp Saturday morning. The guard directed me to hut B.7, and I went in and dumped my kit. I was just about to wash and brush up before going to telephone this girl, when a sergeant came rushing in. "Lieutenant Rhodes?" he asked. "Yes." "We're waiting for you, sir, please come on." He had the sort of voice Sergeant Major Bolding puts on when you miss a target three times in a row. I followed him outside where he had a car and we raced across the camp, over the airfield to where a plane was waiting. Inside the plane were thirty men, all sitting along benches, all wearing parachutes, all looking like death warmed up. The plane took off, and we were at three thousand feet before the sergeant discovered he'd got the wrong Lieutenant Rhodes. Are you still with me?' I asked Joe. He had not drawn on his cigarette for some time. 'Yes, I'm listening,' he said.

'This is a true story,' I said. 'Gospel truth. How I learned to drop and a bigger story of military cock-up you've never heard. The Lieutenant Rhodes he was waiting for was with Alan Cobham's Flying Aces – I once

137

saw them give a demonstration at Yeadon, and this Rhodes character walks out on the wing of a plane, without a parachute. Later he gave a demonstration of free fall with a parachute that took the crowd's breath away. He was supposed to instruct at Manchester. I got aboard a plane in his place.'

'What happened, you came back down again?'

'I got the sergeant in the front of the plane, where the lads couldn't hear me. Lads! One of 'em was a full Colonel. "Have you ever jumped by parachute, Sergeant?" I asked him. "Never sir." "Exactly how difficult is it to learn – no bullshit, exactly how difficult?" "It's not bad at all," he said, "but I'll tell you one thing, sir, if we take this plane load down again without jumping, at least fifty percent of them will never make it." "Right," I said, "teach me how to fall"... It took him five minutes of whispered conversation. When he had finished, I yelled a few sentences of encouragement, pretended to check each man's equipment, smiled at them one by one, then the door was opened, and I was the first to go. They all followed me, each one of them, including the full Colonel, just as scared as I was. When I landed, I had shit down to my knees. So had the Colonel.'

'How many times have you jumped, Major?' Joe asked me.

'Honestly, I forget. Must be, oh forty times. I've jumped twelve times operational.'

'And you never injured yourself?'

'I gave my balls a bit of a wrench once! But I've never shit myself again.'

'I'm scared I'll never pluck up enough courage to jump through the door.'

'Don't worry,' I said, 'I'll be standing beside you, and I'll see you get a push.'

'That was the worst fear,' he said, 'the others I don't mind so much.' Of course he didn't mind. He'd been a hardened criminal, used to walking about during the night with everyone against him. I'd rather walk across a mile of woods at night, than cross a bedroom with a sleeping man in it. A life of crime was not for me. The cigarette tasted like old socks. I stubbed it out on the floor of the barn, lay down on my back, and went to sleep.

The next morning, Joe was already looking better. There was a wall behind the barn, about twenty feet high. When he had washed I told all the men to climb in. They did. He was in the centre of the line, Fred next to him, Arthur Sywell next to him. They looked like clay pigeons at a fairground. I climbed the wall, and stood at the end. 'Righto,' I told them. 'I want every man to shout one two with me, and then we'll all jump. Are we ready? ONE, TWO.' We all jumped. I walked over to Joe and Fred, sprawled on the ground. The rest of the men, including Arthur Sywell, had ended the jump with a forward roll, and were all standing upright.

'That's what it's like, jumping by parachute,' I said. 'We're not going to teach you to jump, you know that already. We're going to teach you to land.'

It was Ben's turn to cook breakfast. The powdered oatmeal biscuit and tins of bully beef tasted delicious.

HARRY LANDON

Harry Landon, born in Norway, came to England with his parents in 1918 when he was three years old and at fourteen he took a job with Lord Laxford as stable lad, near Market Harborough. When he'd worked there for six years, he made third groom. Lord Laxford kept six grooms in those days and four stable boys; there was a stable manager, a first groom, two second grooms, and three thirds. The thirds were the dogsbodies – each had charge of three horses, and God help any if Lord Laxford should happen to rub a white glove over a horse's coat and bring it away dusty.

The thirds took the horses out for walking exercise each morning – riding one and leading two. Since all the horses were spirited hunters, the two on leading reins could be devils to control. Thirds rarely got a canter, and never a gallop – walk and trot, walk and trot, for eight miles each day, usually on the side of the roads around the Laxford estate. Dead boring! Harry didn't mind. He loved horses, and had his own interests anyway.

Also employed on the estate were one head and two assistant keepers. The estate covered four thousand acres of prime Leicestershire and Rutland wood and grassland; it was constantly stocked with pheasants, duck, partridges; the streams ran into ponds full of trout, the pastures were rich in pestilent rabbits and hares. The rabbits, hares, and pigeons 'belonged' by custom to the keepers. The trout, pheasant, partridges, and duck were strictly reserved for his Lordship. Harry robbed them both, irrespective of title. He robbed the gardener, too. The estate had two acres of glass and grew grapes, strawberries, pineapples, avocado pears, and all manner of succulent and tropical delicacies. In season,

Harry helped himself.

Harry was a good-looking lad, full grown and strong by his twenty-first year. Lord Laxford's wife was a pretty woman of thirty, and Harry served her too, in season.

He was in the wood, by the four hundred acre pasture. In the centre of the pasture was a copse and a pond. In the wood were pheasants. Tomorrow, Lord Laxford had a party coming to shoot. Harry crouched at the edge of the wood. Tom the gamekeeper would be out tonight, that was certain. He'd be out until one o'clock, and the other two assistant keepers would take it in turn to watch during the rest of the night. Tom would be doing the rounds. They'd be beating this wood tomorrow, and down the hill to the wood on this side of the home farm. The butts were already in position below the crest of the hill. They'd start the other side of the wood and drive through it, beating the birds before them. Then the birds would come out of the wood, high overhead. The guns in the butts below would be waiting for them, a high shot, up and over. It was the kind of shooting Lord Laxford preferred for the start of the day, heavy flight but a difficult shot, straight ahead then up in the air and over your head. The best time to take them was high over the wood, a forward shot. It was bad form to turn round.

Harry had spotted Tom. Tom hadn't seen Harry sitting on the ground with his back to a tree. Harry could stay still like that for ever if necessary. Tom walked silently along the paths. He could hear the pheasant murmuring in the shrubberies around him. He could walk through a wood, Tom could, and without seeing a single bird could count them in the shrubberies from that murmur alone. And not a bird would know he'd been among them. It's a poor keeper who doesn't know where his birds are. Tom knew they were where they should be, in the shrubberies. No sign of foxes, thank God. One single fox can wreak havoc in the shrubberies – spoil an entire day's shooting in an hour. Tom had an anxious moment yesterday when the hunt headed a fox this way and lost it. One of these days his Lordship was going to have to make up his mind whether he wanted to hunt or to shoot. An estate wouldn't support both. Tom found the fox behind the home farm, down on its belly, wriggling forward, looking down the scent line of the home farm chickens. The smell of chicken must have been thick in its nose. Tom got to within a hundred yards of it before he fired – at that range the .303 shot went straight into its skull. He buried it, of course. His Lordship would have been livid to know Tom shot foxes, no matter how many pheasants they could mangle.

Harry watched Tom walk slowly down the path.

It was half-past twelve. Tom would be going home. Well, bloody well hurry up and go! Harry had a sack, and a basin full of corn soaked in whiskey. He also had a sharp knife and a wire with two sticks, one at each end, such as they use for slicing cheese. Tom was carrying a twelve-bore shotgun, that's how anxious he was. Keepers rarely go out at night with a gun – it encourages poachers to shoot at them. Now Tom was sixty yards away. It was a bright night, too bloody bright, with a high autumn moon. Harry sat against the tree, perfectly still. The base of the tree was in complete shadow. Tom would never spot him. Now Tom had passed across the front of his vision and was heading away from Harry. 'If I get twenty in the sack,' Harry thought, 'that'll be six quid.' It was a fortune to a lad who earned thirty bob a week and had to pay ten bob towards his board. Now Tom was out of sight down the path. No time to waste. Harry moved slowly but deftly, sideways down to the ground then along in the grass. It would have been impossible to see him, there in the grass, even from six feet. Across the rhododendron patch, along the grass – 'thank God they only scythe it.' Then get out the pot and sprinkle the corn on the ground, in a heap. Cover the whiskied corn with fresh, then toss a few handfuls of the fresh corn each one further away, in a line. That's where the sods are, in that clump, over there. Right, corn in your hand, between your fingers, right, flip them, one, two, three, four, five. Good. That one must have landed right on a bloody pheasant; hear the sudden squawk and the fluttering. The pheasant's eye appeared in the leaves of the bush, and then its neck, and then it started forwards along the corn trail. Another pheasant appeared behind it, gobbling at the ground. It tried to pass the first pheasant, which pecked it aside, and then there was a third pheasant, and a fourth and now they were all scrambling along the corn trail until they came to a dead end on a patch where Harry had deliberately thrown no corn. Now they stop and start to cluck and look about them, and other birds, attracted by the sound, come stalking out of the coverts, and now there must be at least twenty birds all milling around. One of them finds the trail and swoops along it, greedy and in haste. The others all follow along the corn trail, and now they've found the heap. Harry had withdrawn about ten feet, motionless in the bottom of a small beech. The birds were tearing at the pile of corn, fighting for each grain. When they were well down in the pile, they reached the whisky corn and not even the reek of alcohol could deter them as they gobbled. By two o'clock, Harry had twenty necks wrung in the sack and was cursing himself for not having brought another with him. The assistant keeper – Mike or John – would be coming up the hill from the home farm. Harry wanted to be clear of the wood by the time he got to the crest of the hill. The disturbed birds were making a helluva racket, searching around for the last grains of corn. In a half crouch, Harry made his way to the corner of the wood. Out of the wood along the hedge bottom into the shelter of the stone wall. Along the stone wall around the bend in the wall to where the open gate led to the back of the greenhouses. Through the greenhouses and he'd be by the back door of his quarters, one bedroom and the communal sitting-room. He'd hide the pheasants under the floorboards of his bedroom, and take them off the estate four at a time, wrapped in a horse blanket. No need to worry about that now. The first job was to get through the greenhouses. One of the undergardeners would be getting up at half-past two to stoke the boilers, and it would be damn silly to let yourself be caught by an undergardener.

Through the door. Path straight ahead but don't take it. Round the side between the two high houses. Camellias in the right hand one in spring time, what a sight! Geraniums and fuchsias here on the left are Harry's favourites. Past the shed where the night watchman used to sleep a couple of years ago when they had all that stealing. Down the side of it.

From inside came the soft murmur of voices.

'Somebody's in there with a woman,' Harry thought. It had never occurred to him to take a woman in there; but it was the ideal place when you came to think about it, wasn't it? There was a sofa bed in there, and the place was heated from the boiler house. It had once been a forcing house or something.

Lord Laxford turned the corner of the greenhouse ahead. He had a shotgun in his hand, the butt tucked beneath his arm. He saw Harry at once.

'So it's you,' he said. 'I wondered if it

might be you.'

The murmuring stopped inside the forcing house.

Harry didn't speak. Still holding the sack in his hands he walked forward. 'I want you on the first bus in the morning,' Lord Laxford said as Harry walked away down the path still carrying the sack.

Harry caught the bus. Lord Laxford shot himself as his wife came out of the forcing shed in deshabille. He would have shot her first had he known that, on that particular night, she had the undergardener in there with her.

Harry caught the bus. He had the presence of mind to grab Lady Laxford as she fainted near her husband's body, and to rush out of the gardens with her. In the ensuing pandemonium, he took her up the back stairs of Laxford Hall, by the route he himself had used several times in the past. He tucked her in bed, but not until she had given him a hundred pounds from her own personal safe.

She was in bed when the butler came to give her the tragic news.

Harry waited until the police had left before he too left, to catch the bus.

He joined the Army the following day, in Bedford.

Once in the Army he started to think about Tom, and the undergardener, about Lady Laxford and his Lordship. He started to wonder what he would do if a woman he had married gave her body to other people. The wonder became a deep-rooted thought, and then an obsession. One day he saw her in a public house in Caerphilly, an officer in the W.A.A.F., dead drunk. She was with a young officer from the 17th/21st Lancers, and his Death's Head cap badge stared out at Harry. She didn't recognise Harry, of course, and Harry didn't speak to her. At the sight of her, the scene in the gardens came flooding back to him, drenching his mind in memory.

He had no chance of going overseas in his present unit.

He volunteered for the Commandos, hoping he would never see her again.

One of our prides was to play a form of quoits with hand-grenades. I encouraged the game in the evening, after training. The meat and vegetable army issue stew came in cans ten inches high, eight inches across the mouth. We would stand a can about sixty feet away; threepence a throw, and the nearest to the can takes all the threepences. To be certain to win the money, your grenade had to land inside the can. Alf Milner made a modest income from the game – at a distance of sixty feet he could put a grenade inside the tin four times out of six.

It was Thursday evening, and though the lads had been told nothing, they knew this week-end we'd be moving out of the camp. We ended training about half-past five, and I went into my billet, took a lengthy shower and used up the last of my Coal Tar soap. From now on it would be army issue carbolic; and not too much of that. I shaved with a brush, conscious that I wouldn't be having many more brush shaves before I got back from this job. It was one of those evenings, cold but clear, clean and crisp as only on the Yorkshire Moors they can be. I felt in perfect form. My civilian batman brought me a supper of soup, stewed chicken, with powdered potatoes, and a hunk of army cheese. The simple foods suited me fine. However, I did open a half bottle of a white wine, and finished the cheese with the last of a bottle of port and a slice of apple pie. I could hear the normal sounds of the camp all about me; sounds that one by one I could recognise, as the lads emerged from the bath-houses, dressed, went to the mess for supper, then came out and either crossed to the N.A.A.F.I. hut for a beer, or settled down on someone's Nissen hut step for a smoke and a gab. Then I heard the clink of the tin as the first grenade hit it. I put on my beret and went outside. The men were playing along a stretch of sanded grass behind two of the Nissen huts. The two huts had been built up on short stilts and stood three feet above the ground at the back end. Don't ask me why the Engineers who built the camp had chosen the only bit of sloping ground on which to put the Nissens – the ways of Engineers have always been a closed book to me! Ben was there, and Joe Stanhope, Harry Landon, Willie Garside and Taffy Andrews. As yet there was no sign of Alf Milner. Whenever he appeared, the groan could be heard throughout the camp.

Ben lobbed one, a beauty landing eight inches from the can. The grenade thudded into the ground, stayed still without a bounce. Taffy's was six inches away. Willy threw one, but it was a couple of feet away. Harry's was fifteen inches and then it was Joe Stanhope's turn. He pulled a grenade out of his pocket and without seeming to take aim tossed it quickly from behind. It rose on a perfect parabola, its angle about sixty degrees from the horizontal, in the sky over his head. Then it started to fall. It was a good 'un, already I could feel that. It accelerated downwards, and there was a tremendous clank as it went straight into the can. It bounced in there, jingled around against the sides, and finally settled. Joe grinned, and held out his hand. They all counted coppers into it – Ben had no change and gave him a shilling and took nine pennies in change. Each win meant a pint in the N.A.A.F.I.!

They were using ordinary issue grenades, already primed and fused. The first thing we always did on training, against the regulations of 'that other Army', was to prime and fuse two grenades which went with each man everywhere. I insisted the men live with live grenades, sleep with them, eat with them. This way they got the feel of them, grew to know and respect them as a man will a pocket knife he constantly hones to keep perfectly sharp. I've saved my life with a grenade, more times than I care to name.

Arthur Sywell came from his quarters, and Sam Levine: I stepped forward into the game. Now we were so many, the threepences went into another M and V can at the throwing line. I put mine in. Joe Stanhope had the first throw, since he won the last hand, but deferentially he waved me forward. I smiled and shook my head. I needed a sighting shot before I could do my best, and this was keen competition with two and threepence in the can! Joe stood on the line, his left foot near the tin, then turned to face his left side down the 'range.' He held the grenade in his right hand then suddenly, again without seeming to take any form of aim, he chucked. It was a good one, but it landed about four inches from the can and skeetered a foot or so past. I took my turn next – a lousy throw, eighteen inches too far, though the line was straight. As the lads threw them, one after the other, I said good-bye to my threepence. Two landed in the can, thrown by Arthur Sywell and Ben. They shared the money between them.

This time I was determined not to be beaten. I stayed at the back end of the firing line, watching each throw. Ben in the can, neat as a whistle. Good old Ben, two out of three. Arthur Sywell wild, at least two foot off. Sam Levine – a good one, but a few inches beyond the rim. Taffy wide, Harry short, Willie close, but not close enough! And now Joe Stanhope; left arm down the range, right hand by his side, up, and chuck. The grenade seemed to falter at his hand, went away on a bad parabola.

'Down!' Joe yelled. 'For Christssake, the pin's out.' He'd pulled out the bloody pin! We all hit the ground as one, faces grinding into the sand. There was a loud clink as the grenade landed on another grenade in the sand around the can, then a skittering noise, and then that awesome silence before the blast. We were all counting.

On the count of four I lifted my head and looked quickly about me. No-one was in sight, thank God! Five, and I pressed my gut even further into the ground. You can hear a thousand grenades explode, but every new one is an eardrum banger, every new one knocks the air out of your body without pity. Six, another quick glance around – when it goes up, if it's anywhere near another grenade, that'll go up too, and there'll be a holocaust of grenade case splinters banshee-ing through the air. Seven seconds can take an awful long time to pass but here was the seventh, wait for it, press down your gut, and pray with that incoherent jumble of words that means only one thing – don't let one of the fragments hit me. Seven. Silence. Absolute bloody silence. Two men coming

154

out of the dining hut! Eight and Nine and Ten. I raised my head. 'Everybody stay down,' I shouted. 'You two men by the dining hut stand perfectly still,' I yelled across the huts. They heard me, stood still, holding back the men behind them.

Quickly I counted the grenades I could see on the pitch. One for Ben, two for Arthur Sywell, three for Sam Levine, four, five, six, seven – where the hell was the seventh? It hadn't gone into the tin, I was certain of that. Where the hell was it? I looked slowly from side to side, in every pocket of ground around the target area. No sign of it. Damn! It must have hit one of the six grenades lying there, and have bounced! Where the hell had it bounced to? I saw the grenade; and the window of the Nissen hut above it opened. In the window opening was Alf Milner.

'Stand absolutely still, Alf,' I yelled.

He heard me, and froze.

The grenade was sitting on a ledge; a piece of timber nailed across the piles on which the Nissen hut was standing. At the back end of each hut was a latrine, separated from the hole beneath only by a piece of sacking. Thus the latrines could be emptied without carrying the stinking pail through the men's quarters. The grenade was lodged precariously on that shelf; any movement, the slightest vibration, was certain to shake it off. Although the detonator had failed to explode it, if the grenade should drop, it was odds on it would explode. With only that canvas, two planks and a bucket of shit between him and the grenade fragments, Alf Milner didn't stand a chance.

The two men waiting at the door of the dining hall were Royal Engineers maintenance men.

'You two Engineers – I want you to make absolutely certain no-one moves within fifty yards of this Nissen hut. Understood?' 'Yes sir,' their voices came back to me.

'Arthur?'

'Yes, Major.'

'Get the men back out of this – take it steady, one at a time!'

'Wilco,' he said, using the army slang to keep his manner calm.

Ben Bolding and Joe Stanhope stayed. Ben because instinctively he knew I'd want him to stay – Joe for reasons I would never know.

'What's the end of those huts like, Ben?'

'Ropey, Major; the shit bin's only balanced on two planks.'

'You've seen the grenade?'

'I've seen the sodding thing,' he said. 'Why the hell did you pull the sodding pin, Joe?' he asked.

'I don't know, sergeant major, I just don't know.'

I knew all right. It was Pavlov's dogs, all over again. That was the way I trained them, to behave instinctively. These were the dangers. Instinct said you held a grenade in your throwing hand, pulled out the pin with the index finger of the other hand, and you threw. One two three. Instinct. Who was I to complain when the system itself took over?

'Save the explanations for later, Joe,' I said. 'No-one's blaming you.'

My big problem was this – what the hell could I do? Removing the grenade was a comparatively simple matter. I should call in the Royal Engineers bomb disposal officer, and he would deal with the explosive. But what about Alf? That grenade could fall at any time, and certainly it wasn't going to make a point of waiting for the arrival of the Royal Engineers. Someone would have to crawl in there, and get that grenade out of there. But who? Leadership, all those fine phrases the Army hands out, said I should do it. But we were leaving on a job for which I'd trained myself and a group of men, and the

life of one soldier, Alf Milner, was less important than the life of the officer trained to
lead that force on the job. Stars and Stripes,
Land of Hope and Glory, and Over the
Sodding Waves. I couldn't leave Alf Milner
there, waiting for the grenade to drop. And it
was a certain fact he daren't move as much as
a toe.

Joe was ten yards further forward than
when I had last looked at him. 'Come back,
Joe,' I shouted. He took no notice.

I started to crawl forward. I hadn't gone
more than five yards when I felt Ben's hand
on my puttee.

'Leave him go, Major,' he said quietly.
'Anyway, you'll never catch him in time.' He
was right. I couldn't catch Joe.

'Take care, Joe,' I shouted, feeling absolutely useless. 'Do you know what to do?'

He paused. 'When I get close enough,
Major, I'll pick the grenade off the ledge
and carry it away from the Nissen hut,
trying not to shake it. Is that okay?'

What a ludicrous bloody situation!

'That's all you can do,' I said.

Sixty feet isn't a long way to crawl, but it
seemed to take him fifteen thousand years.
When he got there, he squatted up on his
hunkers and looked at the grenade. 'Hang

on, Joe,' I shouted.

I scrambled backwards, then rose to my feet and in a crouching run headed for my quarters. I came back out again with my field glasses, walked carefully forward to where Ben was squatting on the ground, then sat down again, ready to drop to the ground should the grenade slip, and focused the field glasses on the grenade. It was about a third of the way on the ledge. The lever had sprung clear; the firing pin would be down, somewhere inside the grenade. Possibly the firing pin had stuck on its way down into the detonator. It happens sometimes; a batch of grenades has too much thick grease on them and if that channel isn't properly cleaned, the pin can stick. But not for ever. The pressure of the spring overcomes the restraint of the grease in time, and the pin snaps into the detonator. That can happen at any time – after one second, one hour, or one year. I searched the ground Joe would have to cross with that grenade in his hands. It was flat, with no sign of obstacles. I focused on Joe. His face was wet. 'Wipe your hands, Joe,' I shouted. They too would be wet. 'Now move one hand near to the ledge below the grenade, so that if it drops you can catch it.' I watched him move his hand. Through the glasses I could see his hand was still wet. 'No, Joe, that's no good, you'll have to dry your hand.' He withdrew his hand and wiped it on his jumping jacket. Then he rubbed it in the sand and wiped it again. When he extended it, the hand was dry, crumbs of sand clinging between his fingers. I lifted the glasses and looked up at Alf Milner. He had frozen, absolutely still. His face was wet too.

'Right, Joe, now move the other hand forward, and pick it up, as slowly as you possibly can.'

I watched his right hand going slowly forward, and then, poised above the grenade, it stopped. 'That's right, lad, take your time,' I said silently. When I looked again through the glasses, I saw the knuckles of his hand were white with tension. 'For Christ's sake, relax,' I prayed silently. I swept the glasses across to his face.

He had set, rigid with fear. He was incapable of movement. I'd seen that look a hundred times, on the faces of normally brave men when asked to deal with explosives. Joe was temporarily paralysed.

Damn blast sod and bloodywell shit.

Two of them. Squatting on a grenade. One with his trousers down, one stiff with fear!

I started to get to my feet, trying to keep

the glasses trained on Joe's face.

'Come back, Fred,' Ben said, loudly. His voice hit my ears with a shock, so intent had I been on Joe's face. I took the glasses from my eyes. Fred Pike had come out of the back of the Nissen hut to our left, and was walking slowly across the intervening space. He must have seen everything that went on. He ignored the sergeant major; walked slowly to where Joe was squatting, absolutely rigid. Fred bent forward and gently but deftly picked the grenade off the ledge. Holding the grenade in both hands he turned, slowly, and walked across the sandy throwing pitch, past the tin target, and out to the side of the camp. Slowly, a step at a time, moving gracefully, barely lifting his feet from the ground, gliding along. About a hundred yards from where we were squatting he held the grenade in front of himself, then in a slow arc but accelerating, he swung the grenade down, twisting it along the parabola so the centrifugal force would help to keep the pin up. He let go. The grenade rose in an arc of forty-five degrees for a maximum distance throw. It landed on the ground in a shallow trough forty yards from him. He turned and walked towards us. I was counting with him. On a count of five he lowered himself rapidly to the ground. On a count of seven, the grenade exploded, whamming its fragments in the air, spending its explosive substance away from the camp.

The boys went wild.

'What made Joe go forward?' later I asked Ben.

'I told him to.'

'Come off it, you never said a word. I would have heard you.'

Ben smiled at me. 'I gave him one of my looks!' he said. 'And that was enough.'

It was enough for Joe, certainly, but what about Fred? He hadn't seen 'one of Ben's looks'.

'What about Fred?'

'That was Dodger,' Ben said. 'He was in the Nissen with Fred. Apparently they were watching the whole thing. When they ducked down, apparently, Dodger said to Fred – "You bloody convicts'll be the death of all of us." That got Fred where it hurt, right in the middle of his pride. He'd have gone for that grenade if it had landed in the shit bucket!'

ALF MILNER

Alf Milner was thirty when he married in 1938. He didn't see the war was coming. In

1938 he also bought a Morgan motor car, his first suit of golf clothes with trousers that buckled round the leg just below the knee, a new set of hickory shafted irons, a gold wrist watch, a gold cigarette case, and a book on etiquette.

Alf Milner meant to go places.

So he should. He'd just come into money. Twelve thousand pounds and a house to be exact. His benefactor had been a widow when he met her, aged forty-five. God bless her, she had a weak heart. Of course, they'd been sleeping together on and off for about six months, but Alf had a lady in Stamford Bridge and it was proving difficult to break with her without returning the money and the presents she'd lavished on him. Finally he 'disengaged' himself by a slow campaign of pretended impotence, and was free to devote himself to the much more promising widow he'd met in the golf club in Virginia Water.

'I adore you,' she used to say to him in bed. 'You're so gorgeously uncouth!' It rankled, and on those nights he would make a point of leaving her just before her moment of satisfaction. She got the message.

Finally, as it turned out to be, she persuaded him to go away with her to Bournemouth. 'Just the two of us, for a week, on our own.' He played hard to get, insisted he had business to attend to, but finally gave in. That was one of the secrets of his method! When they got to the hotel, he suddenly yielded to desire, and put her across the bed the minute the porter had left with the luggage. She was flattered and delighted. That first instantaneous action seemed to set the pattern for the rest of the gay, careless, carefree week and by the end of it she was practically exhausted, sexually more satisfied than she had ever known she could be. The following Monday she died of a sudden heart attack, and he discovered she had left him everything, twelve thousand pounds and a house in Wimbledon. He moved in and shortly afterwards got married to keep himself out of mischief.

With the better part of his windfall he bought a half share in a prosperous garage in Wimbledon, and settled down to a life of business. The money he put in the company was used to expand the stock of reliable second-hand motor cars; he proved to be pretty good on the sales side and the business did well. He was sitting on a little gold mine that, with careful handling, would make him a very rich man. His wife was a small girl, attractive, rather shy, but very exciting when she was roused. Awakening the latent desires of women had been one of his professions in the 'bad old' days. She was delightful. They made a lot of friends in Wimbledon, where a man's income was of more account than his background, and he did a lot of business around the golf course at Virginia Water. He looked every inch a golfer in his buckled knee-breeches and spiked shoes; he was generous to a fault in the club house after a game, and never heard the few members who called him 'uncouth'. Early in 1939 he was put up for the committee – 'Just the sort of younger member we should have to get things moving a bit' – but the secret ballot was disappointing and he didn't get in. Only the club secretary knew the voting had been six for, fifty-two against. He was a kindly man, and even thought of writing an anonymous note to Alf, to tell him he'd be more popular if he didn't monopolise the bar, didn't button-hole the older members with his long and not always very funny stories. He'd also be more than popular if he'd stop looking at the lady members with undressing eyes. However, he couldn't bring himself to pen a poison letter, and Alf retained and fostered many of the habits his book on etiquette could have told him no gentleman ever had.

The outbreak of war came as a complete surprise to Alf; petrol rationing brought about the end of his garage business overnight. He joined the Army more from boredom than from any single patriotic motive. He had a vision of himself in the uniform of an officer in the Fleet Air Arm, or the R.A.F. He could see himself flying away on brief sorties, returning to a glamorous niche in the club at Virginia Water as 'One of our War Heroes'.

It didn't work out quite that way. The War Office Selection Board turned him down for a commission. He just wasn't the type, not even in those days, when anyone who could express himself in the King's English was deemed to have those powers of leadership the country so desperately required.

Alf volunteered for pilot training with the R.A.F. At least, if he couldn't get a commission, he'd get the wings – after all, he could always say in Virginia Water he'd preferred to serve his King in a humble capacity away from the limelight. They'd respect him for that. 'I don't want the easy life of an officer,' he could imagine himself saying. 'I want to get into the thick of it with the lads. Take last night when I took my Lincoln up to knock hell out of Dortmund etc. etc.' It would be all the more impressive if he was merely a sergeant.

They turned him down for air crew training, offered him a job on the ground in motor transport.

One day he was in a pub in Marylebone. In those days, as soon as you guessed the landlord was opening the once a week bottle of whisky, you fought and kicked your way, if necessary, to the bar to get your ration of one double. Alf was in the R.A.S.C. – though he never wore the flashes on his shoulder away from the camp. He started to claw his way to the bar as soon as he saw the first glass of whisky passed backwards. There was a general mêlée, but suddenly the crowd fell back. Standing at the bar was a big man wearing a green beret. An enormous soldier from the Pioneer Corps, Irish by the sound of him, had just challenged the man in the green beret to come outside. The Irishman's companions were pulling his arm. 'Come away, Paddy, he'll bloody kill you. Can't you see what he is, bejesus, wid the green hat an all.' The Irishman was too far gone. The man in the green beret smiled. 'Let him be,' he said softly. 'Give him a whisky, landlord, on me.' The landlord passed one over, smiling that the head-on collision had been averted. Alf eyed the man in the green beret with respect. He'd heard about such men, of course, but this was the first one he'd ever seen. On the arm of the Commando, for such he was, hung a gorgeous girl who obviously swelled with pride in him. An old soldier wearing the ribbons of the first world war and several other wars besides came to the bar and tapped the Commando on the shoulder. 'Bless you lad,' was all he said.

The following morning without a word to any of his mates Alf put in his application to join the Commandos. When the selection psychiatrist asked him why, the answer came out of him before he had time to think. 'I've always been a self-centred sort of chap,' he said, 'and just for once I'd like to volunteer to do something without being selfish about it.' The psychiatrist was a very friendly man. 'Will you mind if I give you a piece of advice?' he said. Alf nodded his agreement.

'You'll go through hell in the next six months,' the psychiatrist said. 'I can see you're smoking too much and drinking too much and not taking enough exercise generally, but stick at it! Go through the training if they'll have you, and come out at the other end with pride. You're the first man who's come in here and given me a perfectly acceptable reason for wanting to volunteer. And, do you know something, I don't think you yourself have quite realised why you are doing it.'

Alf got through the training. The psychiatrist had been right – he'd gone through torture to get his body back into shape. But once that had been done, when burly sergeants had harried him round the Scottish mountains long past the moment when he wanted to die, when he had been plunged into ice cold lochs, had been forced to climb sick as a dog down ropes hanging from the cliff faces of St Ives, when he had been pushed, white faced and vomiting, out of an aircraft with only a parachute between him and perdition, he was able to forget the physical side of things. Then the rest of the training came naturally to him. He had two subsequent moments of great pride. He was on leave in London and a couple of drunken louts were kicking another man in an alleyway off the Euston Road. He ran into the alley. The two drunken louts took one look at his beret, and scarpered.

The other came when his golf club, depleted of regular players but still struggling on, made him an ex-officio member of the committee. He was notified by post and hastened home at the first opportunity. His house was empty, had been ransacked and appallingly vandalised. There remained, however, a note from his wife, posted on with nothing more than a compliments slip from his solicitor, in which she announced, with sickening brevity, her decision to go and live elsewhere with their child, and an officer in the R.A.F. 'Don't look for me,' the note concluded. 'I don't want to see you again.'

Alf came to terms with himself very rapidly, wrote two short letters, one to the garage, one to the golf club. Then, thinking better of that, he destroyed the letters, waited until dark, then rigged a low fuse to the gas-filled kitchen. The insurance company paid out on his house, his wife, his child, his possessions, converting them and his feelings for them into hard cash.

He was never seen in Wimbledon again.

Though there were only four days to our personal D-Day, and despite protests from the War Office team masterminding 404, I let all the men have a thirty-six hour leave, starting at seven o'clock, on the evening of Friday, when they were all driven by lorry to a dance at an A.T.S. camp near Settle. They had all received a prophylactic injection, though we told them it was for tetanus and typhus, and I didn't want to see them again until seven o'clock on Sunday morning.

Two of them deserted.

Arthur Sywell left camp on Friday evening and returned on Sunday morning, with Fred Pike. He'd picked him up on Saturday, at a house in Tottenham where a twenty-five years old girl lived with Fred's illegitimate child. They'd just been in time to catch the night train from King's Cross. Joe Stanhope and Ben Bolding had spent the thirty-six hours together. On his 'dancing night' at Timble, Ben had met a couple of sisters who lived together in a cottage overlooking the Fewston reservoir; Joe apparently, has distinguished himself and earned his keep by chopping and sawing enough logs to last them a whole year.

I planned to spend the week-end somewhere half way between London and Yorkshire, with Sandy.

I rang her on the Friday, from my office in camp. She wasn't at Little Venice, but eventually they found her for me in Chelsea barracks, and put the call through.

'Can you talk where you are, Sandy?'

'Yes. I'm in the Officers' Mess. There's no-one about.'

'I've got something to ask you, but I want to ask it personally. I've just given the men a thirty-six hour pass...'

'Yes, I know, and psychologically speaking, I'm not sure it's wise. Some of them might not come back.'

'I know. That's one reason for giving them the leave. I want the deserters winkled out, right now.'

'You're taking a risk, Robin.'

'I didn't ring you to talk about that. Look, if you came half way, say to Grantham, and I came half way, that'd give us a lot more time together, wouldn't it?'

'You want to spend your leave with me?'

'Yes. Anyway, Grantham will make a nice change, won't it? Book into a hotel there? Nobody will know where we are, no telephones to interrupt us, lashings of grub, set me up for Europe, just what the doctor ordered! And I've got a question to ask you!'

'This question you want to ask, Robin. What is it?'

'I want to ask you in person, not over a ruddy telephone.'

'Robin, is it what I think it is?'

'I'm not going to tell you.'

She was silent. Yes, of course it was what she thought it was. I was going to ask her to marry me. Throughout the whole of the training for 404 I hadn't been able to get her out of my mind. And this was going to be my last job, wasn't it? Why not get married?

'Sandy, are you there?'

'Of course I'm here!'

'What time will you come to Grantham? I've looked up the trains – and there's a four-fifteen if you think you can make it. Otherwise it'd be the six-twenty-five. I'll meet you at the station. I've already made a tentative reservation at the Queen's Hotel, but I have to confirm it by four o'clock.'

'You were taking a lot for granted, weren't you?'

'Was I, Sandy?'

There was another silence. Strange how some conversations exist in two parts, the spoken word, and the unspoken thought. I had thought this conversation would be so simple. Will you come, yes/no? What time will you come, 4.15/6.25? Right, meet you off the train! Sandy wasn't coming to Grantham, and I wondered why not.

'Robin…'

'Yes?'

'I've done a bad thing.'

'You sound like Lenny in *Mice and Men*.'

'I feel worse than that. You've got to understand, Robin, that each one of us is at least two people, often more than two.'

'Are you talking as Sandy, or as an Army psychologist?'

'As both. It's my own fault. I confused the two.'

'Going to bed is a useful therapy for young officers who are about to be asked to sacrifice their all for King and Country, is that what you're trying to say? Well, if you are, come to Grantham as a therapist, come and give me some more of the same treatment.'

'Stop that, Robin.'

'Then say something to show me why?'

'Robin…'

'And don't start every sentence with my name. That doesn't help, you know.'

'Please don't interrupt me. My job was to find out if after all the jobs you've done, you're still mentally sound, and psychologically capable of 404. You've done a lot of hard jobs, and many men would already have been suffering from strain. I had to find out if you were, or not.'

'And where did you look, in bed?'

'The bed was something else. Obviously when I was investigating you, it made my task easier to know you socially...'

'But what about knowing me carnally, as they say?'

'Robin...'

'And don't go on using my bloody name at the start of every sentence.'

'All right. I think you can stand the truth.'

'Too damned right I can, so let's have it.'

'You're angry now, but you won't always be. I'm married. My husband is at home on a leave. I can't leave him to come to Grantham. I don't think we ought to meet again.'

'And that's it, is it, kiss me goodnight Sergeant Major, just like that. How's that for therapy? Is that what they call shock treatment? Why didn't you tell me you were married? Why didn't you wear a wedding ring? What sort of a man do you think I am? I've never had a married women knowingly in all my rotten life, do you know that, because I don't believe in pinching another man's wife. So how about that for bloody psychological treatment? Eh?'

'Robin...'

'Go back to your husband. Get lost!' I said, and slammed down the telephone. I caught my thumb nail on the cradle and ripped it almost down to the cuticle.

I tried to ring her back five minutes later to tell her I was sorry I had lost my temper, but they said she couldn't be found in Chelsea barracks, and would I like to leave a message. There didn't seem any point.

The radio was playing in my quarters. It's strange the way some moments in time seem to solidify, to live as tangibly as an old vase. Someone was singing, 'Maybe I'll live, a life of regret, maybe I'll give, much more than I get, but nevertheless I'm in love with you.'

The Brigadier had told me this would be my last job, and that, if I wished, I could go back to my parent regiment, the West Kents, and take on the training battalion. I'd be promoted to half colonel, and have a comfortable house in Maidstone. He even implied I would be getting an overdue decoration to stand on the chimney breast. I had built castles in the air – Sandy would have been in that house with me, in Maidstone. Now I knew I'd go on and on, job after job, until someone did something positive to end my war. 1943. The war seemed endless, my part of it so ludicrously small.

Before war started I worked for the Leeds Tar Distillers at Knottingley, in the benzene plant as an industrial chemist. I'd taken a mediocre B.Sc. at Leeds University in 1937, and spent the two years before the war watching drops of toluene separate themselves from drops of benzene. Both looked alike, but one boiled before the other – fractional distillation they call it. It was a good life. A three-roomed flat was half a house all to myself on the outskirts of Knottingley. An M.G. motor car took me all over Yorkshire. That's why I'd brought 404 here to train; I'd spread a ground sheet on most of these moors. Summer vacations from University I spent in Germany and France, and quickly picked up both languages in the belief they'd be useful to me as a chemist. They had been useful, but that had nothing to do with waggling test tubes. Friday evening, that Friday evening before the job that was to be the last, I took the Army P.U. and drove it to, of all places, Knottingley. They wouldn't have let me in the works, even if I had wanted to go; now they were making the benzene and toluene into explosives. I went to the pub, my former local, and sat at the bar drinking. A girl came to sit beside me. I think Betjeman's poem inspired me that evening. 'In the licorice fields of Pontefract, my love and I did lie.'

I've always had a conscience about women,

and the uses to which men put them. I had to ask her if I might. She laughed. 'May I kiss you?' She laughed. Later I asked other questions for other permissions, and she laughed again, but 'Why not, soldier?' she said, between the laughter. It seemed to strike a note at the time. Why not, soldier? There were so many 'why nots'. Sandy and I had met and loved, and doubtless she had said 'Why not?' There are many forms of therapy.

Captain Peter Derby was one of the best second-in-commands I'd ever had, a first-class soldier, but he was homosexual. Why not? Fred Pike and Joe Stanhope had been locked away for anti-social behaviour; they had declared a private war on our civilisation, and some judge in all his wisdom despite the war, had said 'We don't need you.' 404 needed them, and the Judge Advocate's Department held a special court in my office to legalise the release of these two men from gaol, to reconstitute them as human beings. Now the army was asking those men to risk their lives for the self-same society that once had rejected them. Why not? Total war is a pattern of expediences, it degrades human kind and humanises animals, lifts suffering like pus to the top of the wound. Why not, soldier? Kill a man if you must, blast away his body with explosive forces that can cut through concrete, but don't insert your pleasure-giving organ into his sister, no matter how much the woman in her might enjoy it. Why not, soldier? Therapy takes too many forms for a simple soldier.

Oh, God damn you, Sandy.

TAFFY ANDREWS

My name is Taffy Andrews and because I'm a Welshman I get the nickname all the time in the Army and not my proper name which happens to be Ianto. In civilian life I own a small printing works in Rhayader which is more or less in the centre of Wales. I take my annual holiday at Bangor. I have a wife, of course, and daughter sometimes subject to epileptic fits of the minor variety. My wife who is a most religious woman believes our daughter was born with the devil in her and refuses to sleep by my side. I've always been a good and faithful husband, as far as a man can possibly be; I've feared God and minded my own business. On Thursdays I close down the printing works, which is mostly concerned with the making of wedding invitations, birth greeting cards, the fixture calendars for the local teams and the like, and I go to spend the afternoon in a small shop owned and managed by Evan Botillone of Welsh birth but Roman extraction, where we drink gassy lemonade to which over the years I have become addicted, and hold conversations on the topical affairs of the day. Evan Botillone, you might say, is my international newspaper.

Well, of course, I should have put all that in the past tense, because War broke out and I joined the Army. I had the intention and the desire to serve in the Royal Army Pay Corps, since I could be said to have a good head for figures but, due no doubt to the prominent position given to my nationality on the signing up form, and an administrative mix-up in the War Office in London, I found myself posted to the South Wales Borderers, stationed in Cardiff, a fate I would wish on no man.

Cardiff, as you may know, is a place of evil purpose and intent. It was not long before my taste for lemonade acquired within the humble portals of Mr Botillone led me to the only places in Cardiff where such liquid could be procured, the public houses. Since these places remain open except on the Sabbath, the opportunities for drinking are unbridled. Once within the walls, I found the temptation to drink something more stimulating than Evan's homecrush to be more than I could bear. Soon, engendered no doubt by the new found self-confidence resulting directly from overstimulation, I began to suspect that life in Cardiff under the aegis of the South Wales Borderers was no more than the tip of a vast iceberg extended as far as the eye could see into far off England. Iceberg, perhaps, would be an unfortunate choice of word – possibly volcano might be more apposite. It was not, however, until I had got a girl on an anti-aircraft site outside Cardiff into what is known as 'trouble' that I decided the time had come for my departure.

The volcano drew me inescapably. I volunteered for the Commando, and was posted a week later to Brighton, over which town I now draw a veil of discretion.

Sometimes I think of the girl on the ack-ack site and hope that any outcome of alliance was not born, as was my true daughter, with the Devil in her. I have given up the drink, since I find it far too stimulating. I used to be a lay preacher in Rhayader, I don't preach any more. There isn't the call for it, somehow, not now.

It sat squat at the end of the airfield, black as the night around it. A bomber. From close up you could see the paint mottled with green in a shapeless pattern of camouflage. How it would stand out against the night sky, the moon and stars that throw its silhouette over the ground below!

I had picked my men. I made Taffy Andrews a corporal. I offered a sergeant's stripes to Sam Levine, but he refused them. Harry Landon and Willie Garside were still the fastest men I could find, and Willie could move like a cat at night. Alf Milner came, eager, dependable, and immensely strong. Dodger Bates, the loner, had finally persuaded Fred Pike and Joe Stanhope to talk to him about explosives, and Frank Farleigh could read Morse faster than any man I knew. Nine men. Arthur Sywell qualified, not only because of Fred and Joe, but because he quickly picked up the technical side of the job we had to do. He could crawl silently, and that was a talent worth its weight in gold; he could shoot a bow and arrow, and knew about locks. Ben, of course, but I wouldn't go without Ben. Captain Peter Derby as my official second-in-command. That was the way the Army liked it.

The Air Force supplied a crew of four, including a despatcher. They also sent a large thermos bottle of coffee and a bottle of brandy, which we left full with the despatcher.

In the hangar before we marched out to the plane, Ben Bolding held our last check. Each man had his own personal weapons, a knife, a bow with twelve arrows all needle sharp, six throwing pins. Each man had his own ration packs, sufficient vitamins and proteins for four days, all condensed, concentrated, dehydrated into a caramel tasting chewing stick that if you weren't careful would give you lockjaw. No man had cigarettes or matches. I was carrying cartons I would hand out to the resistance – any man wanting a smoke could apply to me. We all had morphia and the new elastic bandages and tubes of collodion for pasting over superficial wounds. We had the new powder for preventing infection, clips to 'stitch' together the open sides of deep wounds. We had no radio. Each of us had a pencil torch. Dodger, Fred and Joe carried the explosive. I carried a spare supply. I also had two pairs of women's silk knickers. I found them more comfortable to wear than Army issue, and they took up no room at all in the bottom of my pack.

Ben had the nylon rope, Peter the signal wire, we all had detonators and fuses, carried in wooden boxes, wrapped in cotton wool, in our inside pockets. We were wearing battle-dress, gaiters, Innsbrucker boots, jumping jackets that fasten under your crotch. We wore green berets and scorned the tin jumping hats. I had a piece of wire on two toggles fastened round my waist under the battle-dress sleeve, the sort of thing that before the war was used for cutting slabs of cheese.

The whole equipment was duplicated in three canisters that would be dropped independently on a second pass of the air-craft. Canisters, however, have a way of getting lost. I never trusted them.

We had all been passed by the doctor. We had all been to the lavatory. We were all shit-scared.

It was an old bomber. All the bombing equipment had been torn out of it, and two benches ran along the sides, tucked into the curvature of the side of the plane. It was impossible to sit upright. A one-inch metal rod ran down the length of the plane; from it rings hung like the clothing rail in a garment shop. As each man entered the plane, he took a ring and slid it along the metal rod. Since I would be the last to jump, my ring went first, and I found myself testing its strength. It hung firm and had been well greased. The plane had already been 'warmed up' when we climbed on board. There was no ceremony. There was no-one at the airport to wave goodbye. We filed inside in silence, the door was closed and clipped, the plane taxied out to the runway, destination Belgium. This is it; no generals flashing medals at us exhorted us to valour; no chaplains with a grin full of teeth wished us God Speed. The pilot opened the throttle, the engines roared, the plane lumbered down the runway gathering speed, and then, impossible as it always seemed, the plane lifted up into the air and we were airborne. Each man clipped the hook on the end of his static line to the ring on the rail. That static line would jerk the parachute open when the time came to jump, and it was not a thing you wanted to forget to do. The inside of the plane hung festooned like a Christmas tree without the lights. The men sat back on the benches as best they could, cramped against the walls of the plane. I walked the length, looking at each one, ostensibly checking the static lines. They all smiled at me, in turn, as if I needed comforting. I said each man's name as I came to him, inviting him to make a last comment. No-one spoke back to me.

I haven't written a lot about these men under training, because deliberately I had tried to expunge from my consciousness any individual characteristics they may have possessed. Psychologists talk a lot of nonsense about 'the need to know your man'. I needed to know their capabilities, didn't want to cloud my judgment with my own amateur and half-formed impressions of their characters. I knew they differed, by God how they differed. Taffy Andrews whom I'd made a corporal had been a lay preacher; but that wasn't why he got promotion. I gave him the two tapes solely because he was able to do everything the other men could do a little better than they could do it, and had the urge to be a leader among men. Not a leader of men. I suppose the difference is that between a lay preacher and a qualified parson. Taffy didn't want to rise above them, he wanted to take them with him. It made him an ideal corporal; doubtless it had made him a good lay preacher; but that was something I couldn't know, and therefore didn't want to be influenced by.

186

'Harry?' He smiled up at me, nothing to say. Harry Landon came of Scandinavian stock, big and jovial, the unsinkable Landon. Harry was a good all-rounder, and strong as an ox. But more than that he was a happy man, the sultana in the sponge, the morsel that adds taste to the rest. I had only recently discovered by accident that Harry who, I knew, had been a poacher, was passionately fond of music, knew the scores of most works of the classic repertoire. Thank God I hadn't known about that sooner; one of my set of built-in prejudices was that musicians and music lovers were soft people in general. How wrong I would have been in the case of Harry Landon! It would have been another factor to be overcome, an irrelevant reason for selecting someone in his place.

'Peter?' He too smiled. He knew what I was doing. In my place he would have done the same. Present yourself to each man in turn to give him the last chance to say, 'I don't want to come.' Once that door was open and the lights came on, refusal would become 'Desertion in the face of the Enemy'!

Willie Garside was playing with the rings of the parachute packed on his chest. It suddenly struck me that Willie lived off nervous energy, always on the move, never still, always questing with his eyes, seeking, searching. For what? He moved at night like a stoat, with tremendous economy. Flick flick his eyes always backwards and forwards. Restless. Like a cat. Always licking at himself.

The flak started. Welcome to Europe. The plane rose rapidly jerking at our stomachs, the pilot kicked a rudder, and the whole plane yawed to the right, spilling men on the left onto the floor. They got up cursing, jerking themselves by the static lines, holding on, anticipating the next sickening sideways lurch. Don't let there be a lot of flak. I'd ridden to the centre of France in planes swilling with vomit. Another burst. The plane leaped up in the air lifted further skywards by the explosion of the shell. Then we were in the middle of it, and the gunners found our range. Several holes were torn in the fuselage, one not six inches from my head. Ice cold wind whistled in. All hell was let loose as the pilot dipped the plane in a steep dive and we slid along and off the benches. For a while my head was pressed against the roof of the plane and legs came flailing past me. A boot caught me under the ear; thank God it was rubber shod. The pilot levelled off again out of the flak range, and we picked ourselves up and sorted out our static lines. Ben had caught his neck on one of the bar supports, a jagged cut bled copiously. 'Just my luck,' he raged. We dusted him with powder and stuck an elastoplast over the wound. It was the best we could do; he would come to no harm. The men were cursing the pilot good humouredly. The despatcher put his head through the partition into the pilot's cabin, and shouted at him. The pilot shouted back but his words were lost in the noise. I checked there were no other injuries.

Out of the flak. The plane flew on an even keel, shuddering as it thrust its way through the air. We were near the dropping zone, my watch told me. I stood up, unhooked my static line, and went to stand beside the despatcher. The men knew the time had come. There was silence. The green light came on, winking. Each man checked his static line, pulled it tight against the metal rod to make certain the rings held. Each man swung his line from side to side. The rings clicked like the balls of an abacus. The despatcher opened the side door. There was a sudden roar of engine noise as he opened the door. There was a hand rail at the side of the door. The men stood up and shuffled along to the front of the plane in line, holding the parachutes tight to their chests with the left hand, right hand grasping the static line webbing to make certain it wouldn't jam along the metal rod. I was holding my static line ring in my left hand, standing at the front end of the plane beside the despatcher. Ben Bolding was at the back of the line; our best pusher. If any men were to slip, Ben could push that entire line out of the plane in one run. The light stopped blinking and held steady. We were over the dropping zone.

The red light came on. Peter Derby away, Taffy Andrews, bad exit, off to the side, Sam Levine, Harry Landon, Willie Garside, Arthur Sywell. He turned sharply at the end of the run, swinging round with his right hand on the bar beside the door. Looks into my eyes, 'God help me,' he seems to say. I try to reassure him though there's no time even for a handclasp as out he steps. Arthur's static line flapped back and almost hit me in the face. It had been cut through. There would be nothing to open his parachute. Fred Pike came next and as he swung out and down I thought I caught the glimpse of the knife in his right hand. Certainly I saw his evil smile. His static line held taut, snapping the cord that secured the outer canopy of his parachute, the canopy came off and with it the pilot chute that yanks open the main chute. The main chute opened and Fred started floating down. Dodger Bates okay. Alf Milner stumbled as he went out through the door but the despatcher pushed him. Joe Stanhope jumped, a nervous bundle. The despatcher's arm flashed across the cabin in front of Frank Farleigh and I heard him scream something. I looked down and out of the plane. Joe Stanhope was hanging on the bottom end of his static line, suspended twenty feet below the aeroplane, carried backwards by the tremendous force of slipstream racing past him. Damn, the cord that holds the parachute pack closed had jammed, and the outer canopy couldn't release itself. If it suddenly gives way in that position, he'll pull the parachute against the tailplane of the aircraft and rip it to shreds.

Without thinking I pulled the knife out of my sheath, handed my static line to the despatcher, grasped Joe Stanhope's line where it dangled out of the plane, and started to slide down it. The despatcher must have hooked my ring to the metal bar, and was now holding on to my line, paying it out inch by inch as I went down towards Joe.

Once out of the plane the force of the slipstream hit me, and my grip slid on the webbing. I curled my leg round it, crushing the webbing between the insole of my left boot and the instep of my right foot. Slowly I went down against the buffeting of the wind which threatened at each second to pluck me from the webbing. The climb down seemed to take for ever, though Ben told me later I went down like a monkey on a stick. When I could see my feet almost level with Joe, I swung them off his static line and slid down, holding only by my hands. The pull on my arms was something I'll never forget, the weight of my body trebled by the force of the hundred and fifty miles an hour slipstream. When my face was level with Joe's pack, I could see the trouble. The static line itself had wound round the outer pack of his parachute as he whipped out of the plane, and now he was suspended in a million to one chance loop that clenched the outer pack tight. I had about five seconds of grip left in my hands at that speed. I lifted my feet and pressed them against Joe's parachute pack. As he swung out I could see his agonised face. I pulled with my hands, adding my weight to his weight to jerk his parachute through the knot of the static line. 'Wriggle,

Joe,' I screamed at him, but of course he couldn't hear me. I pushed frantically at his pack with my feet, pulling myself backwards against the static line. I could feel the pack start to slip, but already my hands had cramped, and I knew I would not be able to hold on much longer. I could see what was holding it, the brass ring through which the secondary line, the thin one that held on the outer pack and should snap open under the weight of a man. There was only one thing I could do. I wound my left hand around my own static line, so that the webbing was curled around my left forearm, and then let go with my right hand. The jerk almost pulled my left arm from the socket. I took the knife from between my teeth with my right hand, reached down, and sliced through the cord which held the outer canopy. Joe fell out of the outer pack, downwards. I watched him go. The pilot parachute struggled out as he dropped, and then the main parachute suddenly tugged, blossomed out above him, hiding him from view. At that moment my left hand gave way; I could hold on no longer. I felt the jerk as my static line reached its end, and the pilot chute was torn from the outer pack. The main chute opened, and as ever the shock jarred my stomach. Joe was away to the right of me; I slipped air to try to increase my rate of fall, and veer the parachute after him. Soon I was not fifty feet from him, and below. He seemed to be falling free, his hands clutching nervously on the parachute cords, in the direction he was facing. If he kept his head and landed the way we had taught him, he would get safely down. I could see Ben Bolding silhouetted against the sky on the other side of him. Ben must have spilled a lot of air to get down that swiftly. I looked about me. No knowing where we would land. It seemed to me I had been dangling for ever on the end of that static webbing. The ground came rushing towards me. I had a little trick I did whenever I landed. As the ground came rushing towards me, I always drew myself up a foot or two into the parachute cords. This way, when I landed, I could drop free and the canopy didn't immediately start to yank at me. Usually I was out of the harness before the fold of the chute had reached the ground. It was a good landing. I ran from beneath the chute towards Joe's point of fall. He came in badly, forgetting what we had taught him of course. His legs were apart, one behind the other. Damn fool. He was lucky not to break something. Ben was at his side almost as quickly as I was.

'I was scared he wasn't going to make it up there,' he said, by way of a compliment.

'He had to,' I said, 'don't forget he's got a third of the explosives with him.'

Joe was rubbing himself down, trying to clear the parachute harness. Side by side we unclipped him, then took his parachute and ours and hid them beneath the hedge as best we could.

There was no time to hang about. The partisans would have to take a chance on finding the chutes before the Germans did.

Our destination was twenty miles away, over terrain not quite as difficult as the Course.

But first we had to find the rest of the troop.

I had forgotten all about Arthur Sywell until that moment. Thinking back, I couldn't be certain I had seen that knife in Fred's hand. The webbing of a static line can't slash itself, and Arthur Sywell must have checked every inch of it while they were sitting in the plane. Of course it would be very simple for Fred to seize it as they were running along and slash it, holding the two ends together until Arthur Sywell actually jumped.

But what kind man would do a thing like that? Arthur had told me how sick Fred had been when Arthur picked him up in Tottenham. Arthur, a policeman to the last, had acted on a hunch. He knew Fred had 'scarpered' and doubtless kept in touch with his old colleagues in the police, relying on them to tell him where Fred had gone. Fred swore he meant to come back to camp.

But what could I prove? And anyway, wasn't Fred's knowledge vital to the success of the job we had come here to do? Even if I knew Fred had murdered Arthur, dare I do anything about it until Fred had blown the vault? And, having blown the vault to give us access to so much information that could shorten the war and save so many lives, could I then indict Fred for having taken one life?

These were my thoughts as we found our bearings and set off for the original dropping zone. The code word was TIM, and the answer from the resistance would be BULL.

We had dropped in an area of trees and undulating ground leading down to the Meuse, known as the Hohe Venn. Liège was to our west, the German border and Aachen to the east and north, the Dutch border and Maastritch to the north, the Hohe Venn and Luxembourg to the south-east. Our original dropping zone, I estimated, was on the other side of the range of low hills almost due west of us. We gathered together, myself, Ben Bolding, a badly shaken Joe Stanhope, and Frank Farleigh. Ben had plotted our route with his compass; we were to aim straight across the valley to the woods on the crest of the hill. We set off in single file, Ben Bolding leading at a jog trot. My pack weighed about a hundred pounds. Hanging onto the webbing of Joe's static line had wrenched my shoulder; I felt a dull ache beneath the shoulder-blade I knew would get worse as the night progressed. We reached the wood entirely without incident. Once again, as always on these jobs, I wondered at our ability to descend out of the sky and move about undetected in country occupied by a foreign army. Up here in the Hohe Venn, the countryside was sparsely populated. Between here and Liège, however, the mining areas would be heavily occupied by German troops. The wood sat on the top of the slope, like a crop of bristly hair on a high-domed forehead. Here I estimated we were about a thousand feet above sea level. Behind us the Hohe Venn rose to two thousand feet, the foothills of the higher hills of the Ardennes. The wood was mostly oak and beech, with a few silver birch, but mostly they were poor specimens. This part of Belgium seemed unfertile, a contrast to the plains below and to the north. That, of course, was our principal reason for dropping here – on the other side of Liège, the fertile land meant a farm every five acres or so, the whole countryside dotted with small houses. Not many Belgians could be trusted; the years their country had been used as a convenient corridor by invading armies had not endeared the Belgians either to the Germans or the Allies. Mostly the Belgian people, more than any other Europeans, possibly with the exception of the Dutch, wanted no part of war, or of either army. We had strict instructions to skirt any farm we might run across. From aerial photographs and maps, however, the War Office boffins had created a route that would take us almost into Liège without coming across any known German military installations. We were to cross only two main roads, and the Meuse, and that we would do by our own log bridge.

We met our first trouble in the woods.

A patrol. Of Germans. From the uniforms I recognised them as Fallschirmjaegers, the German parachute troops. Fortunately they were looking the other way, but strung out across our path. From their present positions they would command the valley beyond. In that valley, I suspected the rest of our troop had landed. Right under the noses of the crack German regiment. They couldn't have been there when our plane came over. With the short-barrelled automatic rifles they carried they'd have picked us off like coconuts at the fair. There were eight of them, a German section. We were four, one unseasoned. They were stretched out on the far edge of the wood in arrowhead formation, looking north. I wondered they hadn't posted a rearguard, but when I looked to the valley past them, I could see why: partisans were scuttling about down there like ants, carting away parachutes. 'Damned amateurs,' I muttered. There was no sign of Captain Derby and the rest of my troop. Trust them, they'd gone to ground somewhere. They were professionals.

One of the Fallschirmjaegers had dumped his radio behind a tree. I saw him crawl back towards it. I was crouched in deep shadow where he'd never spot me.

Now the killing starts again. I had lost count of the number of men I had killed. Often, in England, I had nightmares, and all the men I had personally done to death would be ranged opposite me, each with eyes accusing. Of course, the only justification for taking a man's life is that, if you do so, you will never have to take a life again. Each occasion is the last one. If I kill this man I will get to my objective and out again and the war will be that much shorter. It was a specious argument, as all must be that set your life higher than the life of any other individual. Arrogance says that because you can kill another man, you are morally right in doing so to protect your own life. What if the man you must kill to save yourself is another Doctor Schweitzer, or a Thomas Beecham, or a Dag Hammarskjoeld? I had drawn the bow from the sheath down my trouser leg, had bent it to fix the two end caps and the wire. I took an arrow from the other leg. Here we go again. Who is he? What is he, saint or sinner? What am I? I put the cleft of the arrow against the bow wire and drew back. He reached the radio. He had put on the headphones and was about to switch on. I let the arrow go. It's not my decision. I am a servant of my master's master's master, and the servant of God has locked the ten commandments away for the duration of this human cataclysm we call the war. Now there is no 'Thou shalt not'.

The arrow took him, as I had aimed, under his left arm. It would go straight through into his heart. The quickest possible death. That was the only commandment. Kill swiftly, and as painlessly as possible. Only that way can you avoid becoming a brute, only that way can the effect of the bestiality of war be minimised. Each one of us was a professional killer. There were twenty or so partisans in that valley and though later when I met their leader, I might tell him to teach them not to behave like bloody fools, I had a responsibility at that moment to keep them, and my men they were helping, alive. The only way that could be done was to eliminate their aggressors. Cut the cant, I told myself, you mean kill the Germans.

Ben Bolding had drawn his bow, so had Frank Farleigh. Joe Stanhope had not yet learned the instinctive actions. Ben quickly held up three fingers, Frank saw him and flashed two. I would cover. Ben got his first three, one two three, just like that. Target practice, no more. All in the back of the neck. Frank got his two, but his bow twanged; he had the wire too slack. We ran forward out of cover. Two Germans left. Ben got one with a thrown needle at ten paces. I jumped the other just as he was about to empty his rifle into Ben's side. He was tough. I saw the hate on his face; that's where the Germans made their mistake. We taught to kill, they taught to hate first. Often the emotion clouded their vision, slowed their actions just that fraction. We stayed cool; I had no hate, only a purpose and a trained determination. He was tall, dark, about twenty-five, and tough. He bounced up from the ground like a rubber ball, catching me bent, my knife arm forward, off balance. He slammed his knee into my groin before I had a chance to knife him. My testicles seemed to explode with pain. As I went forward I saw his knee continue its swing up into my face. It would have smashed my teeth. I butted forward into his throat, sidestepped and slammed my hand into his neck, just below his ear. As he went down I chopped his neck again. He lay still on the ground at my feet. I was doubled up in agony. Ben came over and put his knife into the Fallschirmjaeger. Never take a chance. 'Let's go,' I said, through clenched teeth, and hobbled away down the hillside. I wanted to find my men quickly, and get them as far and as quickly from that amateur band of partisans.

They were waiting in the wood on the next lip of the valley.

We Tim and Bulled, and I assembled them quickly about me. Captain Derby had broken his leg on landing. According to instructions, they left him; the partisans carried him away on the back of a horse cart. Arthur Sywell had candled. All parachutists hope that's the way they'll go. You jump out of a plane and your parachute doesn't open. Some people say you die of heart failure the moment you realise your parachute isn't going to open; but there were reports in 1943 of a parachutist who did the long drop into the snow on the side of a mountain, slid down the ice-cap beneath the snow and walked out alive a thousand feet later. He was lucky. If you candled on to hard ground they had to dig you up to bury you. I had seen three in my time; now I always packed my own parachute. We wouldn't be digging up Arthur Sywell. Let him die peacefully wherever he was, killed in action. When I got back home I'd tell the Brigadier, and the official machine would go swiftly into action, locating his next of kin. Damn it, I didn't even know who that was. For a brief moment I wished I had taken the time to get to know that much at least about him; but that had never been my method and now it was too late for regrets. Let him die, mourned only by those who loved him; I had the lives of other men to consider. I had a job to do.

What had they said of me? 'That bastard's almost human sometimes.'

'Did you do it, Fred?' I asked him, as we set off.

'Do what, Major?'

The criminal mind. How little I knew about it! What a tortuous mind to seek revenge at such a moment.

'He would have been useful to us; you might find yourself missing him.'

'I'll try not to cry, Major,' he said.

Peter Derby and Arthur Sywell gone. Now only eleven. We set off for Liège, running. We had to be there before daybreak; nearly twenty miles to travel in four and a half hours. It was easy; how many times had we done the Course in training, and I had designed that course with this particular run in mind. Anyway, this was all downhill. The hundred-pound pack bit into my wrenched shoulder. It would be a long night.

Seven miles an hour. Run and walk. How much is that in kilometres? I looked around. We were all going well, despite the weights we carried. Even Joe was going well, Ben had worked on his boots day and night to get them right. Ben, of course, was going well, trundling along like a tractor in top gear, uphill, downhill, the same controlled step, light but firm, fast but stable. When we had been going for an hour I signalled a halt. Five minutes' rest.

We squatted down in the shadow of a wood. Ben, Alf Milner and Frank Farleigh went deep among the trees. We were hull down in a dry ditch, a three strand wire fence without barbs behind us, a long pasture sloping steeply away in front of us. The moon was still up, and we could see the entire length of the pasture. Or so I thought. Willie Garside was on watch on the left, Dodger on the right. I was in the centre, not officially on watch, but as ever permanently, naggingly, alert. I took a strip of dried beef from the pack in the pocket on the left knee of my trousers. It tasted like leather, but I had seen men live for a week on it. It was a trick the War Office dieticians got from the Eskimos. I started to chew. Harry Landon was eight feet from me, lying on his pack jammed against the side of the gully. He had his feet up, and seemed already asleep. I noticed however, his hand was on the handle of his knife, his left knee bent. When he came awake, he'd uncoil as fast as a snake and twice as deadly. That came from his poacher nights!

I had not seen the fold in the hill of the pasture below us, and the patrol making its way slowly along that fold. Now they came over the top lip, advancing in line abreast, eight feet apart. Germans. Dodger and Willie saw them the instant I did. We had three men in the wood. I hissed. Harry came awake, turning as he recovered consciousness, his eyes level with the crest of the ditch. Ten of them in sight, now twelve. To him they must have seemed like giants advancing towards us. I was certain the Germans had not seen us. We could not go back through the wire. Now fourteen. One of us could have done it in total silence, but we couldn't hope all could do it. Any noise, the slightest suggestion of our presence, and the patrol commander would simply call out an estimated range and order his men to open fire. Seventeen. And those rifles would really cut grass. I could see they were all automatic, so close were they. Christ, twenty. And then no more.

Quick glance up and down the line, our own line. Bad news travels fast, don't they say? All my men had seen the Germans.

Only seconds of time had passed since I had first seen the Germans, but already I felt I had been watching their approach for ever. Damn the Brigadier! With rifles it would have been so easy, so easy!

Back in the woods behind us, one of the three men finished relieving himself with the loudest fart I've ever heard. We all heard it, every one of us. The Germans heard it, though to them it was a faint noise on the breeze, unmistakably human in origin. The patrol commander raised his hand. They halted in an arc, the wings about five paces behind the centre. Well trained, as they halted they went down and virtually disappeared into the grass of the pasture. Though I heard nothing twenty safety catches would have been pulled, and twenty rounds, the first of twenty times fifteen in the magazine and other magazines easily available in pockets, were waiting for any slight sound to reveal itself. Willie and Harry were watching me. I had to make a decision. Which way would the Germans head? Would they come up to the wood then go through it? Would they approach it then turn left, or turn right? Toss a coin in the air and you're dead. Make the wrong guess and you have twenty shadows on your tail.

Ben would have to look out for himself and the two men with him.

I pointed right.

We all started to move along the gully.

Now it comes – the long months of training. Remember Timble, all of you, and let no-one stick his arse in the air. Remember Timble and get lower than the proverbial gnat's knackers. This is the real thing, boys, and that's not me out there with a hot rifle – it's a pack of twenty Germans, all with mothers and fathers and wives and sweethearts, and they want to go home when the war has ended, just as you do, all in one piece. So keep your arses down! Somebody behind me slipped and there was a clink of metal on stone. Who the hell is carrying exposed metal? I heard the command snap in the air. He'd got the range too long – he'd overestimated but that's easy when you're looking up a hill. I wasn't wrong about the bindiggers – proper little blood spitters they were, and bullets in the air above us like angry bees spitting in the trees above our heads, splitting twigs, smashing branches, ripping the woods apart in a teeth-hurting ratatatat of fire.

'Keep your heads down boys and don't panic,' I prayed. We ran forward. The patrol commander was good. He detached the last third and the first third with a ten word command, and they spread out like bats' wings and started to move across the front.

They could move faster than we could since they made no great effort at concealment, relying on movement and firepower. They couldn't know we didn't have a rifle between us. I imagine they thought we were a bunch of partisans on a Boy Scout mischief patrol. Sod them! The centre third of the patrol bored forwards, the two wings sped to the side. We were trapped. When we realised it, I signalled the men to stop. Willie was a long time looking at me, and the men behind him detached themselves by a couple of paces, before they saw my signal and stopped. Dead still! Absolutely silent! Breathe through your noses. And Ben, stick a cork up the appropriate arse! Please!

The patrol commander had as good a command of his men as I hoped I had of mine. They stopped seconds after we did, lost themselves behind blades of grass. Six men bunched tighter than I would have allowed. A gap, wider than I would have allowed, eight men, a gap, six men. Check. And his next move would be mate.

I had the first move.

I hadn't the faintest idea of what I was going to do. I hadn't a single clue. Three men in the wood. Or were they dead from

209

that first high fusillade? The rest of us pinned down in a gully not four feet deep. One hundred and fifty yards away from us twenty Germans, who knew someone was there. They couldn't know who but what did that matter? Bullets don't discriminate.

No man alive can throw a knife a hundred yards, nor fire our kind of bow and arrow that distance. What could I do?

The German patrol commander was in no hurry. In his shoes, nor would I have been.

Sam Levine. Hand on my head. Good, he's seen first time. Come to me! Keep your arse down, boy, or they'll circumcise you again, this time from the back. Harry Landon. Hand on my head. On my head you silly bastard that means come to me, fast! When he got there I reached inside his two chest packs, took out a grenade, two grenades, three. Same with Sam. Share the six grenades, two each. Three slabs from Sam. Three detonators from my own field-dressing pocket, three coils of wire from my belt. Hand 'em round, one each. The boys know what to do. Daren't talk, not even in whispers. Press my fingers together, palms of my hands together. God bless you lads, God bless us all, and keep our arses down. Ends of the wire to Dodger.

We set off, crawling. Straight towards the Germans.

I took the group in the centre, Sam on my left, Harry on my right.

Now you're really in it. Body so flat on the ground you can hardly breathe. Left leg fully extended. Draw the right leg up, your instep flat on the ground. Bite with the inside of your instep and without raising your belly more than an eighth of an inch from the ground, push the whole of your body forward eighteen inches. Now your right leg is straight out and you bring your left leg forward, instep flat. Bite in and push. The grass waves all about you like a thousand beckoning hands. 'Here I am, here I am.' You hear your body grind over the earth, each crushing movement like the rustle of a million finger taps on kettle drums. Another eighteen inches forward. One potato two potatoes three potatoes four potatoes five potatoes six potatoes seven potatoes more. Remember when you used to play that game on the pavements when you were a little lad? And Uncle George Willie gave you a bottle of Tizer for cleaning his bicycle, and then bet you a shilling you couldn't drink it in one go. You did drink it, and he never gave you the shilling, and several years later, when he'd got a car and was going out one Saturday night and had conned you into cleaning the car, you found a packet of three in the glove box and punctured all the ends with a pin. Uncle George Willie was killed at Dunkirk and left a wife and two. Were you the father of your own cousins? Now I'm crawling through this grass and I've gone about a hundred yards and its past time to lift my head, and when I do so I'll either see sweet fanny adams, or a dirty big hairy arsed German with his boots pointing at me and an automatic rifle ready to puncture my end. Cautious. No sudden movement. Head slowly up in the grass. Beret's green and that's a blessing. In the daylight you'd have to stuff your cap with grass to break up its hard lines, but moonlight has its own softening effect. Even Mavis looked lovely by moonlight, those long long years ago. Yes. There they are. You can't see them, but you can distinguish the depressions in the grass where they lie. Head down and crawl and now count the steps. No hope to see Harry or Sam. Three individuals, all together with one purpose.

Fifty yards to go. Wet through. Right through to the belly. Elbows and knees wet. Pain in each groin, pain in each instep. Pain in my balls. Pain. Twenty-five yards to go.

Another five yards'll be close enough.

That's another ten of these instep-grinding, groin-pulling lifts, left right left. That's it.

We're here because we're here because we're here because we're here!

Two grenades. Pull out the pin. Hold the handle. Let the plunger go down. Quiet, you noisy bastard. Put in the detonator. No fuse. Put the slab down on the ground. Put the detonator in the hole at the centre of the slab. Now put in the fuse. It fits. Right, take it out again. Careful. Crimp the detonator onto the end of the fuse. Nick the fuse along its side, breaking the coating. That's it, squeeze your nail in. For Christssake don't move about too much. You're only twenty yards from eight Germans, each with two bloody great lugholes tuned to receive the faintest sound. They're just as crap-pants wary as you are. They want to get home, too. Now push the skewer into the ground. Okay Harry? Okay Sam? With luck we'll be able to get back half way. That skewer point is an earth. It carries the current back through the earth. Hardly seems possible, does it, a tiny electric current going to find its way back over a hundred and eighty yards of wet earth. Now stand the two grenades on top of the slab. That's nice. They

213

look well side by side, don't they, like two vases! Each grenade has thirty-two fragments on its outer skin, thirty-two fragments of quarter inch steel that snaps with razor edges all around. All ready? Check! Check everything – wire coming to fuse, fuse stripped, crimped into detonator, back out of detonator into skewer down through skewer into ground, and back through ground to that little box Dodger by now has in his hot hand. On the top of that box is a plunger, and when Dodger pushes down that plunger twenty thousand volts will come screaming along the wire you've been laying out while you've crawled. Guess what twenty thousand volts will do inside that little detonator! All all right! Move two paces to the right, Major, and you can fall out and return to base.

The crawl back took only half as long as the crawl out. It had to – those German rifles were pointing straight up my anus.

Harry had been back quite a while when I got there. His forehead was dry. Sam arrived after a minute, wet through.

No thumbs up, no Victory Roll, or 'up and at 'em lads' grins. Just a little quiet nod. All three of us had been too scared out there for heroics now. I put my pack on again, so did Harry and Sam, we took our positions in line, and I nodded to Dodger. He pressed down the plunger. Twenty thousand volts went screaming down the line, down three lines. Twenty thousand volts hit three detonators with a high intensity spark that shocked the detonators into explosive reaction, three explosive charges went up, and six grenades exploded, as one. The Germans had started forward just before Dodger pushed the plunger. They must have been only five yards from the charges when they exploded. Another pace or two, they would have seen them and some would have lived. As it was, what the grenades didn't get, we got, dashing madly across the green green pastures, faces black, knives gleaming in our hands, the rattle of death in our throats.

Ben Bolding and his two lads caught up a mile later. Alf Milner had missed castration by the thickness of a pencil. Frank Farleigh had been felled by the sergeant major after his fart – it had saved his life. Ben escaped from the wood at the far side, circled the hill, and was preparing to come up behind the flank of the German patrol when our grenades exploded. An hour later we were seven miles away.

Belfière himself picked us up on the other

side of the main Aachen-Liège railroad. Ben Bolding damned near killed him. We were walking down a track between two farms. The rendezvous was to be at the far end of the track. I waited at the rear end. Ben went down it with Dodger Bates and Willie Garside. A tree at the near end of the track was in the shadow of a larger one behind it. I climbed up the smaller tree. From there I could keep Ben in view all the way down the track. He stalked at one side, Willie Garside six feet behind him, at the other, Dodger Bates behind Willie. We were three miles from Liège, and two farms were within a thousand yards of this track. It had been a horse ride before the war, I guessed. Ben was three-quarters of the way down, when a bush fluttered ten feet in front of him. It could have been my imagination; night vision plays its own tricks. Dawn was not far away, and the moon had already gone down. I could see as far as the end of the track but no more. Yes, the bush was fluttering, and there was no wind. I was just going to call my owl hoot, the most ludicrous bird imitation you've ever heard, when I saw Ben raise his right hand to waist height, palm flat downwards. Willie saw the sign and stopped. Dodger went to ground. Ben would be carrying his knife in his left hand. He dropped on the ground and I lost sight of him. Willie would be able to see him; he waited a couple of minutes and then started to advance, his left hand out palm downwards. Dodger stayed where he was, doubtless bow drawn, arrow fitted. Now it starts again, the hunted hunting, the hunter hunted. I felt sorry for the man in the hedge; he didn't stand a chance against Willie and Ben. Willie drew further away from me, down the track, nearer to the man in the hedge. There was a scuffle at the back of the hedge and a man burst into view. Ben came out behind him, grinning. I had heard the strangled cry from up there in the tree. Ben must have had his forearm round the man's throat, about to snap his neck when the sound burst from him. The man would never know how near he was to getting a knife in his kidneys. He was Roget Belfière.

I shook his hand. 'Nice to meet you,' I said. It sounded so ludicrous, but what else can you say to a white-faced man, trembling from the narrowest escape he's ever likely to have.

He didn't speak, but led the way down the track. I could guess from his manner that no-one was about, but nevertheless, we didn't relax our vigil until we were in the barn, a mile from the bottom of the track.

When we arrived I introduced the men to him, then sent Alf Milner and Frank Farleigh out on watch. I was taking no chances. The barn, forty feet long, twenty feet across, was half full of old straw. The straw had been stacked and inside it a dozen small 'boxes' had been created, and a rabbit warren of passages. Twenty men could hide in that straw easily, move from one side to the other, get out of the barn through a dozen holes, up onto the roof, down into the ground. The rabbit warren passages Roget showed me extended outside the barn in the ground, four feet deep trenches covered with wood and sods of turf. The ends of these underground passages were located all round the barn at distances of a hundred feet or more, coming up in copses, under hedges. It was a location ideally suited to our purposes. There had once been a pigeon loft at the top of the barn with four windows without glass but covered with slatted wooden louvres. Anyone in that pigeon coop could look out over the entire countryside.

I hated the need to spend a day in the barn, exposed, vulnerable. Straight in and straight out – that was my way; but on this job there wasn't the time to drop in and get to the objective in one night. We couldn't have landed any closer to Liège than we did for fear of being spotted coming down. The journey had to be broken somewhere close enough for us to get to the location and do the job during one night, and that meant holing up during the hours of daylight. More than that, however, it meant entrusting yourself and your men to the care of other people. The burden of command is weighted by the amount of responsibility you must leave with other people. I had never approved of involving the Belgians in what we had to do – I would have preferred to make our own way to the target, relying on our own planning and skill to get us out again.

This job, dammit, couldn't be like that. Time and distance were against us. As Ben would have said, it was a right cow!

Ben was sniffing round the barn like a lost ferret. He came across to me. I could tell he was dissatisfied.

'We're taking a right old chance here, Major!' he said.

I shrugged my shoulders. He must know I had considered the dangers, but the alternative of hiding in the hedgerows near the town was too tricky. We'd done it once before, near Innsbruck in Austria. It was in the thick of winter. When the time came to get to Innsbruck to do the job, half the men were incapacitated by frostbite. I wasn't taking any such risks again. Lying about in hedge bottoms is no way to prepare men for the rigours of a job. They needed to relax, needed to be warm, to get some food in their guts. The barn was warm and cosy, seemed safe enough and was reassuringly easy to get out of. By the first light of day, my men were all hidden in the straw caves, doubtless fast asleep, except for the two on guard.

Belfière and I went over his briefing, over and again. He checked my specially drawn maps and aerial photographs; all were substantially correct. At nine o'clock Ben Bolding came from his hiding place, his hair filled with straw, and went to find Harry Landon and Willie Garside to relieve the two guards.

'That man has a built-in alarm clock,' I thought.

It was a love of his men, a deep feeling of compassion for them, that wouldn't let him rest totally while other men watched for him.

'You are not afraid, monsieur?' Roget asked me.

I turned to him. He was afraid, I could see that, and respected him for it.

'Yes, I'm afraid, but I've learned to live

220

with it.'

'So have I,' he said, 'but it's not easy when you grow older.'

My shoulder throbbed, my testicles ached from the Fallschirmjaeger's kick. Life, at that particular moment in time, was not very precious to me.

'Go, sleep,' he said. 'We'll keep watch. But don't forget to wake up again. Your canisters will soon arrive. We can unpack them and bring them in, but it's you who must ignite them!'

'Watch the detonators,' I said.

'I was watching detonators, mon enfant, when your sacred Mother was looking for her first hatpin.'

I slept like a log without dreams, until four o'clock.

WILLIE GARSIDE

Did you ever hear of the Flying Gages, before the war? I was the gripper, you know, the lad who swings out on the bar up there in the top of the tent and catches the others, the flyers. Of course in those days it was more gripping than catching – all this diving and jumping, that's modern stuff. In '38-'39 we had a great act. Of course we weren't brothers and sister like the posters said; Ronnie and me had started in the halls with a double-knockabout comedy act. That wasn't setting the house on fire and the bookings was dropping off and then one week in Bradford we met Amy who was doing an acrobatic act with her sister Elsie, the two Roses they called themselves, and Elsie had got pregnant and that left Amy on her own. Ronnie seemed to take to her from the first, though meself I couldn't see what he saw in her, and when Elsie went out of the business because the gin and epsoms didn't work, Amy come in with us and we got a booking in Potters One Ring in Morecambe. Ronnie and me travelled a waggon in them days, but it wasn't long before I was kipping on the grass outside since I've never seen the fun in watching two other people having a go and anyway it isn't healthy with a third party, is it? And then to cap it all, when we was down in Sittingbourne they went off together after the matinée up to the Registry Office in Chatham and made it legal. Which was hunky dory by me since she was coming on nice in the act and there wasn't too much of her to grip.

Like I said, I was the gripper. I'd climb the Jacobs up to the top, spotlight on me if they could get it to work which wasn't often, and swing backwards and forwards on the lead trapeze – we call 'em bars. I'd do all the usual that looks hard but isn't if you keep yourself fit and sleep with your hands outside the blankets, hanging from my knees, from my toes, from my heels, you know, all that stuff. I'd take the applause for that lot and while the customers was clapping Amy and Ronnie would get up there and the light would switch on to them, again if they could get it to work. We had three bars. One at the far side, one in the middle I hung on, and one on the platform where Amy and Ronnie stood. The bar at the far side, away from the platform, had a thin rope on it, and you could pull that rope and get the bar to swing. No, I'm getting ahead of myself. The next part of the act was that I'd start swinging the bar I was on, then Amy would get out on the bar by the platform, and swing down to meet me. I'd grip her, and we'd do a bit of clever stuff of her whirling around beneath me while I hung by my knees. We'd do the toe to toe hang, you must have seen that, and we'd do the bit with the rubber between the teeth and her twisting. When she'd done I'd swing her back up to the platform, and then Ronnie would come down for the heavy stuff, some very fancy swinging. Meanwhile, and now we can talk about that third bar I was telling you about, Amy would have that third bar swinging on the end of its thin rope, judging it just nice, and then I'd throw Ronnie and let him go. The audience thought every time he was a goner. There'd be a gasp from below, maybe a scream or two, because the light was on him and none on the swinging bar, and as far as they could see he was heading nowhere, fast. We never worked with a safety net, you see. Well, almost out of nowhere there'd be this bar. Ronnie had done his two and a half by this moment and he'd come out of it straight and grab the bar. And they always went crackers below. If you never hear that shout when they think you've cheated them out of a fall, you've never heard nothing. Half of 'em with you, admiring your skill, half of 'em against you, but all of 'em shouting blue bloody murder. Well then Amy'd take off and I'd grip her, give her a couple of fancy whirls, throw her to Ronnie, and that was that, end of act. We was fully booked, I can tell you.

Now I've got to have a bit of a digression on the personal side of things. Ronnie and Amy was doing very nicely and since I've never been one much for the girls – not that

I'm bent or anything – everything between the three of us was grand. Sometimes they'd be a bit stiff in the joints after going at it all night, or whatever young married couples do, but thank God there was still no sign of 'em needing a pram.

I used to go downtown a lot, wherever we were playing, looking in the shops, going to the pictures if we didn't have a matinée, and buying steak. I've always had a right hunger for steak. Well, one day I was coming out of the butcher's when I ran into Amy and being sociable, I asked her into the boozer for a drink. We had a couple or three and that was that. Honest. Nothing more than a couple or three drinks in a boozer and me with three pounds of steak in my lap. Back to the circus we went at midday closing time and I thought no more about it for a while. I was sharing a waggon them days with a lad who rode a one wheel bicycle and was booked around the same circuit we was.

I was just frazzling up my steak when Ronnie comes stalking in the waggon and without saying a word he cops me one right across the chops. Then he looks down at the front of my trousers and knees me right up the crotch. It damn near crippled me. 'You didn't wash it off properly,' he was shouting.

225

'I can still see the stains.' 'What bloody stains?'

Well, the long and the short of it was that marriage had made him a jealous sod and somehow he'd got the impression I was having it off with his Amy. When he'd smelled that couple or three drinks on her he assumed I'd got her drunk and had shoved her over in the grass on our way back. It had never entered my head to touch her. I tried to quieten him down, but he was like a dog with the rabies. We did the show that night – well, that's the first rule, isn't it – but it was bloody awful throwing her about and him looking daggers at me, handing her up and down knowing every time I touched her he was thinking I was having a quick feel at something that didn't belong to me. What's more, it got worse and worse. All the time he watched her and watched me, and nothing we could ever say would ever convince him I wasn't slipping it into her the minute his back was turned. He even tried to change the act so's he could be the gripper but I wasn't having that.

This is how serious it was – I even took a little Arab girl from a balancing troop to try to show him I wasn't interested in Amy. One night after the show I asked him and Amy to come to the waggon later to have one, and arranged it that when they came up the stairs, this little Arab girl and me, bless her heart, was on the job together. Damn them both, I thought when they came into the waggon, and I went right on and finished it before I got off the bed, pretending I hadn't seen them; the paranoid sod turns to Amy and says, 'Oh, aye, been having a threesome, have you?'

That was when I knew we'd never change him; and we couldn't go on the way we were. The dead funny thing is that, all this time, Amy and me hadn't so much as looked at each other. We daren't. Somehow, though, his jealousy brought a link, like a bond of sympathy between us, and we began to be right good friends. Oddly enough, for the first time I could see why Ronnie'd fancied her.

One Thursday after the matinée when we had no evening performance I made up my mind to have it out with him for once and for all – tell him that if he didn't pack this jealousy lark in, once we'd done the week in Northallerton, I would bugger off on my own. As a gripper I could work any act, anywhere. Their waggon was parked on the outer ring. It was about eight o'clock. Their light was on as I walked across. Ronnie was a great reader; he'd have a book spread out and Amy'd be sewing and I'd slip her the wink to go and see her Aunt Fan, and Ronnie and I'd have it out, once and for all.

I walked up the steps of their waggon. I didn't knock, well, you don't, do you, in that mood? 'Now look here Ronnie!' I was going to say. But she was stripped off on the side of the bed. She'd been having a bath in the tub and the water was still steaming, and she was sitting there naked on the side of the bed cutting her toenails.

She looked up, saw me. 'He's gone down the town,' she said. 'We've had another flaming row and he copped me one and now he's gone down the boozer. He says he'll be back after closing time and cop me another one.' She showed me the bruise that was developing. On her neck. It wasn't the first she'd had since he started this jealousy caper. I felt so sorry for her, being knocked about by a brute as ought to know better, and her so gentle and tender and soft to the touch and loving and arms about me and crying softly on my shoulder my neck my cheek and then biting my lip and before I knew it I was in her, right up to the hilt. What she was doing to me and I was doing to her I didn't ever want to stop. And it didn't stop when it should have, we both knew that.

When he come home she was lying on the bed asleep; of course he checked up on me and I was playing cards with the bike lad and it must have looked as if we'd been playing all evening. I should have had it out with him that night, but I couldn't. Not with her the way she'd been and me not wearing anything I should have been. I was going to tackle him the following night, after the show.

Friday night we did the show as usual, and I could feel her hot and soft when she swung down to me. When we got to the twisting bit, she slipped the tip of her tongue in my mouth, ever so quick. We got through all that, and then he came down, like a ton of bricks. I brought him round and round, lifting him, spinning him, dropping him. She'd started the far bar swinging, and I went into the last sequence. The final part of it was three whirls, right round the bar, before I chucked him. It's the gripper decides how far a flyer goes. You have to vary the chuck according to how far you think the bar will be on its arc when he gets to it. It was my intention to chuck him just that bit too far, right out of our lives. I'd thought about nothing else all day. It was an easy solution to all our problems, wasn't it; I mean, he was out of his mind with jealousy. Here it comes, the last swing, into the arc, pull a bit to correct, straighten him, and let go. At the last minute, I couldn't do it. I don't know why. I could have chucked him right out of our lives. But at the last minute, I held him back and aimed him straight for the bar. It was beautifully timed, like all my throws. He came out of the loop and the bar was there, between his hands. His hands clasped the bar – the crowd was roaring as usual – the bar took his full weight and he started to swing away from me on the first part of the pendulum and then he started to scream and when the pendulum swing reached the far end and he should have came back his hands slid from the bar and he went down down. When they picked him up his thigh had been driven up into his ribs and his spine had snapped.

She'd spread Vaseline on the bar.

The forensic police lads found her pot, compared the two, came up with some of her hairs in both. You probably read about it in the papers? Luckily war broke out before they got her to trial and she died anyway having the baby. All I can think about is the way she felt that night, and the way she looked stark naked cutting her toenails.

The baby died too. That's why I joined.

Willie Garside was sitting near to me, stropping his knife on a piece of leather he always carried. I had seen him do it before, in Yorkshire; he sat there, leaning slightly forward, the end of the strop under his foot, the other end pulled tight in his left hand. He was stropping the knife backwards and forwards, looking not at the knife or the strop but at me. First wakening moments carry the hallucinations of sleep, he looked nine feet tall and proportionately broad, a giant. As my eyes took back their focus, he slowly shrank to size. He saw me waken, smiled, and made an involuntary movement to get to his feet. I waved him down. My mouth tasted of the straw of the barn, and my body had sweated while I was asleep; I felt the sweat run in my crotch and under my armpits and was, momentarily, sorry for myself.

Ben Bolding had eyes like a hawk; he must have seen mine flicker open from across the barn. He walked over with an earthenware bowl of coffee made with the concentrated powder we had brought with us as a gift for the partisans. He had sweetened the coffee with condensed milk from a tin, also a gift. Ordinarily it would have been undrinkable; at that moment it tasted like nectar. I sat up and drank it slowly. It was hot and would have burned my mouth; I blew over the rim of the bowl to cool it, watching Willie Garside. 'I shan't let him do any more jobs,' I thought to myself. This was the fourth time Willie had been with me, once in Holland, twice in France, and now in Belgium. 'He won't survive any more,' I thought. I could see he was running on the edges of his nervous system. He'd get through this one all right, but next time out he'll crack. 'What are our chances this time, Major?' he asked, when I had drained the coffee bowl.

'Chances of what, doing the job successfully, or getting home alive?'

The Germans didn't keep prisoners alive if they were caught wearing a green beret. It wasn't yet official, but we all knew the Germans were as scared of us as we were of their Fallschirmjaegers. Later in the war, the German High command made the fear official, and orders were issued to kill on sight any man wearing a green beret.

'Both?'

'We'll do the job successfully, of that I'm certain. If I hadn't been certain of success, I would never have started.'

'How can you be certain?'

'Willie, I don't know. I've been on many jobs, as you know, and there's always been an element of certainty about them. Not necessarily a certainty the job will go all right. Sometimes I've looked at a man and been certain he would not survive. Call it a premonition, if you like, though I prefer to think it's the information stored away in my mind that works out decisions for itself. You see a man in training, and you realise he takes chances. You know that each chance he takes is a risk, a small percentage figure, if you like. If a man takes too many risks too many times, the percentages add up to a hundred.'

'And your mind does this adding up?'

'I don't do it consciously.'

'Do I take chances?'

'No more than you should do.'

'Where do my percentages stand?'

'Nowhere near a hundred, I imagine – I don't know, it's not something I think of consciously. Is there any grub?'

'Marvellous. One of the girls cooked it. Boeuf à la mode. I'll get you a plate.' When he came back he put the plate in front of me. Boeuf à la mode! It was bully beef, cold, minced in with oatmeal biscuit. At least it had been warmed on the smokeless fuels we'd brought with us.

'You think I'll survive, do you?'

'Yes, if you don't do anything silly, and you're not the man for that.'

'Will the job go all right?'

'Yes, it will.'

'How can you be so sure?'

'Willie, I don't know; look, you're a religious man, you and Taffy Andrews. How can you be so sure there's a God in heaven above?'

'We have faith.'

'I have faith, if that's what you like to call it. You're all good men, you've all been trained to do what we have to do, the job has been well planned, and I have faith in you!'

'But could it go wrong? A bomber might drop one on this barn within the next five minutes.'

He was beginning to exasperate me, but I tried not to show it.

'Give me that knife,' I said. He handed it over to me. The edge of the blade was as sharp as a razor. I held the knife by its handle, point towards the ground. I flipped the knife up in the air, whirling. The knife began to fall, still whirling. I clasped suddenly with my hand, and was gripping the handle of the knife. It was a party trick if you like, but we'd handled knives for so long they had become part of my nature.

'There,' I said, as I handed the knife back to him. 'That could have gone wrong, couldn't it? If it had gone wrong, you'd see the blood on my hand, wouldn't you?' I held out my hand. 'Look, Willie, no blood. The kind of faith I'm talking about is a blind conviction if you like, but you go on with it because it works.'

'But what if it doesn't work?'

I could see what was bothering him. 'It works because I am not afraid of what will happen if it doesn't work. All things are possible, Willie, if you master the simple techniques involved and are not afraid to put those techniques into operation. You can't do that if you're worried about what will happen if a thing doesn't work. I couldn't have put my hand fair and square in the path of that dropping knife if I had been thinking about what would happen if I didn't grab the handle. I knew, from conviction, that I could do it, so I did it. I also knew that, if I didn't do it I'd cut my hand badly, but I didn't think of that when I was doing it. That's what I mean by "blind conviction". Don't look at what will happen if a thing doesn't

235

work, since that will often be the very factor that will prevent it working.'

'You're taking a terrible risk, Major?'

'I'm taking a terrible risk just breathing. The air could be full of disease. I don't know it isn't. There could be a dead cow behind that straw, and this air could be full of cholera, ever thought of that, Willie?'

He looked about him, uneasily.

'Look, you're a Godly man, Willie. Think of it this way. We can't go it alone. We need to draw our extra reserves of strength from somewhere, and I'm prepared to admit they come from God. Right is on our side, Willie. We're the goodies, the Germans are the baddies, and good will prevail. We shall prevail, Willie.'

He understood that.

'And all the killing...'

'The killing has to be a part of it. God and the Devil are absolutes, Willie, and good and bad can be absolute only if death is accepted as part of it. We're like trapeze artists who work without a net so the audience will know we accept that failure means death.'

'I was once what you call a "trapeze artist",' he said quietly. I knew he was. I once overheard him talking with some of the boys – what did you do before the war stuff. I guessed, however, that his memories of the circus life were something he could do without.

'I know you were. I thought the symbol might mean something.'

'There was killing there, too, and taking chances all the time. We trusted our own knowledge; we practised so many times we knew there could be no falling from the top bar. This job we can't practise in the way we could that one. We can train, but it's not the same thing, is it?'

'There's a long drop and death waiting for us, if we fail.'

'There was a long drop, there, and death too, but it had nothing to do with training or practice. It had to do with people, and trust.'

'And wasn't that something you could practise?'

'No, it wasn't. I had a man in my hands twice on most days, and at any time I could have thrown him that bit too far. There was a time once I thought I had a perfectly valid reason for throwing him that bit too far. It would have been the unsolvable murder, because no-one ever could have said I did it deliberately.'

'And did you?'

'Throw him too far? What do you think,

Major. Did I?'

Willie had come a long way with Ben and me. We'd given him a lot of confidence in himself, we'd taught him to do things he would never have attempted. We'd even taught him to speak the King's English, or our rather limited versions of it. I had to cast back my mind to when I first knew him, shortly after he joined the Commando. It wasn't easy to get through to him in those days. He was a bitter man. At least, I thought him bitter at the time but might that not have been remorse, fear?

'No, I don't think you did it,' I said. 'That's not a chance I can see you taking, Willie. Certainly you take chances, but you always can calculate the risks. Beneath it all, you're a careful gambler.'

'You're right, of course. When it came to the point, I couldn't throw him that extra bit. This is the fourth job we've done together, Major, and there's always been killing. I've always accepted that, and I don't think you've ever seen me hold back. But one thing scares me in a way I'll never be able to explain. One time, it may happen I have my knife out ready to flip it but when the time comes, I may not be able to do it – just as I couldn't flip that man that little bit too far.

Even though I had the best of reasons – a damn sight better reasons than you can give me now.'

'When that time comes – the time you can't flip the knife – you're dead, Willie, and there's nothing I can do to help that. We don't carry safety nets. I only hope that, when the time comes, you won't take the rest of the lads with you.'

'That'll be your responsibility, won't it, Major?'

'Mine, or the sergeant major's or the corporal's, or even, if you have the lowest Army number among any who are left, your own responsibility, Willie. Anyway, let me make one thing quite clear. If I thought there was any danger, any danger at all, that when the time came to stick your knife into somebody you'd hold back, I'd kill you myself, here, and now. You're not the only one on this job, Willie, and I have an equal responsibility to every one of them.'

We sat there, silent.

He believed me, that I could tell. There was nothing else I could say to comfort him. At least, nothing I could think of.

'Now I've got to go,' I said.

I had to leave him, for nothing more

dramatic than to relieve my bladder. Damn it, I'm not a priest, or a psychologist. I can't fight those inner battles. I can teach, train, lead, do, but I can't justify except in terms of the actual outcome of what we did. When Willie had an armful of signals data to take back to England, he'd get the message; he'd race home like Moses down the mountainside, hand over the folders of information with all the smug wisdom of a divine truth.

It was dusk. Sandy was wrong – this was the worst time, not four o'clock in the morning.

I went back inside the barn and reviewed the details of the plan for the thousandth time. Of course it would work. Why shouldn't it?

Ben came over and sat beside me.

'Calm before the storm, eh, Major?'

'I hate waiting about.'

'So do we all.'

'You've checked the equipment?'

'Yes.'

'Given Belfière his stuff?' At every drop, when we became involved with partisans, we took as many supplies for them as we could. I always felt like a trader going into an Indian settlement with a box of beads. Mostly they wanted grenades, weapons, ammunition, but we always made up 'gift' parcels of chewing-gum, boiled sweets, cigarettes, pipe tobacco, medicines, coffee, sugar, condensed milk. Each parcel was always individually wrapped so that it could be hidden quickly. The girls who wrapped them put messages inside. The personal touch. It helped.

'Yes, I've given him his stuff.'

'What did he say?'

'Thank you.' Ben laughed. He knew me so well. I was always grouchy just before an action. Bless him, he never showed he noticed.

'There is one thing that's bothering me,' he said when I had finished my routine ill-humour. 'This business of a simultaneous explosion. Can we talk about it?'

'The plan's all set, Ben.'

'I don't like it,' Ben said. 'The whole success of this little lot depends on those two explosions happening simultaneously. It only needs one person to become suspicious and try to look in that vault and we've had it.'

'What do you think will go wrong?'

'They're a bunch of sodding amateurs, this lot. You should have seen the way they brought in the detonators, laughing and joking like a Christmas party. I just don't think it's safe to rely on them to create an explosion exactly at four o'clock.'

241

In this matter of explosives, Ben was the amateur, not the Belgians. Most of Belfière's men had worked in the mines, had been handling explosives since they were boys. We were fresh trained to them, and had not yet lost the respect of fear. I could see Ben's point, however. Discipline among the partisans seemed entirely spontaneous, entirely voluntary. They were a democracy, a committee trying to work by majority vote. This job needed a boss.

Already there had been voluble arguments about the best way to tackle their share of the night's raid. Some must die. They were going to draw the Germans away from us, and that meant exposing themselves. In that barracks down the road were a thousand Germans, and once the alert was given, the small band of partisans could be surrounded and picked off one by one as sitting targets. Belfière seemed to have no prearranged plan of final escape. His decoy tactics were simple, based on the time-honoured fire and movement. One section covers with fire while the other section moves.

It can be a good method, since it gives you complete mobility and we ourselves had used it many times. It does, however, demand an instinctive knowledge of the men you are with; you need to know that any move you might make, in whatever direction, will be covered. It was inconceivable that the partisans could already have achieved that much understanding. Though they had all worked with Belfière many times, many of them had not seen each other before. All knew this district well, of course, and could lead the Germans a Pied Piper dance down the profusion of back alleys and short cross-streets; but the vast number of German troops in the area could quickly surround the handful of partisans, and squeeze them out like drops from a lemon. The Germans had all the advantages; they were not concerned with damage to property and if they caught a number of partisans holed up in a house, or even a street of houses, they had sufficient heavy artillery available to reduce the lot to rubble. And they would do so without hesitation, such would be their venom. The Germans had been taught to hate, and hate generates total destruction.

My task was to estimate the chances of a simultaneous explosion taking place. If that could happen, I knew Roget Belfière was experienced enough to draw the interest of the Germans away from us. That was all I asked, that we be given just sufficient uninterrupted time to blow the vault, get in, and get out again. Belfière was going to have to mount a 'do or die' action.

I was glad Willie had not asked me to estimate the partisans' chances of survival. Only a lucky handful would get away. It was a calculated risk; Roget Belfière must be given credit for knowing what he was doing. My concern was with the explosion. I could not let anything else matter to me.

There were no practical difficulties. Our canisters had arrived safely and we had four times the amount of explosive we needed. I had planned to leave the spare charges with Belfière.

'We can't signal to them, to give them a cue?'

'It would be dangerous. We have no radio; it would need to be done by lights, and imagine this little lot flicking lights about,' Ben said. Chaos begins at Dover!

'All right, Ben, we'll change the plan slightly. You don't trust the Belgians to do it exactly on time, we'll do it ourselves.' I had brought with me a dozen aerial and other photographs against just such an eventuality. We went through them together. One showed a length of the road by the bank. It had been taken from a window high up on the other side of the road. Ben grunted with satisfaction as he gazed at it. 'See that,' he said, pointing to a small square darker than the rest of the pavement, almost under the bank wall. There was a gas lamp on the pavement edge beside it. 'I'll bet that's a manhole cover for a gas main,' he said. 'Dodger could do a lot of damage under that cover with a couple of blocks of P.14. We could drop a wire over and down the side of the wall, and Dodger could wire into the detonators and put the manhole cover back. No-one would ever see the wire hanging.'

I looked at the other photographs. One showed the back of the bank, and the parapet which went round the top of the walls, at the bottom of the mansard roof. There would be sufficient room for a man to crawl round the inside of that parapet, concealed from view from the road.

'If we carry a wire from our own box over this roof, we could drop it down to Dodger.'

'That's right. And if we made the two wires of equal length the explosion would be absolutely simultaneous.'

'And what about Belfière's explosion?'

'Let him do it. The Germans won't know which way to go. When they see that gas main fracture, they might very well forget about explosives; they might think the gas main has blown itself, and they'll leave the repair of that to the Belgians.'

It seemed a feasible plan. Backwards and forwards in my mind. What could go wrong? Where were the dangers? Dodger of course would be vulnerable on the road, but he shouldn't be there for long. That'd mean him carrying two blocks of explosive already detonated in his pocket, lifting the manhole cover and lowering in the explosive, connecting two pieces of wire, putting back the manhole cover with a chink of free run for the wire. I 'did it' with my mind's eye, timing the actions. It should take him not more than thirty seconds for the job, say thirty to get there, thirty to get back off the road. A minute and a half of danger.

'Get Dodger,' I said. Ben brought him over and Dodger sat down, bent forward, eager. This was a job for a loner, a man who could work best by himself.

'Change of plan, Dodger.'

'Yes, Major.'

'I need a man to go out on his own.'

He smiled that secret smile of his. 'Some of us prefer it that way!'

'Some don't. Some like another person to hold their hand.'

'Most people are lucky, Major, and find a mate somewhere. I never did. That's one reason I volunteered for the Commando, that's why I wanted to come on this job!' He looked around the barn, noting each of our lads among the crowd. 'I think I've found it here,' he said quietly. 'There's not one of the lads I wouldn't rely on.'

'But you're still willing to go out on your own?'

'Let's put it this way. There are times I still prefer to depend on nobody but myself!'

One false move and that explosive would go off in his pocket. There wouldn't be enough of him left to scrape off the wall. 'It's a volunteer job,' I said, 'but how would you like to walk down fifty yards of road, carrying two slabs of P.14 in your pocket, lift a manhole cover, set the P.14, connect a wire, replace the manhole cover, and walk back again?'

'What type of manhole cover?'

'Steady on,' I said, 'there's one small difficulty.'

'I know,' he said. 'The detonators would have to be in the slabs, wouldn't they? Trip yourself, or even stumble, and you'd be playing a harp.'

'It's a volunteer job,' I said.

'Shall I stick my hand up?'

247

'You won't need to, lad,' Ben said, and put his hand on Dodger's shoulder. According to the manual I ought to have made a speech about esprit de corps, shaken him warmly by the hand, and made an appropriate mark about initiative on his record sheet. I said nothing. You don't say thank you to a man at a moment like that.

Together we allocated the explosive charges. Dodger would handle the one in the street on his own, Fred and Joe together would work under the signal data vault. Dodger's explosion would make as much noise as possible, blow the gas main, and start a fire. Fred's would be as silent as possible. Ben gathered the men about me, and quietly I rebriefed them. Roget Belfière sat in on the briefing, since he would need to relocate some of his men. It was ten o'clock in the evening. All our men had slept well, none had any last minute aches or pains. We were not due to move off until twelve o'clock, but already we were caught in the pre-operational fever, the subdued excitement I knew so well. Glances became significant. Men looked at watches, at each other, and every glitter said: 'It won't be long now.' The smell of imminent danger was in the air, and no-one could sit in one place for any length of time. They checked and rechecked items of equipment, and those secret death-dealing devices each man made a part of his confidence. Ben I knew carried a spring loaded dart gun made from a part of a copper aerial. Only three inches long and thin as a pencil, it fired a two inch needle fifteen feet with deadly accuracy. I myself carried a one-sided Ever Ready razor blade in the heel of my boot. I must have looked at it twenty times while we waited. Dodger had lead weights tucked in the overhangs of his trousers. He'd taken them in a bet from a guardsman. To Dodger they were a defensive weapon.

They had all slept well, and the time crawled by towards twelve o'clock. The partisans assembled in ones and twos and threes, and I withdrew our sentries. Roget replaced them with his own men who knew all the faces. I sent Harry Landon up into the pigeon coop, to watch all around. From time to time I looked up at him; each time he gave me the thumbs up signal that meant no enemy within sight.

All the partisans had been checked and rechecked by Belfière, and though there was no reason to suspect them, unconsciously I found myself comparing them to my own men. All my men had washed, they all looked neat, tidy supermen. I saw several of the partisans eye them and whistle silently in admiration. I swelled with pride for them; they were all obviously so fit, disciplined and tough. Four partisans were girls, in their early twenties I would have guessed. One was a woman of about fifty, short, fat, dumpy. She wore spectacles, and her hair was done behind the nape of her neck in a tight bun. Roget brought her over to me. 'May I present Artoise,' he said. I recognised the code name. I shook hands with her. Her grip was like the clutch of a steel vice. 'Shot putt champion of Louvain University,' he said. I could well believe him. She had a nervous giggle; I invited her to sit down, then sat down on the straw bale facing her. Roget sat down. It was one of those awkward moments. I could hardly ask her if she was in good health.

'You're a brave man, Major,' she said.

'It could equally well be said, and with more reason, that you are a brave woman,' I replied. It unleashed the giggle again. 'Gallant, also?' she said. We were speaking French, the language of gallantry. I shook my head. 'It's true,' I said.

'England has become our big brother,' she said. 'You keep your eyes open for when the bullies try to beat us.'

'And sometimes, with your brave assistance, we beat the bullies back again?'

'That's the truth,' she said.

'Artoise will conduct you to the vault yard,' Roget said.

'I shall be charmed.' It was a game, played to pass away the time left to us, to speed the passage of these intolerable minutes.

'The Major has brought you a present, Artoise,' Roget said. Her eyes gleamed. I could have wished it had been a piece of feminine frippery. 'A box of Mills bombs,' he said, using the First World War name for them. Small hand grenades, they broke on explosion into half-inch square fragments, the most lethal grenade invented. 'Artoise likes Mills bombs,' he confided to me, 'they keep in her hand for the shot putting.'

'I'll bet you're very effective with them,' I said.

'I try to do my best. None is wasted.' She dug in the folds of her garment and produced one that must have been lodged in her brassière. 'I learned to throw so that I could take part in the Games,' she said, 'and the Games were supposed to bring International Brotherhood of Men, and peace. Now I use the throwing in war. Que c'est drôle.'

The humour escaped me, but I laughed

251

with her as she giggled.

By deft sleight of hand, she caused the grenade to vanish again as quickly as she had produced it. She rose from the straw bale, shook my hand, and left me.

I looked up at Harry Landon, got the reassuring signal. Now the barn was filling up, and I felt ill at ease. I was used to doing jobs on my own, with just a few men. This gathering seemed more suited to a Sunday afternoon outing on the river. They were all apparently light-hearted and almost gay. I could see no trace of depression or tension, of the sadness that always seemed such a part of a partisan's make-up. In the barn Roget had a cache of arms in one of the underground passages; as each new person arrived he was issued with a rifle or a machine carbine, ammunition, a pistol, the grenades we had brought with us, the shells of two inch mortars, two inch mortar barrels. Some of them had never seen the grenades before. I winced as I saw Roget's lieutenants demonstrating how to prime them, handling the live detonators as if they were cigarette ends. If one of those grenades should explode among so many men at such close quarters, we'd all be lucky to get out alive.

Ben, Joe and Dodger were sitting in one

corner, splitting the packets of explosives, preparing them for the charge. Frank Farleigh and Alf Milner, oddly enough, were playing a word game on scraps of paper – Jotto, I think they called it. Five letter words, each man guessing the word the other is using. I had tried, but hadn't the patience for it. I knew it relaxed them, took their minds away from our imminent operation.

Willie Garside, Fred Pike, Lance Corporal Sam Levine and Corporal Taffy Andrews, were playing a game of cards. Ben was chatting to one of the Belgian girls. She seemed to be from the Flemish north part of Belgium. She probably spoke no French – they'd need to communicate in German. Ben could get by with sign language, if necessary.

The card players finished a hand and seeing me sitting alone, Sam Levine left them and came across. I beckoned for him to sit down on the straw bale adjacent to mine.

'I wanted to ask you something, Major, but there doesn't seem to have been the opportunity.'

'Now's your chance, Sam.'

'It's all right, is it, Major, about me not taking the stripes to make me up to Sergeant?'

'Of course it's all right. Why shouldn't it be?'

'Well, I mean, I thought that maybe you might think that, because I didn't want to be made up, well, I might not be keen, like…'

'Sam, I brought you here with me, didn't I?'

'Yes, Major, you did, and, like I'm grateful for that, but I was just a bit worried in case you and Corporal Andrews might think…'

I knew what was bothering him. What a damnable thing it is not to be able to speak your thoughts, how lucky are people with that gift. 'Look, Sam, if you're worried about Taffy, you needn't be. Taffy and I have talked together often about promotion, and we both feel the same way. A section corporal is a man who can get on with the men, live with them and represent them. If you like, he's their trade union representative. It's a particularly difficult job, and a good corporal is hard to find. Taffy is a better corporal than you'll ever be. That's why I gave him two stripes. There's a certain type of man who should be a sergeant, and many good corporals have been ruined by promotion to sergeant. I think you'd make a better sergeant than you are a lance corporal. Can you see what I mean?'

He could see it, but that brought us back to square one.

Would I be wise to take the risk of speaking

my mind just before the operation started? Wise or not, I decided to do so. 'You're not a good lance corporal, Sam, because you're a Jew, and you let all the lads know it.'

His face set hard.

'None of us holds it against you, but I won't lie to pretend it doesn't make a difference because it does. Soldiers will only accept their own in the ranks with them. They'll accept a Jewish sergeant, or Jewish officers, but in the barrack rooms alongside them, they like their own kind.'

His face had not altered.

'I could never be a private soldier,' I said. 'Once they heard the way I speak in the barrack room, once they learned I'd been to a University, I'd never be accepted as one of them.'

'Ah yes, Major,' he said, truculently. 'But that's all right. You're a gentleman.'

'And you're a Jew.'

'That's right, Major, and there's a world of difference between them.'

'We're both outcasts, you know.'

He would have spoken, but his thoughts had not formed. He sat there, his legs spread before him, his hands dangling nervously between his knees.

'You can't alter it, Sam.' The three card

players had wandered idly to where Ben was talking animatedly to the Flemish girl. Soon the other girls joined in. It was a lively party, quiet, but without an apparent care in the world. Ben was behaving outrageously, flinging his arms round each of the girls in turn. They for their part were laughing good-humouredly at his antics.

'Look at the sergeant major,' I said. 'Neither you nor I could do that. Those girls and those three men accept him completely, because they see in him a common streak. He's one of them. It doesn't matter that he's the sergeant major – he's one of them. If you or I went over there, we'd be so tongue-tied and self-conscious, we'd embarrass the whole crowd.'

'I've never wanted that sort of ability,' Sam said.

'Of course you haven't, because you've always been an alien-outsider. The mistake you make, if I may say so, is to want what you can't have. You cannot be totally accepted, so why try? I don't. I know some officers ask men to call them by Christian names. I don't. It wouldn't work. It doesn't work for any officer unless he's got that common streak and shouldn't be an officer anyway. Take what's rightly yours, Sam, and

256

don't strive for what you shouldn't have. Be what you are, and profit by it.'

'I'm a Jew,' he said, and at last there was a vestige of pride in the statement.

'You're a Jew,' I said, 'so why not be a sergeant Jew?'

'I think I will, Major, if the offer still stands.'

'Of course it does.'

A crafty look came across his face. 'Retrospective?' he asked. I laughed. 'Yes, retrospective, so you can get the extra pay, you Jew!'

'You're wrong about that group over there, if I may say so, Major.'

'In what way?'

'Are we off duty?' he asked, again with that crafty look.

'As far as any man can be in the middle of an operation.'

'I'll bet you my first week's pay as a sergeant, I can go over to that group and pick out one of the girls, and have her behind the straw bales in thirty minutes!'

'That small one, with the black hair?'

A gleam came to his eyes. 'You're on, Major,' he said, got up, and walked casually over to the laughing group.

I had noticed she was a Jewess as soon as

I saw her, but wasn't it part of my duty as a gentleman and an officer to make life easier for him! Thou shalt not cause another man to commit adultery, even when he needs it to bolster his ego. According to the Bible one of them would need to be married before it became adultery – the Bible says nothing about Thou Shalt Not Fornicate.

I went out for a stroll outside the barn.

It was an evening typical of late November, the air crisp, the trees redolent of the fruit left for wasps and moist bark. I was alone in an alien country, surrounded by friends and foes. Perhaps I was sorry for myself, sorry I hadn't it within me to take a laughing girl behind the straw bales, grasp at the moment of human contact before the inhuman dangers of the night to come. In times of danger, privation, hunger, the population always increases, they say. You'd think babies would be conceived more readily in times of plenty. I was going to break my way into a vault, and from it extract information that would help to stop the fighting. I would kill without question any man who stood between me and that objective. It was a fragrant night. A night for the sudden odour of tobacco out of doors, or a girl's perfume, a night for shaving close to the chin, and driving a car with the hood down so the cold air would lap your ears. Lamps seen from far off across a valley, twinkling like laughing eye lights, and comfortable chairs in front of chess men, Irish whiskey in a tall glass on the table beside you, a jug of hot water and the squeeze of a plump lemon; the feel of a long scarf against your cold chin, a glance down at the coloured stripes, and the reassuring knowledge you belong. Snug down on a sofa in the joint Common Room with a girl who says 'stop it' and means something else; that first half the landlord draws and says 'You owe me fourpence from last night' and you know you're where you've been before.

I was standing in a hedge bottom by the end of the track, where the road bends round to Reaville. They rolled past me on the road, truck after truck after truck, a convoy moving in to replace a convoy moving out. Possibly the men crouched along those bench seats, clasping a rifle between their knees would be among those destined to die tonight. It was that kind of night, after all, a night in November, cold, grey, half-lighted, no stars nor moon, nothing but a grey cold death night.

I shivered and went back to the barn. Ben knew I wouldn't stay out for more than an hour.

We set off at midnight. In our packs we had brought raincoats which we wore. We took off our gaiters and let trouser bottoms hang over boots, our only disguise. We didn't want to be caught wearing complete civilian clothing. Dodger pocketed his lead weights.

We left in twos, one soldier, one partisan. We made no attempt at concealment once we came to the edge of the town, but walked through the suburbs talking to each other. Several times we were passed by German motorised patrols, but no-one took any notice of us. Why should they? In the suburb of Minsal, bicycles had been left waiting for us at several inconspicuous points. Mine was a lady's bicycle; the pedal had been bent at some time and clanked against the frame every time it turned round. Artoise and I rode side by side. She occasionally clutched my saddle. Soon we came to the factory area and more people were about. There were more Germans, too. Away from the principal roads, down back streets and back alleys, we took a route longer than the directions, but safer. We finally abandoned the bicycles in a scrap yard, about a quarter of a mile from the Signals Data Storage Centre, to be reclaimed by the partisans to whom they belonged. We walked the last few hundred yards down the mean streets of the industrial quarter. At the bottom of one street the main road we couldn't avoid crossing carried a steady flow of traffic, workmen going on shift by bicycle, German patrols on motor cycles and in cars. All the way we talked, quietly but continuously. There is something less suspicious about people who talk together, especially a man and woman. Mostly we talked of sport, about putting the shot, her life at Louvain University, my youth, her experience, my world still to come, her world dying about her. All my sentences began, 'After the war'; most of hers 'Before the war.' Often she referred to 'La force de ta jeunesse dorée'. 'When that force is gone,' she said wistfully as we walked along, 'your whole life becomes a compromise between what you wish and those things of which you still remain capable; the number of your capabilities decreases every year, like the roll call of your blood relations.'

'But surely, you have an increasing experience; new knowledge?'

'To do what? To know how to become

more unhappy, to know of the many things you miss from life, and will never live long enough to see again? Ah, les salles boches, ils ont volé ma jeunesse.'

The youth they had stolen was ended long before the war, but I couldn't tell her that. She was dreaming of potency, of achievement without doubt, gone like yesteryear but still unforgettable. 'You've had a wonderful life,' I told her. 'Yes I have, and now where has it gone? Now I fight and kill, and my only prayer is that next time there is an opportunity to fight, Roget will not pass me by as a fat old woman, fallen into a monstrous decrepitude!'

Striding along beside me I doubted Roget would ever dismiss her as decrepit. 'This war,' she said, 'is hell.'

I agreed with her too quickly.

'Oh, not in that way. The war will go on for ever. It is our hell on earth. We have caused a cataclysm that will never end. When the actual fighting has stopped we shall find we have destroyed ourselves. Like fruit trees after a storm, we shall find we shed our fruit and grow no more.'

'And God will let this happen?' In her voluminous clothing I had noticed a cross on a steel chain when she extricated the grenade.

'God has flown to another world on another planet, leaving us to kill each other.'

We crossed the road between the traffic, turned right, and walked along an alleyway. I was shaken by the finality with which she had spoken. At the bottom of the street a narrow alleyway led to another street. We started to walk down the alleyway.

A German soldier walked towards us from the other end of the alleyway. We kept on. We would meet at the centre. I smelled her fear sweat. Her hand clenched and unclenched behind her back as she walked along, though you could not discern a lack of confidence in her stride. When we reached the German she continued to walk forward in the centre of the alleyway. He pressed himself against the boards remembering, from who knows where, some relic of courtesy. She passed him. He moved out in the centre and came forwards. Now it was my turn to press into the boards. His eyes glittered with cruelty. He raised the butt of his rifle and jabbed it as he went past, into the pit of my stomach. I doubled over, the bile of suppressed hatred rising in my gorge. Then he stopped and turned round.

'Where are you going?' he bellowed suddenly in German.

Artoise turned round and spat her Flemish at him. He couldn't understand her. 'Where are you going?' he repeated. 'Speak German, or I'll have you shot.'

Again she talked rapidly back at him in Flemish, with no trace of fear or servitude; rather did she imply by her tone of voice, 'How dare you challenge us.' She brushed past me in simulated fury and brandished the papers with which she had been provided against such an emergency. It said that we were mother and son, workers entitled to our rations and to move about the district. He glanced only cursorily at it. Artoise eyed him up and down, every bit as arrogant as he was, though she had the look of a bitch accustomed to making dogs crawl. Two of the fly-buttons of his trousers were undone. A gleam came to her eye. She reached out and flipped the buttons. His hand shot down in an involuntary gesture to cover himself. He glared at her.

'Not much Strength Through Joy left there, is there?' she asked him in her bad German; then 'Nichts Kinder machen,' she said. It was a phrase the girls used to torment the Germans – don't make any children. Use me as you must, like a rutting animal, and I'll stay here like a log while you

264

grunt out your satisfaction. But don't leave any small part of yourself inside me, don't breed any more beasts like yourself, Nichts Kinder machen! He glared at her, turned and marched away leaving us unmolested.

'He'll be late back to camp,' she said to me, giggling at her little triumph. 'He's been in a brothel; he'd better hurry.'

'You approve of the brothels being open?' I asked her, disgusted despite myself.

'Of course! The girls do valuable war work. They get plenty of information out of these German louts – it's amazing what a man will tell a girl when he's been between her knees.' I was still shocked.

'That surprises you, doesn't it? You're not the first male hypocrite I've met,' she said angrily.

We walked along the alleyway in silence, then suddenly she stopped and turned around. She was still angry. 'Here's something else that will shock you,' she said. 'Every so often we put a girl in there with a venereal disease. You'd be surprised how many of the Herrenvolk we succeed in infecting before they find the girl responsible. The girl works overtime, and they keep a score on the side of the bed. One girl got over two hundred on her score sheet before we lost her!'

'What happened to her?'

'Hospital, in Germany, then labour camp. With luck she'd be able to kill herself some-where along the route.'

I don't know when I've been more revolted. Somehow I was able to discount everything we did, everything we were trained to do – this involvement of young girls in this fashion, deliberately spreading vile diseases known to man, was something I couldn't tolerate. She must have seen the look on my face. Her mouth set in a grim pudgy line – at that moment she looked, not like the shot-putting champion of Louvain University, but the Madam of some back-street whore-house.

'War is a dirty business, monsieur,' she said, quietly but with an intense venom. 'The first to forget that fact are the soldiers themselves. To them, war becomes a team game, our side, their side, and who's going to win. Nobody is going to win this war. Every single human being is being degraded by contact with this war. All the men can do is kill, devise new methods of killing, and kill again. The women have to drag out an existence – for many of them the enemy is no more tang-ible than bad breath because there's no toothpaste, dirt, disease, no milk for the children, brutish rape, broken limbs, and a complete lack of sanitary towels. In these circumstances death itself can appear a wonderful release. But you, of course, being a man, would understand none of those things. For you, it's up to the team, Long Live the King, and kill, kill, kill!' She walked on.

Half way along the alleyway, a closed boarded door was set in the wooden hall. She looked up and down the alley then turned suddenly and opened the door. We stepped through into a yard on the other side. The yard was filled with timber recovered from derelict buildings. The smell of sawn wood hung over the yard, smells of sawdust and varnish. Under a shed at the far side of the yard were piles of old furniture, sofas with stuffing torn from them, wooden backed antique chairs. The furniture maker himself waited under this shed, sitting in an old armchair, smoking a pipe. At least he was holding a pipe in his mouth but when I got to him I noticed the bowl was empty, and his eyes were rimmed with sleep. Poor devil, he had been sitting there all night, merely to ensure the Germans had not laid a trap for us. Artoise introduced me to him and again I shook hands. We crossed his yard. Under the eaves of the long shed was a door, set high against a wall. A pile of furniture with a wardrobe on the top had been stacked against this wall, carelessly it seemed, but in such a way as to make an innocuous ladder to the door hidden inside the wardrobe; we had the strange experience of climbing into the wardrobe, which had no back, and climbing through the door which opened within it. Through the door a gully between two roofs was about two feet wide and lined with asphalt material. On each side the roofs of the buildings below rose steeply. The buildings below were furniture storage sheds.

We walked boldly along the gully between the two roofs, a distance of about two hundred feet. At the far end, the roofs ended sheer and beneath us, about three feet down, was the top of a wall. We crawled along the top of this wall, and suddenly there it was in front of us, like a forgotten oasis in the middle of a desert. I had seen the small yard many times in photographs – it was about fifty feet square and entirely surrounded by walls. Apparently the ground of the yard was owned by the cabinet maker; before the war it had been his intention to roof it and extend one of his storage sheds by knocking out a back wall. To our left was the back wall of the bank building; there were no windows on this side of the building except a small grille set at floor level about two feet high and four feet long. Behind the grille was a wooden door. Straight ahead of us was the back wall of the Signals Data Storage Centre, with no windows, and made of solid concrete we knew was four feet thick, reinforced by steel rods. To the right was yet another wall, again no windows, and behind that wall a yard larger than this one in which motor vehicles were parked during the day. The Data Storage Centre was not in constant use; a small staff came on during the day and worked on the top floor – they were not due on duty for another five hours, or so we had been informed. The photographs we had received of all this area, smuggled out by the partisans, had been taken from this wall on which Artoise and I were sitting.

Artoise was to stay with me as 'liaison officer' during our attempt to crack the vault. I imagined Roget had disposed of her in that way; she was too important to him to be risked in the cut and thrust of street fighting. Certainly I had discerned an extra affection between them when the partisans had been milling about in the barn, like two older people watching with tolerance the innocent peccadilloes of the young.

There was, strangely, no way into this yard, other than over the wall on which we were sitting. The concrete Data Storage Centre sealed it completely from view. It was ideally suited to our purposes.

Artoise and I were the first to arrive. Two by two the others came. As soon as each partisan saw my men launched into the cabinet maker's yard, they left to take up positions near the road below to draw the Germans off after the explosions. My men ran along the gully between the two roofs and dropped down off the wall into the yard. Corporal Andrews and Sergeant Levine ('You owe me a week's pay, Major') carried a steel manhole cover, provided by the partisans; I had noticed it in passing in the cabinet maker's shed. Harry Landon broke open a door concealed in the ground. Beneath it a short flight of improvised steps led into the space the partisans had dug under the vault to extract the petrol cans. All the preparations we had requested had been made. A heap of sand, gravel and two bags of cement stood in one corner of the yard, doubtless smuggled here after dark sack by sack. There was also a water butt, three quarters filled and beside it four twelve-inch diameter baulks of timber each about three feet long, and an enormous hydraulic jack.

Fred Pike arrived, closely followed by Joe Stanhope and Ben. They had carried the explosive. 'No incidents?' I asked Ben.

'None at all. It was a cake walk.'

Fred looked at the manhole cover appreciatively; Taffy and Sam carried it down the steps into the cellar, then came out for the timber baulks. I hadn't spoken to Fred since my one question in the woods; he had had the sense to keep out of my way other than to attend the briefing sessions I had given them all. I knew his role in this job was paramount, but I kept on seeing Arthur Sywell's static line flapping at me, and the evil grin on Fred's face as he jumped out of the plane. Damn it, I couldn't work out the rights and wrongs of Fred and Arthur, Fred and the job, or Fred and me. Of one thing I was certain; once this job had been completed satisfactorily, I wouldn't want Fred within a hundred yards lest I yield to a sudden paroxysm of fury and clamp my fingers around his windpipe.

Frank Farleigh and Alf Milner didn't arrive. I gave them ten minutes, then sent Artoise to look for them, or for information about them. Frank was quiet, immensely strong and reliable. What he lacked in imagination he made up in method. He wasn't the sort of man to be caught out in a careless mistake. Alf Milner was a here-there-and-everywhere sort of a man, not the sort to be taken easily.

When Artoise came back I could see from the look on her face that both had been taken.

'How did it happen?'

'One of our girls,' she said, 'had a punctured tyre! Your man Farleigh stopped to help her.' Trust Frank; natural gallantry would be the one thing to penetrate normal caution. I blamed myself – it was a human emotion I had overlooked. We should have trained with girls! 'When the next group of two arrived they tried to get the bicycle off the road quickly...'

'...instead of riding on and ignoring them.' That would be Alf's way; see a mate in trouble, bustle about trying to help him. Alf wouldn't care about the woman; he'd see Frank stuck there and immediately his every-which-way-mind would seek some method of getting Frank out of difficulty.

'...and a patrol came. The girl who caused all the trouble with her puncture got away and reported to Roget.'

'Where will the Germans take them?' I asked.

'The headquarters at Beerenbarracks. Roget has already sent an ambush. With luck they'll get away and you'll see them here.'

'I won't. They all have strict instructions. Any man taken is on his own, and must not compromise this operation by coming here. No, if they get away, they'll head for the coast, or for Sweden or Portugal.'

'Won't they go to the aeroplane coming to pick you up?'

Damn Roget! No-one was supposed to know about that aeroplane except he and I. Of my own men only Peter Derby and Ben knew the landing location. If any were captured I didn't want them giving away under torture our one escape route. Artoise and Roget must have been closer than I thought. Damn the war and women!

'They don't know where the aeroplane is going to land. And what's more, you shouldn't know that, either.'

Her face lit up with mischief, but I was in no mood for coquetry. 'Roget and I are very very close,' she said. 'A man needs a woman at a time like this.'

'Is that why you kept the brothels open?' It was a mean hard thing to say, and I would have withdrawn the words had they not already spilled hot from my mouth. She was shocked, hurt, but not angry. She gestured with her hand, an ineffectual movement to brush away the stupidity of all of mankind.

'That you think yourself some sort of bird of paradise, some species of god to be able to dispose of women as you do! Voilà une femme, eh, Dieu, a portion of which I will serve myself, like some small but tasty snack, a veritable appetite breaker?'

I cannot adequately translate her vehement French, the pent-up bitterness which escaped from her. It was true. I had thought of her as a woman of consolation, a morsel to quench the appetite. I put my hand on her arm. 'I beg pardon of you,' I said. 'No, beg pardon of Roget, that you think he is a man who needs to spill his secrets into a woman's bosom like a frightened child beneath the pillows. We discussed the matter of your landing an aeroplane, since I have a certain topographical knowledge, and I was the one to suggest the landing place, since only I knew it.' We were standing at the edge of the gully, above the wall. She had her back to the yard. I had mine to the cabinet maker's shop. 'Stand perfectly still,' she said, her voice silent, but edged with menace. I had no idea what she intended. I stood still. She reached into her clothing and produced a grenade.

'Stand still,' she said. She let her hand swing gently behind her, and then, with a quick up and over movement, she flung the grenade into the air above my head. I turned round rapidly. A German soldier was walking along the gully towards us from the cabinet maker's. In his hands he held a machine carbine that pointed in my direction. He made a quick upwards jerk with the machine-gun to indicate I should raise my hands. His hand was tight around the stock of the machine-gun. At that moment the grenade Artoise had lobbed in the air came down on his shoulder. The gun was jerked from his grasp by the sudden impact. The grenade lay at his feet. I dashed forwards. When that grenade exploded it would awaken the entire neighbourhood. I skittered along the gully. The German had gone down on one knee, scrabbling for the gun and the grenade, eyes staring out of his head. As I neared him I kicked upwards. The force of the blow under his chin snapped his head backwards and he fell over. I picked him up in one swing and dumped his body on the grenade. Only two seconds left. At least his body would stifle some of the noise. Artoise still stood where I had left her. I went back towards her in one long low dive, scooping her backwards off the end of the roof. Then we were falling. I contrived to twist and landed backwards, body flat on the ground. I pulled my head up tucking my chin on my chest and, as my shoulders hit the earth, I yanked myself over in a backwards roll carrying Artoise with me in a flurry of skirts, throwing her sliding along the earth. The backwards roll took some of the impact of landing but the vertical drop had an impact that had to make itself felt somewhere. It did. In the shoulder I had wrenched coming out of the plane. Men came rushing out of the cellar. Anger made me forget my pains. I picked Artoise from the ground, a shaken bundle of clothing and pushed her against the wall. Then I stopped. The grenade had not exploded.

'Just your damned luck,' I hissed at her, 'the grenade was a dud. If that bloody thing had exploded, you'd have given the entire game away. And now we have the job of defusing the damn thing.'

'How could it explode?' she asked, not a bit abashed by my violent treatment of her, 'I didn't pull out the pin.' I climbed back up the wall and raced along the gully. As I had supposed, the German was dead. I dragged him off the grenade. The pin had not been pulled. Artoise climbed the wall after me. I threw the grenade to her; she caught it deftly and tucked it in her clothing. I dragged the German towards the end of the gully, then paused, and crawled up and over the roof to my left. I wasn't going to risk the gully door in the cabinet. Another German in the yard below was menacing the cabinet maker with his machine-gun. An isolated patrol, they must have followed the last man to arrive into the wood yard.

The German was too far away for an accurate bow and arrow shot. I cursed. Artoise had come crawling behind me. She raised her head slowly against the side of the roof and saw the German.

'Now throw the bloody thing again,' I said, 'and still don't take out the pin.'

'Oui, mon Dieu,' she said, a mocking look on her face. She took out the grenade, hoisted herself where she could get sight of the German, and launched it. By God, she was deadly accurate with those things. The grenade rose silently in the air then came down on a long slow parabola, turning and twisting in its flight. The German was watch-ing the cabinet maker, his head slightly forward. The grenade hit him on the back of his neck beneath his tin helmet, a perfect rabbit chop. He fell forward on his face. The cabinet maker looked around bewildered. I leaped off the roof, and dashed over to him. The German was out cold. The back of the top of his spine was bent at a curious angle.

'Who are they?' I asked the cabinet maker.

'Two men going back to camp. They had been out on late night pass. They saw the last two men come in, and were suspicious.'

We dragged the soldier out of sight behind the furniture in the shed. The partisans would dispose of the bodies later. I climbed back up through the easy route in the wardrobe. Artoise was ransacking the German soldier's pockets.

I left her to it. I had an explosion to attend to.

The manhole cover had been inverted and filled with explosives, packed tightly packet by packet. Detonators had been placed in the explosive and the wires led downwards through the two small holes in the manhole cover, shaped like a bowl six inches deep, two feet in diameter. It had been made of half inch steel to support enormous weights. On the clandestine radio we had asked Belfière to supply such a container; Fred was delighted with it. He was chuckling with pleasure when I came back into the cellar. As soon as he saw me he fell silent. I examined the charge. Around one of the detonator tips he had screwed silver foil from a cigarette packet. We had not brought it with us among the official stores, and for some time English cigarettes had been packed without foil.

'What's that?' I asked Fred, suspicious.

'That's what got me my pardon,' he said, cockily. 'It makes sure we get through the concrete.'

'What is it?'

'I don't mind telling you, now. It's a delaying fuse. All this explosive on the outside will go up first. There should be just enough to cut the concrete, if it's as thin as you say. That second charge is delayed a fraction of a second until the shock wave comes back, and then the second lot, here in the centre, goes up, and punches the plug of concrete out of the hole. By using a double charge like this, you get double the kick of the first part of it. But your timing's got to be dead right. If your second charge going up meets the reverberation of the first charge coming back, you'll be in a helluva mess.'

I left him to it. The timber baulks were placed under the manhole cover, and then the pack was placed in the centre. The jack was slowly pumped up, its central ram about ten inches across lifting the manhole cover tight against the concrete floor above.

In the cellar we had been working in four feet of space since on our instructions, the partisans had concreted the floor the previous week to tame the pressure of that ram. Slowly we pumped, the ram rising imperceptibly with each stroke. I cursed the loss of Alf Milner; he was carrying the compressed air cylinders with which we would have been able to ram the cover up under the floor within a few minutes. I checked my watch. The time was three o'clock and we had a charge to lay in the road. Finally the ram extended from the floor to the bottom of the manhole cover, jamming it tight against the ceiling. When those charges exploded, all the force of the blow would go upwards through the floor. It wouldn't come downwards because of the ram and the steel manhole cover, a ram to tamp home the explosive, and a delayed action fuse to increase the cutting impact and keep down the noise.

As soon as the explosion was set we climbed out of the cellar and over the wall, coiling the wire with us. In the space between the two buildings we set the plunger I had carried, and Dodger went with his explosive back over the gully.

I had to climb to the roof of the building to our left, the bank onto which the vaults had been built.

The wall was forty feet high.

Ben took the iron spiked grappling hook from his pack and looped it on his nylon cord, through a metal pulley ring. The nylon cord, strong enough to support an elephant, was too thin to grasp effectively. He coiled the nylon cord at his feet, then swung the grappling hook slowly in an arc increasing from twelve inches to three feet. When he had the grappling hook whirling to his satisfaction, he let it go upwards. The grappling hook rose up through the air at the end of the double length of nylon cord, landed on the roof, slithered down the sloping mansard to the gutter, then caught on the gutter brick. The shank of the grappling hook came over the edge of the brick, but the double prong stayed on the other side, as the boffins had assured it would. Ben pulled on the nylon cord, and the shaft of the grappling hook, about a half an inch thick in soft iron, bent over, doubling the grip of the hook on the top of the wall.

I said a silent prayer for the efficiency of

Belgian bricklayers – my life would depend on the strength of the mortar holding that brick wall in position. Ben pulled one nylon cord and the other snaked through the pulley attached to the hook. Attached to it was a thicker sisal rope, up which I could climb with ease since it was knotted every foot. I went up to the top as quickly as I could, then crawled along the roof gutter to the side of the building. Here the roof gutter turned at right angles and I was able to crawl forward until I overlooked the road.

Below me was a gas lamp, illuminated. Damn, it should have been out!

Near the wall on the pavement beneath me, though I couldn't see it without bending over, was a cover for the gas main. Dodger's task was to lift that cover, dump his prepared charge inside the hole, and pass the wire up to me. I had a reel of stout cotton, with a metal ring on the end. I lowered it over the edge, felt a short tug on the thread, then, a second later, another tug. Dodger was there. I heard a clang as he put the cover back and then the third tug.

I started to pull the thread and the wire up the side of the building.

A motorcycle patrol came roaring down the street, the blacked out beam of its headlight illuminating only the path in front of the bike. I heard the squeal of the brakes as the bike's brakes were suddenly applied.

Dodger exposed on the street spoke no German.

I heard the man in the sidecar call out, 'What are you doing there?'

Dodger must have been thinking quickly.

'Look at the drunken devil, he's having a piss!' the driver called, and laughed.

'Nevertheless, I'm going to have a look,' the man in the sidecar called.

I craned my neck cautiously over the edge of the wall. Dodger was staggering drunkenly towards the motorcycle combination. The man had risen to a half-standing position in the sidecar when Dodger got there. Dodger was still urinating as he walked, and both men were fascinated by the performance, laughing at his stumbling attempts to maintain his balance.

'Don't point that thing in here,' the driver said, laughing.

It was the last thing he ever said. Dodger lifted his hands and cracked the passenger's tin-helmeted hat against the driver's throat. The passenger he chopped with the blade of his hand against the side of his ear. He ran round the motorcycle combination, lifted the driver off the seat and dumped him, with the other man, into the cab. Even I could see that both were either dead, or so near death as to be incapable of recovery. I had wound the thread until I could grasp the end of the wire. I pulled the ends of the wire gently until I could feel the pressure of Dodger's hand. He had dragged the motorcycle against the kerb, under the lamp. It appeared as if the two men sitting one behind the other in the sidecar were waiting for the driver to return.

I went back along the roof, paying out the wire, then left, along the gutter and down the rope. Ben took the wire from me, lashed two more pieces of wire to it and taped them, and we climbed back over the wall into the v-shaped gully between the roofs. There he connected the wires from the street to the wires from the vault, and wound them onto the terminals of the plunger.

The time was five minutes to four o'clock.

'Where're Fred and Joe?'

'They've gone back into the cellar for a last check.'

'There should be no need for that, if they've done the job properly.' At that moment their heads appeared over the wall and they climbed up beside us.

'Can I be the one to blow it?' Fred said.

I let him. 'Matter of pride,' Ben explained.

There were two minutes to go. Fred and Joe were lying some distance from the front of the v-roof. Their work was done.

Harry Landon was lying flat on his stomach at the front, nearest to the explosion. Behind him Willie Garside, Sam Levine, Taffy Andrews, the Company Sergeant Major, then me.

Dodger Bates was taking care of our route out. The partisans should now be assembled in the road in front of the bank. As soon as the explosion occurred, they would set off down the road, ready for the first Germans who would certainly be in the road outside the bank within minutes, in time to see the partisans escaping, or so they'd think. Certainly no-one would notice or pay heed to our explosion in the cellar of the vault when they saw and heard the tremendous impact of the one in the street and the dramatic flare of the gas main, the tongue of flame that would follow it. Ten to one the Germans would call out the Belgian disaster squad from the town hall maintenance department, and several of Roget's men were in that squad. They would take their time about repairing the main.

One minute to go. Everyone is in position.

Somehow Artoise had given me confidence in Roget Belfière and I knew all his men would be in position, his diversionary explosion ready for firing. Alf Milner and Frank Farleigh taken. Hope they'll get away, but there's nothing you can do about it. For them the long dreary walk home on their own. Once this vault is blown and we have taken the files we want, we'll be off running. Already they'll be warming up the plane in England that is coming to take us home. Marvellous thought; with luck we'll be eating a hot breakfast in camp; waited on hand and foot. Without knowing any details they'll sense we've been on a job, and ply us with hot food and sympathy to assuage their U.K.-bound consciences. Half a minute to go. There'll be no hot breakfast for Peter Derby. With luck he'll get someone to put him back together again, and hide until his bones knit. Then for him the night walk, the hedgebottom and haystack route out of Europe. There'll be no patching Arthur Sywell; he's taken the long drop, and Fred's lying in this gully behind me. After the job is over, I shall have to make a decision about him. Smirk, Fred, you won't get much longer; you haven't got away with it, no matter what you may be thinking. Fifteen seconds to go. Damn it, my balls tickle. Scratch 'em now, there won't be time soon. Ten seconds to go. Last quick check, all in position. Roget's watch is synchronised with mine. Suddenly I had a fear; I hope he's remembered to wind it up! Mine had a sweep hand I watched count off the seconds. Five four three two one tap Fred's foot. Press it Fred! Press it Roget! And an almighty boom! From the street! A boom that yanks the tiles on the roof and clatters them down again, a spume of dust and rubble lifts off the road up in the air higher than the roof and the noise comes whipping over the top, hugging the rattling tiles clacking back as the post explosive suck plucks the air down again, and then the crackle of a soaring sheet of flame licks into the air high about the bank, dies down again, and now the roar starts as bricks and masonry loosened like stacked cans come rattling down amidst the screeching banshee of the metal edging and cover of the gas main. The cover itself was thrown twice as high as the roof top and spun lazily downwards, smashing through the tiles on the far side of the roof. I turned to Fred. 'It didn't explode, you dumb bastard,' I shouted at him. From the cellar of the vault I'd heard no sound. 'It didn't go off!' I screamed above the roar and the crackle of the street flames.

He was smiling that lazy insolent smile.

'Go and look,' he said. The first four were already over the wall and I followed them. The hole in the floor of the vault might have been cut with a tin opener, so neat were its edges. I hadn't even heard the explosion, so well had the charge been laid. All the sound had been absorbed by the four feet concrete walls, all the explosive shock upwards, two short arm jabs of a shattering power that punched the plug of concrete straight up through the floor. The walls and the ceiling of the vault itself were splattered with crushed concrete, thick with dust and powder. The fog however quickly dissipated itself as we went in coughing. Fred followed me down and stood looking at his handiwork. It was a beautiful job. He fingered the edges of the hole, neat and sheer. The men scrambled through the hole into the vault itself; I followed them. Filing cabinets stood all round the walls of the vault. None was locked. I lost no time with the files. I had a specific job to do, and with Taffy crossed to the door of the safe. We had to jam this door to prevent the Germans getting in to realise the vault had been opened. There'd be damage to the floors and the ceiling of the room above, but this would be put down to the effect of the gas main explosion. The jammed door would be attributed to the same cause. I grinned as I thought of the planners in London. I'd make a point of telling them of our emendation to their plan. That'd wipe the smug smiles off their faces.

'Back outside, Fred, and you too, Joe,' I said. For this part of the operation, their place was on top of that wall, receiving the folders the men would push up to them. In the absence of Peter Derby, Ben had now taken over command of the files; his would be the job of selecting what would go, what could remain behind. He had been shown prototypes of the sort of document we were looking for.

Taffy was studying the safe door. We had seen photographs and models of most well-known safes in use in Belgium at that time, and some of the more common German safes. A safe 'expert' had briefed us.

This door extended the full height of the room, and was three feet wide. It projected into the room; it must have been two feet thick. All the mechanism was exposed at this side, presumably to facilitate maintenance. A plate, however, was screwed on to the actual lock. Taffy had brought a small kit of tools with him. He unwound the canvas belt and laid it on the floor. I gaped at the safe door, aghast. Of all the models we had studied, this was not one. I started back out to get Fred. 'Hang on a minute, Major,' Taffy said, 'it's an adapted Sicherstein.' It was. On a Sicherstein vault lock, a wheel operates a worm gear screw that pushes steel roller bolts into the edge of the door seating. There are three roller bolts, each two inches in diameter. In this adaptation, additional worm gears had been incorporated to push further bolts, not only into the side of the door opening, but also into the top and the bottom. A slab of steel, doubtless fitted with roller bolts inside also rolls backwards into the frame of the door between the hinges, so that the door could not be lifted out that way. He unscrewed the plate that covered the locking mechanism, an electromagnetic pulse bar cylinder type. When the correct setting was dialled on the outside combination, a cylinder moved along a solenoid and twisted to present another face. Only when the correct second number was dialled would the cylinder move one notch farther open. There were eleven codes on the cylinder, eleven combinations that needed to be 'dialled' before the cylinder would come to the end of the solenoid and the spring-loaded 'key' could come forward to engage into the worm gear, and permit the wheel to withdraw the bolts. The spring-loaded 'key,' a metal plate two inches by four inches by a half an inch thick, was held on a ball bearing spindle by one nut. We unscrewed this nut, slipped the key sideways and off. No matter what combination was dialled, no-one would be able to unfasten the lock, since the wheel outside would never turn the rollers. We screwed the combination cover back on and started to help Ben and the men. They had already collected a small pile of folders on the floor by the hole.

I dropped out through the hole and climbed the wall to the top of the bank roof. I crawled round the gutters beneath the mansard roof until I could look down on the road. The fire from the gas main was still burning, surrounded by Belgian workmen. They were shouting to men at the other end of the road, obviously waiting for them to turn off the gas supply. They seemed in no hurry. From my vantage point on the roof I could see across the road and down several of the streets that abutted it. The crackle of rifle fire was everywhere in the back streets, and from the frequent boom of grenades the battle seemed to be moving from the road, and already was at least a half mile away. Lorries came hurtling down the road carrying German troops, but none seemed to take the least notice of the Belgian work group below me. Over the arms dump, where Roget had planted his explosion, a black pall of smoke hung in the air and I could see the flash of mortar bomb explosions in the half light. It would soon be dawn, already vision was lengthening. The partisans would need to move fast to escape encirclement. Already I could see the flash of lights in streets about a mile away, behind the partisans. The Germans were bringing further reinforcements to block the back way out. I slid back down the rope and then with an upwards flick, disengaged the grappling hook from the brickwork. I climbed the wall, and ran along the gully. Bless her, Artoise had not moved from her position on guard at the other end. 'Tout va bien?' she asked, excited. 'Excellent.' 'I may go now?' I could see she itched to join the partisans. I took her hand. 'I'm sorry I said what I did, about the brothels,' said. 'That is the past,' she said. 'Think only of the future and escape.' She swarmed through the door into the cabinet and that was the last I ever saw of her.

Something was wrong. A job is a chess board with every piece memorised on its square. Two of my pieces were missing.

I ran back down the gully. Fred and Joe were gone. How could that be with Artoise on guard all the time? Perhaps they had gone straight up, over a roof. Silly bastards! What could they hope to gain by leaving us now.

Rats and rabbits have an uncanny hearing system. Criminals doubtless have antennae in the mind which pick up signals we don't hear. Certainly I had survived many times because, in an otherwise silent night, my inner antennae warned me of physical danger. This was not imagination. It was a specific and clear knowledge of actual danger. Fred must have felt it, and had decided his chances with the Germans were greater than his chances with me.

He and Joe had vanished without a trace.

In the road outside the bank I heard the clamour of a fire bell. No doubt the partisans among the Belgian disaster squad had hoped to add to the confusion by turning out the fire brigade. I heard an ambulance drive up, its siren bleeping a high-pitched wail. The burning gas had spread a thick smoke over the street, and there were metallic flashes in the flame. From streets at the other side of the road I still heard the explosion of grenades, but gradually they were moving further away. I glanced at my watch. We were ahead of time.

Dodger came scrambling down the gully. He was smiling.

'You should have seen that motorcycle after the explosion,' and as he spoke the fire suddenly died away. 'Someone must have turned off the gas,' he said.

'Have you seen Fred or Joe?'

'No, they didn't pass me. Have they scarpered?'

'Yes.'

'That Fred,' Dodger said in disgust. 'He was a queer one. He was a damn sight more interested in that bank there, than in the vault. Asking questions about it all the time he was, in the barn.'

'What sort of questions?'

'Oh, you know, Major, what was in it, how you could get inside, all that sort of stuff. He kept going on about it to the lads, how we was a lot of mugs messing about with signals data when there was probably gold and jewels in that bank for the taking. And then, here's another thing, he nicked Captain Derby's escape money.'

Whenever we jumped into Europe we were always given a pack containing money in German, French, Dutch and Belgian currency, for use should we need to escape through the country. We were also given a belt full of gold sovereigns. 'I saw him putting the money into his own pack,' Dodger said. 'I'd give him hell for it, but there was nothing I could do, not if he was to finish this job. I'd 'a killed him.'

I had a sudden certainty of what the buggers were about! I leaped back off the wall and ran to the corner of the compound. The lads were just starting to lift out the signals material. I waved Dodger to come and give them a hand. In the corner of the yard was the iron-grilled door, only two feet high and four feet wide, doubtless a ventilation door for the bank cellars. The iron grille had been severed recently by bolt cutters. I pulled the grille back out of the way and gently pushed the wooden door. It opened. The flimsy lock had been jemmied. That's what they had been doing when supposedly they went back to check the charge under the vault.

I slid my body through the door, five feet into the cellar beyond. The room into which I dropped was used as a cleaning store and general brew-up room. There was a stove in the corner whose chimney went up through a side wall. By the stove was a coffee-bean grinder, and on a shelf rows of coffee bowls. There were no beans in the grinder, and it appeared not to have been used for some time. A divan in the corner of the room seemed to have been used more recently. The door at the far side of the room was open slightly. I went across to it. A light was on in the cellar beyond. Joe and Fred had un-packed the surplus explosive we had brought with us, and Fred was tamping it to the ceiling, just as he had tamped the vault. This time, however, he had no manhole cover, no hydraulic ram, though I noticed he had 'borrowed' the four baulks of timber we had used in the vault. God. They had been busy! Two of the baulks just gave him sufficient height, one on top of the other, to hold a heavy metal washing-bowl – doubtless from the sink near the stove – in which he had placed the explosive. The wires trailed from the edge of the bowl and were coiled on the floor.

Relying on the general confusion in the streets, Fred and Joe were going to blow a hole in the bank floor and get out what they could. Then, doubtless, they'd make their own way out of the country. I turned to climb back out of the cellar. Any activity, any thought, any movement which did not increase the chances of success of our mission I regarded as treason. There it was, black and white. We were on a job, the job was all important.

I once knocked a French Commando unconscious to prevent him going to see his mother on such a job as this. She lived only two streets from a power station we were to blow; but I wouldn't let him go. If I had known about his mother, I would never have taken him with me. He volunteered to come of course, in the expectation of five minutes by his home fireside. It didn't work. By the time he recovered consciousness, the fuse was lit and we were running.

I was half-way out of the window when I felt the impact of a gun barrel in my kidneys. Fred was standing behind me.

'Not so fast, Major.' I fell gently back, dusting my hands.

'You sound like a cheap American gangster,' I jibed. His face flushed. I moved hard and low and fast, but Ben had trained him too well. He moved sideways avoiding my knee and chopped with the gun against the side of my face. I felt the trickle of blood down my cheek and slammed against the wall as he followed up his blow with a kick behind my knee. Groggy, I whirled to try to back hand him, but he saw my open hand and drove his fist containing the gun hard into my adam's apple. I choked, gasping for breath. The adam's apple is a killer's target. Waves of pain ran through my head and I felt myself going under. He grabbed my hair through the beret and held my head up. I was powerless to resist. This is it, my brain flashed, a sideways chop with the gun across my upper lip beneath my nose. He shook my head roughly. He was a tough fighter we'd trained well, but we hadn't managed to instil the killer instinct into him. Thank God. I got to my feet.

'Don't try anything again,' he said. 'The sergeant major taught us all he knows. Now walk through into the other cellar, quickly and quietly, and I'll be behind you, *Major!*'

I did as he told me. He'd been a good pupil and Ben was a good teacher. I was finding it hard to breathe and had no strength at that moment for resistance.

'Now connect those detonators and do it right since Joe will be watching you and I'll be standing back here ready to shoot.'

I started to work connecting all the wires that came out of the bowl into the two wires that would go back to the plunger. 'Where did you get the pistol?' I asked. It was a colt .45.

'I've had it since Yorkshire.'

I looked at Joe as I worked. He was uneasy. I could see he didn't share Fred's enthusiasm for what they were doing.

'What do you hope to get?'

'Gold, and jewels, if you must know.'

'And then what?'

'We take our chances. Every day you hear of prisoners-of-war who get out of Germany and back to Blighty. Well, if they can do it, I'm damned certain we can. Do you know how many times I've been on the run from the police? Don't worry, we'll get away, and with all them jewels, we won't be heading for England, though – we'll bribe our passage down to Africa, somewhere nice and hot for a change, and sit out the war in peace and comfort.'

He was right, of course. They could get away. They were professionals at escaping, and Africa is a big continent. Cargo boats still came up the coast and touched at Lisbon. They could get down to Tenerife; money is the best passport, especially if it happens to be in gold.

'What if the Germans hear this explosion?'

'They won't. You didn't even hear the vault go up, and you were listening for it; all these idiot partisans running about chucking grenades, and Old Dodger knocking off gas mains. We'll be through that floor up there and out again like a dose of salts.'

'And what about me?'

'That, I'm afraid, is the one thing that bothers me. According to the watch, the lads will be taking off any moment now. You've told 'em that nobody is to waste time looking for anybody who's missing, so they'll bugger off without you.'

'Where to? I'm the only one who knows the route home.'

He laughed. 'Don't kid yourself. Half the partisans know it, and they must have told the lads.'

I had connected the wires. One pressure on that small box and the whole lot would go sky high. I was sorely tempted to blow the whole lot now, but I knew I couldn't until the men were all away with that signals data. I daren't risk the explosion being heard before the men were away.

'Joe, get over here.' Joe went and stood beside him. I looked at my watch. The boys would be leaving. Ben would doubtless think that for some reason I had gone ahead, relying on him to get out what was left of the troop according to our disciplines on time.

Joe and Fred were standing beside the door.

'Another little point we have to consider, Major, is that your lads have arranged a little lynching party for Joe and me. They think we don't know, but I could sense when I got back into the barn after my sentry duty that they had something up their sleeves. So you see, we've got to wait here until they've gone, and we can't have you prancing about, can we? You're just the sort of blood-and-guts bugger who'd get a couple of men and come after Joe and me, or tip off the partisans to do the dirty work for you. So I'm afraid that, just as soon as your lads get out of earshot, it's curtains for you, old lad. Or should I still call you Major, since we're still in the Army?'

Joe was sweating, and beads of perspiration stood out on his upper lip. 'Remember the static line, Joe,' I asked. 'I could have left you dangling. You wouldn't have lasted five minutes.'

'Very good attempt, Major, but it won't work, will it, Joe?' Fred said. 'Joe knows when he's well off.'

'You only got me down because you

needed me on the job,' Joe said.

'You and your jobs,' Fred said, 'you've made me sick, poncing on about England, Hope and Glory. Well, let me tell you this, Major bloody Rhodes, we only agreed to come on the job in the first place because we reckoned it was a good way of getting out of England, and there'd be a bit of loot in it. I knew when that prick Sywell turned up at the prison, it had to be a bank job, or a safe, or a vault.'

'Joe, I could have left you dangling there. You'd have died within minutes.'

'Well, what do you want me to say, thank you?'

'It's not true the lads want you, Joe,' I had to persist.

Joe looked at Fred, thinking. Bless God, was I getting through to him?

'It'll be because Fred slashed Arthur Sywell's static line, Joe. The lads have got nothing against you, believe me. I would know if they had.' It was a lie – I hadn't even known the lads knew about the static line. Frank Farleigh must have seen it dangling there when he was waiting his turn to jump and I was climbing down Joe's line. 'It was a stupid murder, Joe, and that's what gets the lads. If Fred could do it once, he could do it again, to you!'

Fred lifted the colt in a demonstration of strength. Joe was looking at him, doubtless wondering to what sort of man he had tied himself. Bank robbers are not normally violent people. 'That sod Sywell was lying to us,' Fred said, his voice raised, 'he said we'd be given a pardon, but I know damned well the minute we got back he would put us straight back into Durham.' It was a stupid lie, but he was doing what I had seen so many times, working himself into a frenzy so he could kill me. Few men can kill in cold blood; that's why army sergeant majors teach raw recruits to yell as they stick a bayonet into a straw-filled dummy, why men yell as they dash across a field in a bowel-opening charge. He started to raise the gun. I had about ten seconds.

'I could have left you dangling on the end of that line, Joe; at that altitude with that wind blowing, you would have frozen to death in no time at all. Five minutes, Joe, that was all you had, and I risked my life to climb down that static line to you.'

'Because you needed me for the job,' Joe said.

'No, damn it, because you're a human being, and I couldn't see you go like that.'

Now the gun was level. Fred's finger began to pull on the trigger. He'd deceived me, he didn't need the anger, he was perfectly capable of killing in cold blood.

Joe's hand flashed upwards in an arc knocking the pistol out of Fred's grasp. I rocketed forward, my arm outstretched, a battering ram that took Fred in the chest, staggering backwards out of the cellar through the door, clutching the green box in his left hand, me following. I hit him a short-armed curved jab with all my force behind it aimed under his jaw bone up into his head, my knuckles fully extended. I heard the awful crack and knew I had broken his neck. The speed of my impulsion carried me on. He fell backwards already dead and I tripped over his feet and stumbled on him. His head hit the floor. I tried to stop my hand but in that instant knew it to be impossible. My hand descended on the plunger of the little green box, and the whole cellar was filled with the muffled punch of an almighty explosion.

There was no bang, at least none I could hear. Suddenly there was an immense pressure on my body, my lungs, even my eyeballs. The air, intensely heavy, squeezed my chest. The only noise was a dull crunch like that of a heavy boot on dry snow; and then the post explosion suction began and I was gasping for breath in air filled with dust fine as French chalk. The explosion slammed Joe to the ground and scraped the side of his face. His skin, and doubtless mine, was pock-marked with impregnations of sharp black powder particles. I dragged him to his feet, and tried to push him out through the window, but he had no strength in his arms to lift himself.

'Sit with your head between your hands,' I told him. 'I'll make my way along to the cabinet maker's yard and wait there for you.' I had to keep my promise to get him out and back to the plane alive. I climbed through the window. The men had all left on time as we had planned. The sand and gravel and cement were still in the corner. Soon, the partisans would clean out that vault as best they could and re-cement the floor. It wouldn't pass inspection for long, but might give the decoding experts in Essex a few more vital hours. I climbed the wall of the compound, walked along the gully mentally checking to see the lads had left no traces of their passage. The mark of an Innsbrucker boot sole was stamped in a patch of mud in the gully. I cursed, and scuffed it with my hands. When I dropped down into the cabinet maker's yard he was sitting in a small shed in which he kept a few machines, such as planers, circular saws. He had made himself a cup of coffee; when he saw me appear, he poured some for me into a bowl, and I swigged it gratefully. The men had left on time, he confirmed, in good spirits. They had asked about me, but he hadn't seen me since the incident with Artoise and the Germans. It took Joe five minutes to come to his senses. I was just going back to fetch him out when he appeared in the wardrobe at the top of the pile.

'You better?'

'I'm all right now, Major.' He looked horrible.

The cabinet maker looked out into the alleyway; no-one was about. I shook his hand. It was all I could do. I craved the eloquence of a Churchill adequately to thank him, to tell him how much I understood the enormity of the risk he took. It was easy to be a come-and-gone soldier; he had to sit in his yard, and if ever the Germans suspected we had used this as our route of entry and exit, the Gestapo would tear him limb from limb. Roget Belfière would give me his name and address and when I was able I would communicate my gratitude to him. 'Bon voyage,' he said.

'Merci.'

Over his wall, into the alleyway, and turn left. Run for a hundred and fifty yards, turn right, run for a hundred yards, along another similar alley, turn right again. Small door. Open it. Inside, a yard. In the yard other bicycles. On the bicycles, out through the front gate left along the street away from the explosion. To our right we could see the barricades; the Germans had surrounded the entire area but we were outside the cordon, the partisans drawing them in the other direction. In the distance I could hear the muffled explosions of grenades, and now the heavier boom of small calibre guns. As we rode along, Joe came level with me.

'Major, about the cellar...' he started to say. I cut him short, wanting no explanations.

'What happened down there you can forget,' I said. 'Our job is to get back home quickly, and we have no other purpose in life at this moment, do you understand? When we get back, I shall put in a report saying Fred was killed in action. Just that. I shall never mention your part in it, understand?'

'I understand, Major,' he said, 'and thanks.'

We caught up with the last two men after

a mile on the bicycles. I tinkled my bell in our prearranged signal to identify us, but by now there were many people about on bicycles, early workers going to the factories. Sam Levine looked with concern at my face as I rode up beside him. The gash Fred had cut it in with the colt had run with blood, but the powder blast had caked it – it would be as good as a dressing until we got home. Now the streets were becoming light and the false dawn before the rising of the sun spread a grey November light. I was beginning to feel the first traces of physical tiredness; mentally I was as alert as ever, but the wrenched shoulder, the fall from the wall, and Fred's attack, had taken a toll. I never had difficulty on a job, never took any of the pills the Medical Corps offered to combat sleepiness. To me, the job was everything, and I had no fear of collapse so long as we were active. But my bones ached, and I thought with longing of the hot breakfast and bath I hoped would await us.

Tomorrow I would need to travel to London for a debriefing; that would doubtless include a psychological examination. I would see Sandy again. Half my mind flicked over the fearsome possibilities of that meeting; the other half clung stubbornly to the job.

Perhaps Sandy would have been replaced at her own request by some other psychologist. They were all the same, all tainted with the academic passion for experiments, no mater what decent human emotion they sliced to shreds for their microscopes.

'Everyone safely away?' I asked Sam.

He nodded eyeing my face. 'What happened down there, Major?'

'There's no time to tell you now. Fred Pike's dead.' I saw the gleam of satisfaction on his face. 'Data spread out, as planned?'

'Yes, except the sergeant major's carrying Alf Milner's load, and I have Frank Farleigh's.'

'Right, off we go.'

'Yes, Major.'

It was a good thing that they would have left me, or so I told myself. But it was also such a horribly bad thing. You crush emotion from yourself; fight to crush it in other people. You stamp out human foibles, refuse to accept their existence. 'After all, he's only a human being, sir,' had been said to me so many times, and I had been enraged by it. I refuse to accept that any man is 'only a human being'. The human ethos is the finest of all the Creations, capable of infinite ability. The very phrase 'only a human being' sought to reduce the marvel of humanity to the level of animals. Man is capable of anything, providing he believes that to be true. How many men who believed they couldn't cover five miles, had I loaded with a hundred pound pack, and shown them they could cover a seemingly endless succession of five mile stretches at unbelievable speeds? How many times had I taken men into the Highlands of Scotland on a hardening course, and kept them off food and water for days while scrambling up the sides of mountains, swimming through ice-cold lochs? The human being is capable of anything he believes in; it had become my credo. How galling now to realise that anything could include leaving me behind. Well done, chaps, good show, you bastards.

In the distance, I heard the boom of guns, the wide-mouthed ones that fire house-destroying shells. Doubtless the Germans had pinned a section in one of the houses and were busy shooting away the walls. Joe and I cycled together along the road, and turned right. Mean houses were beside the street, men and women, on cycles, some walking. For them the working day starts soon; for us we hope it is nearly over. 'Keep a regular pace,' I had ordered, as if it was a nine days' bicycle ride. Ben and the rest should be ahead of Joe and me; Sam and Taffy were behind. We rode all the way along the street, just two more workers on bicycles. Turn left, then almost immediately right again. I had rehearsed the route a hundred times in my mind, as had all the men. We could have cycled it blindfold. Above all, to any watching eyes, we must appear to know where we were going. There must be no hesitation, no pausing at the end of long mean streets.

The Germans were waiting just around the corner. Ten of them. One section. They had a tripod-mounted machine-gun and automatic rifles. The machine-gun was hidden behind a car, the men with the automatic rifles lying along the back of a lorry. One of the men carried a radio and had the earphones clamped to his ear, the microphone in his hand. They were looking straight down a long street, the one I had intended to use. The radio operator called out to the section corporal and we saw them all tense. A section of the partisans was being driven, or so I gathered, into the far end of that street. The Germans would let them come part way up the street and then open fire. It would be massacre. I signalled to Joe to dismount. We wheeled our bicycles slowly forwards. All my training, all my instincts told me to get out of there, as fast as I could, but somehow I could not bring myself to do it. Over the rooftops we could hear the explosion of grenades – doubtless ones we had supplied to the partisans. A wreath of smoke spilled up and over the houses down near the bottom of the street, and we could hear the explosion of larger shells and the whining of mortars. Poor bastards in among that lot. I could sense others behind me, a small crowd of people all with bicycles or walking to work. The German corporal looked round, saw us and muttered something I didn't catch to his second-in-command. He jumped off the back of the lorry and came towards us. He herded us together in the lee of one of the buildings. I signalled quietly to Joe to stay on the periphery of the small crowd. Where we were standing we could see down the street. The crowd was silent; they knew what to expect. Typical of the German mind to want the Belgian people to witness the massacre. A salutary lesson, their Teutonic minds would say. They could never comprehend how firmly it resolved the will to resist, how strongly it would fan the flames of hatred. I felt rather than saw Sam

Levine and Taffy ride up behind. They joined the crowd, inconspicuous as ever. To run for it would have been fatal.

Six of them, four of us. They have one machine-gun and four automatic rifles, we all have a knife each and two grenades. No, I'd taken Sam's two grenades up there on the hill by the wood. He was looking disinterestedly at my face, or so it seemed, chewing his gums. I knew he would be alert for anything I might suggest. He took his hand out of his pocket. In his clenched fist was a grenade. He put the fist back in his pocket. Good, he'd acquired two more grenades in the barn. Trust Sam!

Taffy was watching Sam.

We were now standing behind the machine-gun, about ten feet from it. The men with the automatic rifles were on the lorry just behind the car shielding the machine-gun. We couldn't throw a grenade in such a confined space, with that crowd there.

Taffy had worked his knife down his sleeve. I saw its point in the palm of his hand.

Ten feet's a long way to jump with a knife.

One of us for the machine-gun, but that leaves only two for the four men on the back of the lorry. I couldn't rely on Joe.

I looked at Sam, looked away from him at the machine-gun.

He nodded. He'd understood. He'd take the gun.

He looked at Taffy, then at me and at the back of the lorry. Taffy understood. He and I would take the back of the lorry.

I dropped the knife out of its holster beneath the raincoat I wore and felt it in my hand. Trouble with a knife is that it can be bloody awful to get out again, sometimes. You slam it in, and it can get stuck, held by the suction you create with the blow.

Knife in the left hand. Jump up on the back of the lorry using the right hand and arm as leverage. Left arm on a wide arc in beneath his shoulder blade, that's the quickest. Right elbow forward so that if the other German turns round it'll go straight in his eye.

'Grab hold of my bike,' I whispered to Joe, 'and be ready to go like hell.'

'What are you going to do, Major?'

'Watch, and be ready to move, fast.'

Look at Sam, look at Taffy, look down the street.

A group of partisans had just turned the corner and had started up the street, running past each other, facing the other way, except for the two in the front who were looking up the street. The corporal growled a quiet 'Achtung' – but there was no need. Everyone had seen the target.

The partisans came on up the street. At the bottom corner, a group dropped a Bren gun on its tripod and started firing short bursts along the side street down which we couldn't see. The German machine-gunner wanted to shoot, but the corporal insisted he wait. More and more partisans were in the street – by now there must have been thirty. Then I saw the black-haired girl Sam had been with in the barn. He saw her at the same moment, looked despairingly at me, and I nodded. We were about to spring when the corporal, losing his nerve, yelled 'Fire.' The machine-gun raked along the street, a slow rate of fire, each shot made to count. Then the men with the automatic rifles opened up. Rat Tat Tat. The rate of fire was higher than that of the larger machine-gun.

We were too late. As the firing began, the section corporal turned his automatic rifle to cover the crowd. There was nothing we could do. One by one the partisans were chopped down by the rapid fire, one by one they fell on the pavée, in the doorways, across the window sills. As soon as he heard the fire, the Bren gunner tried to turn his fire up the street, against the Germans, but the bastard who invented the Bren never allowed for a fast turn when he stuck the blasted tripod legs up at the front end. Before the gunner could turn through twenty degrees, the German machine-gunner sighted on him, and held a long slow burst that whipped down the street and cut away the Bren gunner's head.

I thought Sam would go crazy when his girl dropped, a blood red mass where her chest had been. There was nothing I could do, now, with that automatic rifle pointing at us. Sam turned against the building and was sick. The corporal jeered at him.

It was all over in a few seconds and twenty or more Belgians had been slaughtered.

The corporal glanced down the street, then waved us all on in silence. No-one spoke. We rode silently past, me with Sam, Joe with Taffy.

'We were just that bit too late, Major,' he said. There was no hint of reproach. 'Sorry about the spew.'

'Forget it,' I said. 'Anyway, it wouldn't have worked.'

I changed places with Taffy. I wanted to

keep Joe by my side. Taffy and Sam dropped behind, Joe and I went as fast as we dared to catch up on the schedule. Here is the turn to the left. Down this quiet street. Here the turn to the right, following the mental map. No hesitation. Here is the barracks. Unavoidable, but at that time of the morning, the sentry should take no notice of us. A platoon of soldiers was forming up in a hurry on the street outside the barracks; reinforcements against the partisans. The street widened in front of the barracks; we rode past them averting our gaze in simulated respect. I bent my foot so the cleated rubber soles of my boots would not show; Belgians were not well shod by that time in the war. Joe nearly knocked down the German sergeant who stepped backwards without warning. The German bellowed at him, but I willed Joe to keep on going, muttering 'pardon monsieur' as it came my turn to pass him. The sergeant mollified, turned his early morning spleen against the platoon laggards. How dearly I would have liked to heave a packet of P.14 amongst them, but that was not my task. I had abdicated all responsibility for the safety of the partisans. It had not been an easy thing to do. We could stop our bicycles at this approaching corner and lob a grenade back amongst them. Hold it in your hand long enough after you'd pulled the pin and it would explode on impact. I bet I could get twenty with that one throw. But it must not be. We turned at the end of the street, went along for a half mile, and were in the country.

It would be a fine morning for November when the sun eventually struggled through. Now the air was heavy with dew, the fine penetrating moisture that pierced your clothing. Thank God we were on the move; we'd have been miserable crouching beneath a hedge.

I pinged on the bicycle bell, three times. Joe heard the signal and stopped. He got off his bicycle and examined the front tyre. I halted beside him as if to commiserate. Ben, Harry Landon and Willie Garside ahead of us had been stopped by a patrol in an open pick-up truck, and two men on the pavement were searching our lads. Two men in the open back of the truck, hunched in overcoats, had machine carbines on their laps.

'We'll have to have a go at 'em,' I told Joe. Our men were carrying signals data. 'We'll go from the outside of the vehicle, okay?'

It wasn't okay, but it had to be done.

'You go first, eh, Major?'

I outlined my plan to him, we mounted, and set off down the road. Ahead of us was a T-junction and the patrol had our men on the right-hand side at the bend of the road. We were riding up the right-hand side, of course, and would pass near the open truck. I rode ahead of Joe. Our men were standing with their hands on the wall, and the Germans were searching them. The two men in the back of the truck didn't look particularly alert. How I longed for a rifle; it would have been child's play to pick them off. As I drew nearer I felt the old taste rise in my mouth, that here-we-go-again bile of too constant killing. It would be worse for Joe, since he'd never done it before. The men in the back of the Mercedes glanced along the road towards us but took no notice. Huddled in greatcoats, they were too somnolent to care.

The two by the roadside were opening the briefcase Harry Landon carried strapped to his wrist. In it, I knew, were Signals Data Centre papers. I rode my bicycle slowly forwards. The soldiers in the truck paid no further attention to me. At the cross roads I slowed, dismounted, turned the bicycle left, between me and the truck. I pinged the bell twice. The man at the back of the truck leaned out to see nothing was coming down the road, then waved me on. I had shifted the grip of my left hand to the centre of the handlebars, my right clasped the back of the saddle. In one swing I lifted the bicycle clear of the ground and tossed it onto the back of the truck, entangling the two guards. The chain wheel caught the face of one of them. I followed the bicycle forwards, reached through the frame to grasp a machine-gun, jerked up the muzzle and sprayed the two men conducting the search. It was a wild burst but the Germans dropped instantly. So did Willie Garside. Ben Bolding sprang to the side the moment he heard the crash of the bicycle against the back of the truck after the two warning 'pings.' He came round in a fast arc and grabbed the machine-gun of the man nearest him. I sprang back just in time as he sprayed both men in the back of the truck, the bullets whipping savagely past me, flying off the bicycle frame.

Willie had taken a bullet through his side, below and to the left of his heart. A through-and-through wound; it would give him hell for a day or two but was not serious. I ripped the bandage from my field dressing pocket and pushed it into his hand. He was only half conscious. I jerked him upright, sat him on his bike, and with Harry on one side and me on the other, we rode away hell for leather down the road. Banging my bike onto the truck didn't seem to have injured it. I would have liked to take the truck, but didn't dare risk a change of plans at this stage. Anyway, the lorry was only two miles away, and we could keep Willie going for that distance. Joe rode in front with Ben, completely bemused by the speed of what had happened. He was carrying Willie's briefcase, and that gave him a sense of purpose. Half a mile down the road which ran through well tilled farm fields Willie seemed to get a new lease of life. 'I think I can manage now,' he said. We let him pedal ahead until he was level with the others, and Harry and I dropped back a hundred yards. We were not challenged again. I looked back. Sam and Taffy had almost caught us up. I waved them on and Harry and I dropped behind them.

The lorry belonged to the German Army. It had been 'borrowed' on false papers from a Vehicle Repair Depot. The engine sounded like it; at first I doubted it would get us to our destination without breaking a valve stem. All the others were inside the back of the truck, hidden beneath the closed canvas. When Roget Belfière saw us arrive, he slammed down the bonnet and got into the cab. He was wearing only overalls and would pass for a mechanic. We threw our bicycles over the tailboard and climbed in; I took a rapid count; all were there. The driver let in the clutch, and the lorry coughed into movement, rattling and clacking its way along the road. There was safety, however, in the noise it was making. Several German patrols passed us, and through the canvas cover I saw each give us a derisory grin. Belfière had chosen a lorry with a doubtful engine deliberately; ten miles past where we intended to abandon it was the Vehicle Recovery Depot for this area, the lorry's graveyard. The engine must have consumed oil like whisky; black clouds came belching from the exhaust up into the air, sucked into the back of the lorry. 'If we don't get there soon,' Sam Levine said, 'we shall all be sick as dogs.' We rolled the canvas an inch or two all round to blow the smoke from the back. It helped a little but not much.

Eight miles down the road, the lorry turned off down a cart track, towards a farm, through a lane into a valley behind low but steep hills. The farm belonged to one of Roget's men. We climbed down, and the driver took the lorry away. For him a long slow drive around the town, to abandon the decrepit vehicle somewhere on the other side. If it ever got there.

We spread out in the hedge bottom, and waited. Only ten minutes to go, so close had our timing been. The valley had been fertile land before the war, ploughed for crops. Since the war, however, it had been allowed to go back to grass. The actual field was unusually large for a Belgian farm, and ringed with trees. On the hills above the field partisans had been sitting all night to warn us of any German infiltration. They had been luckier than their compatriots in the town. There had been no signs of activity. The morning developed its early promise, and the sky was clear. The nearest anti-aircraft battery was on the outskirts of Liège; the plane would come in low, and go out hugging the hills, hedge-hopping across Belgium. Only when it had reached the sea would it be safe to rise, and for that we had two hundred miles to go, through a corridor of fire-power.

We patched Willie's side with sulphanilamide powder and a field dressing. 'You didn't need to shoot me to prove what faith is, Major. I believed you already.' He grinned.

'Sorry I shot you,' I said, 'that damned gun kicked left. The armourer ought to have a look at it before he re-issues it.'

'You ought to have left him a Weapon Report.'

He knew the wound was not severe, though it had begun to ache furiously. A wound is a surprising thing; in the abstract the thought of a bullet ploughing its way into your body is terrible; when it actually happens, and it had happened to me four times, the effect is very small. The first shock of course is sickening, since you do not know at that moment of impact what damage has been done. The fear of crippling is worse than the fear of death. Many men would prefer to die by a bullet than be maimed to live afterwards in a cripple's wheel chair. Once you realise, however, that the bullet has passed through you, you can accept the wound. It doesn't lessen the pain, but makes it acceptable.

Willie was quite cheerful, but that too was normal. The immediate aftermath of a bullet wound is always a rise in temperature and the feeling of good humour that accompanies it; only later when the white corpuscles begin to fight back does the temperature go down and with it your morale. That's when the aches suddenly become intolerable.

Roget looked sombre as he came across to me. I didn't relish the thought of our conversation.

'What was it like?' I asked him.

'Pas bon, pas mal.'

I had to ask him. 'How many did you lose?'

'I saw twenty. There were others.'

'Artoise?'

He nodded. I had an inkling of how much she had meant to him.

'You have all the signals data?' he asked.

'Yes.'

'Alors, ça vaut tout.'

Was it worth all the lives so generously offered, so wilfully squandered?

The whole operation had been Roget's idea. But for him we could never have known about the Signals Data Storage Centre. But now, would he still think it worthwhile?

'You think so, Roget?'

The dullness went from his eyes. 'I am absolutely convinced, Monsieur le Major,' he said firmly. 'Though the deaths are matters of an infinite regret.'

'Especially that of Artoise!'

'Yes, if you'll permit a little sentiment. Artoise was of my generation, she could understand me without the constant need for explanation. The young ones are fierce, but they ask me too many questions I can't answer.'

'Like, why should we die for a group of Englishmen?'

'Ah, no, you mistake me! Like why should we not die, so long as we can take the Boches with us. Death is not a problem to the people of your generation, Major. You haven't seen sufficient of life to fall in love with it. You've not become greedy for it, as we old ones.'

'And Artoise?'

'There was a time when Artoise was greedy for life. Recently she had wanted to die.'

'She told me. Not that she wanted to die, but that life had become a hell to her, that God had left us to our own devices.'

'She must have admired you very much, monsieur, to be able to say those things to you.'

He did not cry. The old man must by now have shed so many tears he was dry of them. I could say nothing to help him. We had flicked death too often, too close to too many people for me to be able to commiserate with anyone; for us death had become an acceptable necessity, a factor you included in all your calculations. The circumference of a circle equals two pi times the radius, but no-one can ever know exactly how big pi can be. You divide one well known number by another and the answer is an imprecise, approximate 'pi.' We could divide the known advantage to us of the signals data by the known risk we would take to acquire it, but the unknown factor, the number of deaths we would suffer along the way, would always elude us.

'She died quickly?'

'Yes, a bullet.'

'That's a blessing.'

'Yes, the only one.' For a moment he doubted. He put his hand on my arm and looked questioningly at me.

'We are going to win the war, Major?'

'Yes,' I said, with parrot-like sincerity. 'We are going to win the war, Roget. Thanks to you, and Artoise, and hundreds like you...'

'When will you start the second front?'

'Next year.'

'This signals data? It will help?'

'Undoubtedly.'

'Tell them about us, won't you?' The people in Europe always asked us this – tell them about us. Sometimes we were interviewed by a journalist after one of our jobs, and we tried to 'tell them' about the people locked in Europe. It never worked. We could never get the human interest right; the stories were never complete. We knew these people for such a short time, in such a false way. Cowards became heroes, heroes revealed themselves to us in the one lifetime's moment of cowardice. I had learned to suspend judgment.

'Yes, we'll tell them.'

I left him then, and drew near to my own men, my own kind. I could understand them, and feel comfortable in the knowledge of their needs. With Roget I felt like a man who watches another slowly dying of an illness he cannot diagnose.

Roget's men, or what was left of them, were guarding the valley. They may appear a rag-tag-and-bobtail crew, but had earned our respect. We owed our lives to them individually, collectively, and on behalf of all those who lay crumpled on the pavements of Liège.

'The plane will be down in five minutes,' I said, glancing again at my watch. 'You all know the drill. He'll come in badly since he can't run back and manoeuvre for take-off. The sergeant major and Dodger will help the pilot turn the plane round by chocking the wheels. I want all the rest of you out of sight until that plane is ready for take off, and then you run over that field like bloody rabbits.

Harry, you give me a hand with Willie. We shall be flying low all the way to the coast to avoid the heavier ack ack, so we may get a bit of small arms fire up our backsides.'

'Do you mind if I walk home, Major?' Dodger Bates asked and the others laughed. He might stand a better chance on his own two feet; he'd walked out of Europe three times already and he knew the long way home.

'That's up to you,' I said only half-jokingly, 'but there'll be breakfast waiting for us in England, served by some of those W.A.A.F.'s they keep on airfields especially for returning heroes. And then there'll be leave, after you've had a pay day, of course.' Each man was entitled to sixpence a day danger money – they'd draw an extra shilling for this little trip.

'I'll ride,' he said.

FRANK FARLEIGH

'It's always the same when *I* ask for anything,' Frank said to his Mother as he towelled himself dry. 'You always say, I'll have to ask me Dad, and he always says I'll have to ask you. And then there's never any brass. It isn't as if I wanted the earth, is it?

All I want is a bit of carpet in me bedroom to put next to me bed, something to put me feet on when I get out of a morning.'

Frank had been back home from the Works for an hour, eaten his supper in his muck, which his Mother didn't like, and had washed himself, as he always did on a Friday night, in the large tin tub in front of the fire in the living-room that functioned as kitchen, sitting-room, bathroom in their one-down two-up back-to-back house in Hunslet. 'Getting ideas above your station, you are,' his Mother said. 'Just because you're earning two pounds ten a week.'

Frank was wearing his navy blue suit with the chalk stripe, double-breasted, with deep lapels, and a metal spring along the collar line to stop the lapels bending over. Frank couldn't stand creased lapels – they gave a jacket a scruffy, slept-in look.

He put the collar on to the back stud sticking from the back of the neckband of his shirt. He laced the tie into the collar and came and stood before the fire, trying to fit the two tabs of the front of the collar into the front stud. His thick fingers fumbled at the stud. His Mother watched him and then stepped forward in pretended exasperation. 'Here, let me fix it; you'll have the collar

330

black bright before you've even worn it, the way you're going on.' She stood in front of him and gently prised the two tabs onto the long stud. He put his arms on her waist, feeling the straps of her pinny between his fingers.

'What is my station then, old love?' he said.

'I don't know with you, you're that forward with yourself,' she said. 'You'll be going down to the dance hall tonight, and meeting some smart lass, and the next thing you know you'll be buying her port and lemons. Nobody never bought me no port and lemons, except at Christmas. The next thing you'll find she's living at Armley and you'll have a long walk home all that way.'

'Maybe she'll be worth it?' he said.

'Nobody's worth it, all that much,' she said. 'There's hundreds of nice girls round here, and they'd be glad to meet a nice smart lad like you that looks after himself a bit and dresses nice, and there's not one of 'em would think of ordering anything but a glass of stout. Yes, and they'd hang on to that for an hour or two.'

'Can't you see, Mum,' he said, as she clipped on the second tab and stepped back to let him knot the tie, 'that's not what I want. I want the best I can get.'

'That's the snare-and-delusion,' she said quickly. 'The best you can get is what you've been brought up to. It doesn't do no good to set your sights too high, young lad, and if you don't soon learn that, you'll come a nasty cropper. The higher they fly, the heavier they drop, that's what they always say,' she said. She picked up the heavy tin bath half full of water, carried it over to the low stone sink, and placed it there. He made no move to help her – had he tried she would have stopped him. After all, he was wearing his best, wasn't he? She took the overalls he had discarded, and dropped them in the still warm water to soak. They would stay in there until the water was cold. Heat was something you didn't waste. She took his shoes from the bottom cupboard, got out a rag and a tin of Cherry Blossom, and began to polish them for him. He sat on the hard chair and picked his toenails clean with the prong of a fork before putting on his socks.

'Can I borrow Dad's cig case?' he asked. She got up and opened the oak bureau which stood against the wall. From it she took the curved gunmetal case, opened it, closed it again, and handed it to Frank. 'You mind that now, it was my wedding present to your Dad,' she said.

'I know, love, you told me.'

'Just so long as you value it.'

'Honest, love, I'll guard it with my life.' He scratted about in the overcoat he wore to work and pulled from it a packet of Gold Flake cigarettes. He opened the packet and took out the cigarettes one by one, and slid them beneath the yellow elastic of the cigarette case. She put his shoes in front of his feet and picked up the empty cigarette packet. 'Gold Flake, eh? Going up in the world. What's wrong with Woodbines?'

'On a Friday night, love? Go on,' he said, 'have one.'

She hesitated. 'Go on!' She slowly took one.

'Aren't they big?' she said, and put it on the mantlepiece next to the rent book and the vase in which she kept her hair grips.

'Aren't you going to smoke it, then?'

'Not yet,' she said. 'I'll save it for later when I've got me feet up. That'll make a nice treat for me of a Friday night.'

'Well, don't go giving it to our Dad!'

He stood in front of the mirror and brushed his shoulders where the white dust of dandruff showed against the navy blue of his jacket. He put the cigarette case in his inside pocket, a box of matches in his outside pocket. He lifted the silk handkerchief higher in his pocket, rearranging the folds. He took his navy blue overcoat from behind the door. In the pocket was a white silk scarf he wound round his throat. She stood up. He had tied the scarf like a muffler.

'Not like that,' she said. 'Let me show you.' She undid the knot in the scarf and draped the scarf round his neck, tucking it beneath the lapels of his overcoat so that only a half an inch of it showed. 'That's how they wear 'em,' she said.

'Go on, how would you know!'

'I saw a photograph, in the papers. That's how Adolph Menjou always wears his scarf.'

He was standing at the far end of the ballroom when first he saw her dancing by, in the Valeta.

'That's her,' he thought.

He waited four dances until they had an excuse-me waltz. He was all right with the waltz.

'Where do you come from, then?'

'Roundhay,' he said.

'My my, posh up there, isn't it?'

'It's all right.'

'All right? I wished I lived up there.'

'Where do you live, then?'

'Armley.'

'What you doing after – I mean, would you like a drink?'

'Fast worker, are you?'

'No, but with these excuse me's, you never know!'

'We could have a drink. I'll have to tell me friends.'

'That's all right then, isn't it?'

She asked for a glass of stout. He insisted she have a port and lemon. 'It makes me drunk,' she said, giggling.

'Well that's all right then, isn't it?' he said. 'How you getting home?'

'Last tram.'

'I'll come with you, if you like.'

'That'll be nice, but how'll you get home? It's a long way from Armley to Roundhay.'

'I'll get a taxi.'

'Posh, aren't we?'

On his way home he passed his Dad, sitting by the brazier, drinking his mashing. His Dad made room for him on the box outside the little wooden hut, poured half his mashing into a pot he fished out of the hut and made both up with more water from the kettle.

'Brought you a present,' Frank said. He

got out the cigarette case.

'Here, you look after that. It was a present to me from your Mum.'

'I know,' Frank said without exasperation. Somebody always has to say something. Whenever you bring out the fag case, somebody has to say 'Careful of that, it was a present.' Every time you put your hand on a girl's chest she says 'Cheeky.' If you're lucky enough, as he had been that night, to get it up her skirt, she has to say, 'Keep your hand to yourself,' as if you were going to take it off at the wrist and leave it there for always.

'Gold Flake, eh? Going up in the world, aren't we?'

'Go on, it's Friday night. Smoke yourself to death!'

'Seen this?' his Dad said, tapping the newspaper he'd been reading when Frank came along. 'The way they're talking, you'll be in the Army before you know where you are. You can go in my old mob, the King's Own Yorkshire Light Infantry.'

'I bloody well won't – you can keep your footsloggers.'

'They was good enough for your Dad.'

'Well, they aren't good enough for me.'

'Ideas above your station, that's what you've got my lad.'

When he came home from the Commando training his Dad was sitting in the kitchen, washing his feet, and his Mother was getting the tea ready.

'Well, they've filled you out a bit, haven't they?' she said.

'How long you stopping?' his Father asked.

When he was ready to go back, seventy-two hours later, his Father came to the door with him. 'Here,' he said, and pushed his cig case into Frank's hand. 'Tek this with you.'

'You look after that,' his Mother said.

'I know, it was your wedding present to me Dad!'

The plane came in low over the hill, a beautiful landing. Even had he bounced in like a yo-yo, it would still have been a beautiful landing. The sergeant major and Dodger ran into the centre of the field and when the plane had taxied to a halt they chocked each wheel in turn while the pilot turned the plane round in its own length. I grasped Roget's hand. A wordless farewell when it came to it, and we dashed across the field 'like rabbits', opened the door and scrambled up the ladder. The plane was a twelve seater, and unusually, all the seats had been left in. There were whistles of approval. Dodger, irrepressible as usual, bounced up and down on one of the moquette seats. Beneath each was a parachute of the civilian 'ring on the chest and count ten' type. It was a V.I.P.'s plane temporarily seconded to less important duty. I suspected the hand of Brigadier Steele, especially when I saw a bottle of unblended malt whisky on the rack.

'They mean to take us home in style,' Dodger said. There were two pilots and, bless the Brigadier's heart, or was it Sandy's touch, a sergeant from the Royal Army Medical Corps, who took immediate charge of Willie. Roget waved as the plane took off. As we raced over the ground, not more than a hundred feet in the air, hedges came whipping towards us at frightening speed. Several times we passed over military units; the sporadic rifle shooting didn't seem to threaten us.

Then the fighters came. Two Messerschmitts, streaking down from the skies, behind us, guns chattering death and destruction. A line of shots perforated the top of the cabin from back to front, but miraculously no-one was hit. Our plane banked steeply to the right and then to the left, then climbed. Down there we were sitting ducks. We were tossed in a heap in the aisle and against the walls of the cabin, then the other way as the pilot banked again. Up and down, side to side; he did everything but turn the plane inside out. Meanwhile his co-pilot, talked urgently on the radio. I couldn't hear what he was saying, but soon saw the results; four Spitfires, guns mounted forward firing through the propellors, jumped on the tail of the Messerschmitts, and suddenly in the air about us, plane after plane, dog chase dog, dived and soared, zoomed and chattered death. One Spitfire spiralling rapidly, the pilot hanging on the thin thread of a mushroomed parachute. Then a Messerschmitt exploded on the ground with no parachute above it. The other Messerschmitt rolled and climbed, dived and flattened out then headed east like a cat with dogs on its tail. We headed west into the dawn of a peaceful morning. Soon the Spitfires returned from the chase; one flew ahead of us, waggling his wings, and streaked off into high cloud. The co-pilot was still talking to him; the Spitfires were our escort. Bless the Brigadier, he had not told me he was providing fighter support to get us home.

Sobering thought, we'd never had a fighter umbrella before, and suddenly I realised the V.I.P.'s on board this plane were contained in the manila folders, stamped with the Most Secret sign of Wehrmacht. Now we were flying about two thousand feet and anti-aircraft shells exploded in the skies about us, sudden bursts of stars that reminded me of Guy Fawkes' nights so long ago. Each time the blast tapped the plane sideways we bored into a cone of vacuum that shook the plane up and down with the sickening undulations of a crazy fairground big dipper. There was nothing we could do about that save to strap ourselves in and pass round the whisky bottle. At least the plane appeared to have a metal floor. The men didn't seem to mind the anti-aircraft explosions; each time another came close enough to rock us they cheered wildly. They were all talking nine-teen to the dozen. Up here we were free, the dank November night an illusion behind us.

Ben unstrapped his seat belt during a lull in the ack ack fire and came to sit beside me. He had brought the whisky bottle with him, and I took a generous gulp. It tasted wonderful; two more gulps and I wouldn't need any breakfast.

As he sat down, he let out a sigh of relief,

like a fat woman who has just unfastened her corsets. He strapped himself in, rested his head against the moquette seat head rest. The window beside my hand was armoured glass. I looked through it at the ground below. The plane was making a good speed, soon we would be home.

'You know you get a feeling sometimes, Major?' Ben said.

'Yes.'

'Did you get it this time?'

'No,' I lied.

'I did,' he said, 'and I thought you had. I never thought I'd make it this time.'

'Nor did I down in that cellar,' I told him about Fred.

He sighed again. 'Well, it's a good thing,' he said, his relief evident, 'that feeling has given me a bloody awful time on this job, and now I've learned to mistrust it. I shan't have such a bad time again.'

'Assuming there will be another job.'

He turned to look at me. 'There will be another, won't there?'

'Do you want one?'

'Not yet, of course. I want some leave, and I want to unwind. I wouldn't mind going back to America for one of those demonstration tours, if you could fix it. But there'll be jobs after that, won't there? I mean, Major, what's the alternative?'

'The barracks, at Maidstone. They've practically offered me the job of commanding officer.'

'I couldn't be a regimental sergeant major,' he said. He was right. He couldn't be. I couldn't imagine him parading across the square with a pacing stick in his hand, left right left. 'I wasn't talking about R.S.M.,' I said. 'I could have a word with the Brigadier. I reckon you'd make a passable War Substantive Second Lieutenant, acting Lieutenant, Temporary Captain, doing a Major's job as my second in command. The war would be over for us. You could take a commission, move into the Officers' Mess. These "fair maids of Kent" they talk about! It can't be all talk!'

I had caught his interest. Ben would like to be commissioned officer. Oddly enough, I felt, and knew the Brigadier would share my feeling, that Ben could be anything he set his mind to, whether frigging about in the ranks as a private soldier, a non-commissioned officer, or a fully commissioned officer; warming his backside by the fire in the Mess, or leading his men into the sort of action we had just completed.

'Give me a swig of that whisky, if you please, Major. That's something I shall have to think about. Maidstone, you said? It's a most agreeable county in the Spring, Kent is.'

I passed him the bottle, and he gulped at it.

I put my hand on his arm. 'No nonsense about this, Ben, but I think you're a bloody good man to have on a job like this, and Maidstone would be my way of saying thank you.'

He lowered the bottle out of his mouth, his face red but not, I knew, from drinking. 'The feelings' mutual, Major,' he said, unbuttoned his seat belt, and went forward to where the lads were obviously telling of their adventures behind the straw bales.

I remembered Roget had told me that all four of those young girls had been killed, but didn't tell the men.

We term sleep a death, yet it is waking that kills us, and destroys those spirits which are the House of Life. Sir Thomas More had said it. At two thousand feet in that plane, listening to soldiers relate without malice, the things those girls had said to them in the heat of passion, remembering Roget's face as he told me of the death of Artoise and the

343

girls, I felt I almost understood what Thomas More had meant. If this is living, let me die, let me live again after death as I live in the death of sleep, and let me never wake again to this horrible life.

Sam Levine staggered up the plane, just a little drunk. He stood by my seat and swayed, fixing his rather watery owlish eyes on me. 'Retrospective, Major?' he asked yet again.

'Retrospective, sergeant, and I owe you a week's pay.'

He saluted. It was a sincere gesture. 'I shall do my best to merit the trust which you have placed in me.' I smiled.

Joe had been silent since we climbed aboard. Sitting alone on a pair of seats near the front door, he had fastened the parachute to his chest, and the seat belt around his waist. Beside his right hand was the door. The R.A.M.C. sergeant was at the back of the plane with Willie Garside. Since the plane was now on an even keel, I walked down the plane, collecting the folders of signals data together. It was an impressive bundle and I could imagine the delighted faces of the Intelligence and Signals experts when we arrived. The plane banked slowly in a steep turn, heading right, northwards for home. I took Sam Levine's papers from him and added them to the others in my haversack. I was about to go forward to collect Joe's when he unfastened his seat belt and stood up. In his hand was the pistol Fred had used on me. Damn! I had left that for the partisans to take when they removed Fred's body. Joe must have pocketed it while he was sitting in the cellar, recovering from the effects of the explosion. His face was white, drained of blood.

'Get back, Major,' he shouted. The pilot glanced back, saw what Joe was holding, and pulled back the stick to put the plane into a climb. 'Level off,' Joe shouted, bracing himself against the back of the seat. I would have darted forwards but the motion of the plane was forcing me back. 'Level off, or I'll shoot the Major.'

The pilot looked back at me. I nodded. No point in provoking Joe. There was a rifle at the back of the plane, clipped in a rack on the wall. With luck one of the lads would have seen it. Joe didn't stand a chance. All were armed. By now one of them would have drawn his bow and arrow and was waiting for my cue. As soon as the plane levelled.

Oh no, this is too bloody ridiculous. Oh Christ, here we go again, I thought. What was Joe playing at? He must have known he didn't stand an earthly chance of getting away with it, whatever it was. It has to stop sometime, waving pistols in people's faces, the death, the stench of fear, shattered bones, pulverised flesh, the blood-letting. It has to *stop* sometime!

We've finished the job, I thought, an immense resentment welling inside me. I've taken the lads over there, we've done the job, and most of us have got back. I couldn't hold myself responsible for Peter Derby or Arthur Sywell, Fred, Alf, Frank, Artoise and all the unknown Belgians. I've done my share of the job; I've finished; I'm going to Maidstone, the Brigadier has promised me that.

But Joe, the silly bugger, was still pointing that pistol at me, and someone would have to kill him, and there was a chance, an outside chance, that he could kill me. Oh damn, when's it all going to end?

'Knock it off, Joe,' I said, trying to insert all my authority into my voice, 'put the pistol down.' Our Father which art in Heaven above; if only he'll listen to me now he can get back to England alive. If he doesn't, he's already dead.

But when, when's it all going to end?

'Come here, Major,' Joe shouted. I walked to the front of the plane and sat on the front seat. He placed the barrel of the colt against my temple. Damn it, we had taught him too well. No-one could take a chance at shooting him now, since the reflex action would be bound to jerk that trigger, and he had the safety catch off.

He reached his hand behind him and dragged open the side door.

His face was still white, though doubtless with the fear of what he intended to do. It's one thing to jump out of a plane as one of a stick, quite another to take the long drop cold. Everyone in the plane was silent. The rush of air through the door almost blew me from the seat and I felt his hand waver on the gun against my temple.

'What are you hoping to get by jumping?' I asked him.

'I've got it already,' he said. He reached a hand in the pocket of his jumping jacket, and brought out several diamond necklaces, pendants on gold chains. He thrust them back into his pocket.

'You went up into the bank?'

'It seemed daft not to, when Fred had gone to all that trouble to blow a hole through the floor.'

Blind, blind! Just because Fred had been the overt one of the pair, I had underestimated Joe. It was a damned old cliché, but nevertheless true that still waters run deep.

I couldn't attempt to dissuade him. I knew he could jump; we'd trained him, and once down there, in France, he stood a better than average chance of getting away to the south. Once on the Mediterranean Coast, with that amount of convertible wealth, he could disappear completely. There must be about eighty or ninety thousand pounds' worth of diamonds in that pocket.

Let the poor bugger jump! Why not? He's helped you do the job, and first priority is to get this signals data home. That's what you came for, not diamonds and a study of the criminal mind. Let him jump! If he can get away with enough money to lose his need for crime, so much the better.

'Okay, Joe,' I said, 'but listen to me. We're flying low at the moment, and you're wearing a manual parachute, so don't wait for the count of ten before you pull the ring. Count two, understand me, only two. You'll be well clear of the plane by then. This time, when you get near the ground for God's sake put your ankles together, and land with your feet in the same line; not like last time when your legs were at ten minutes to four.

Do you get that?'

He looked at me. He had expected resistance. What the hell, I had other things to do.

'Right, lad; keep her dead steady pilot, right, off you go. And Good Luck!'

Bemused, he turned, paused and jumped.

Ben Bolding came running down the plane with his parachute on, the rifle in his hand.

'Did you see what he had sticking out of his pocket, Major?'

Damn. I had seen it, of course, but with the barrel of that colt sticking into my forehead and the sweat of fear running into my eyes, I had not paid attention. He was carrying a set of the Signals Data Storage Centre documents in a folder plainly marked with their origin and the German word 'Top Secret.'

'If they pick him up with that in his pocket,' Ben said, 'they'll know where he's been; the way he lands, I wouldn't rely on him to get down safely twice in succession.'

Damn! 'Parachute,' I shouted. Sam Levine grabbed one and handed it to me as I passed him my own pile of signals data. 'Fly round in an arc, pilot, and lower,' I shouted as I struggled into the harness. The pilot banked the plane losing height, spiralling. Joe's 'chute had opened perfectly. I took the rifle from Ben. This was something *I* had to do. It had been *my* mistake. I couldn't risk having to chase Joe through the French country-side. I aimed the rifle, pushed forward the safety catch, drifted towards Joe's hanging figure. Aim off for wind out there, air speed, rate of descent, aim off, and squeeze the trigger gently; now! Joe jerked once, slumped and hung in his parachute lines.

'Take over, Ben,' I said. 'I'll come with you Major. You know the old Army principle of two being the minimum number.' It was true, the Army doesn't recognise one man in action; every guard ever posted has to be two men, every patrol composed in units of two. 'Right-o. Take over, Sergeant Levine.'

The reception party was all arranged in Essex. The men had the signals data. They would get a hot breakfast and a pay day.

I looked at Ben. 'Here we go again,' I said. He nodded, tight lipped. I jumped. Once again I felt the pull of the parachute above me as it mushroomed out into a cloud.

Ben jumped. His parachute failed to open. He candled, past me.

The publishers hope that this book has given you enjoyable reading. Large Print Books are especially designed to be as easy to see and hold as possible. If you wish a complete list of our books please ask at your local library or write directly to:

Magna Large Print Books
Magna House, Long Preston,
Skipton, North Yorkshire.
BD23 4ND